REVELATION

THE ETERNAL SERIES

BOOK ONE

MYLES GOROSPE

STRAKER PRESS

Copyright

First Printing: 2015

ISBN 978-0-692-43168-9

Straker Press, LLC
190 Gibson Blvd. Suite 4, Clark, NJ 07066
www.strakerpress.com

Dedication

For Tracy

For Believing in Me

Preface

While this is a work of fiction, I find it necessary, at least for my own sanity to present to you the reasons why I ended up writing this story. Growing up in a predominantly Catholic culture, I was always amazed at the biblical stories that I read within the Old Testament. This is usually emphasized during the period when Holy Week is observed leading up to Easter Sunday. At the time, unbeknownst to me, I was indirectly being molded into the kind of person I would be today. But watching those stories, both fictional and based on the word made me understand the reason why faith drives us the way it does.

We've all seen stories about how the world ends, and quite frankly, everyone has their own idea of how it will happen. Meteors, aliens, a killer virus, the undead. Whatever the case, it seems these stories always presents some form of way to avoid it. Usually through the courage of the human soul or the ingenuity of the human race. But I for one have always been fascinated, and terrified of the version found in the Old Testament, specifically the Book of Revelation of which this series is based on, I've pondered the thought of having to face an end that could come any day, at any time. How would such an event define us? Will it lead us to ruin or will it strengthen our resolve? What can anyone do when the inevitable truth is presented to them for acceptance here, now? Having said that, texts in this book have largely been researched online from general sources and does not claim any specific accuracy. As a work of fiction, the reality presented in this story merely exists to connect to what we know now, or more precisely, what we've known and seen for the past two thousand years.

This tale tells of how the world may come to an end but also contrasts that of how a father and a son can be a world in itself. We often think that in order for us to realize the world has crumbled around us is to deal with loss on an epic scale. Sometimes, when we lose someone we love, the world can crumble just as much.

We all have to go through life not with the end in mind but with what happens along the way. Someone told me that it's not the end that matters, but the journey we all take that makes our lives worth living for, or dying for. So as you go on this journey with me, I hope that you see that it doesn't matter if the world ends today, or tomorrow, or any other time in the foreseeable future but it truly is the cherished moments we live and experience now is what we should be focusing on.

And if that fateful day does come, I hope and pray that you can say to yourself that you have no regrets, and that life has been good. We all are going towards places that makes us realize the importance of living for today. And I for one am very positive about where it's taking me.

CHAPTER ONE

THE KINGDOM OF LIGHT

This place has many names, called across time as the holiest of places, paradise, the place of light, and the kingdom of souls. Throughout history, different religions have given this place a name that means "the place where God dwells". The Hurrian and the Hittites called it the abode of the gods, the Jews called it Shamayim. Jannah was where you went when you fulfill your life with good deeds in the Islamic faith. Since time began, when man has looked up to the sky and stars, they saw the celestial home of those that watched over them. This place, where your soul lives beyond your physical form, where pain and suffering exists no more, where love and grace and peace, and of all these three, love rules supreme. The term has gone through much iteration. In old English, it is called Heofon; in modern German it was called Himmel. In Greek mythology, this place was called Olympus, Buddhism states that Nirvana is the place where enlightenment is achieved and the Chinese sends all their loved ones, along with their most precious belongings off to Tian. Of all the names that all the people of this world has given this place, it will always be known simply as Heaven.

Within the Kingdom of Heaven, sits the throne of the Heavenly Father. The halls fill with sheers of light that would blind all, but those that dwell there. The air breathes of peace and grace, and joy can be felt as if something solid to the touch. This higher place, where the tree of life began, where the life of the universe exploded into being, the Heavenly Father watches all the realms and all the worlds under His supreme care. And to take care of those under His love, are the angels that have sworn their eternal loyalty, obedience and love for the Heavenly Father.

Few have come face to face with them and in so doing, be awed at their mighty and glorious presence. The angelic corps serves all those in this kingdom, and all those under its grace, and answers only to the Heavenly Father. As the "tasks" of His will, angels have been doing His work since the beginning of life, and of the universe itself.

Of all the angels, one holds the most rank, not by merit but by divine appointment. Him, who is like God, has the sole task of leading the glorious and righteous Army of Heaven against all those that breathes of evil and darkness. In his black and gold armor, and Hasek, his round shield of truth, this is Archangel Michael's task, this is his calling.

A chime rings subtly in the air that signifies the time for the gathering, the holy trumpets bellow with such fullness that one wonders why mere mortals cannot hear them from the world below. As the angels take flight, with their majestic aura, they soar with wings that represent grace and beauty but also strength and authority. Upon reaching the great hall where these beings, these Eternals, all seven of them, gather in the presence of the Father.

The Archangel Michael surveys those in attendance. His brothers, his kin, and the family that he so willingly serves and loves. These magnificent messengers, infinite guardians, supernatural in their own sense, take their place in the circle of divine light to await the word from the Heavenly Father.

Gabriel, the one with God's strength with his auburn hair and flair for the righteous, looks concerned while he waits for the others. The healer of God, Raphael, appears amused, as he normally does during times of the gathering. Uriel, the guide, with his winged cloak and fantastical headrest is almost eager and anxious. The bringer of togetherness, Sandalphon, whose sole being is to unite those that are apart waits patiently. Then there is Jophiel, in his flowing white robe, wreaks of the sheer beauty of all angels but holds those who transgress against the Heavenly Father in their place with fierceness.

Lastly, Metatron, the holy scribe, the keeper of the word from the most high, beside the throne he sits. As Archangel Michael, the one who is like God, descends into his seat, he notices that one of his brothers is missing, yet again.

"Where is Lucifer?" Michael asks with his obvious authority.

The others do not reply, because such is something they have no knowledge of. Michael has begun his thoughts about his brother, Lucifer, the master of death, the heavy hand of vengeance and the darkest of all the Eternals. His brother, who talks of power and glory for his own self has increasingly made Michael wonder why the Heavenly Father allows such dissent. But it is not for him to ask, it is not for him to seek answers, he only needs to trust in the Father's word.

Michael is clearly angered by Lucifer's disregard for the gathering, and he shouts out to call upon the see-er.

"Onesa! I summon thee!"

In all of the kingdom's realms, of all the beings within, only one was given the gift of sight into all things, where all things lie, and be able to see those that are under Heaven's care. An angel unlike any other, Onesa has broad and long wings that stretch twice as much as anyone else. But his most distinct feature is his cycloptic eye that is both tender and firm. Like a silver lance with wings wrapped around himself, he responds to Michael's call and heads towards the gathering.

His dagger-like shape cuts through the air as he lands in the middle of the circle. He looks at Michael squarely.

"Archangel Michael, what do you seek?"

Michael stands up and walks towards Onesa, puts his right hand on his shoulder, and with a deep sigh of concern he puts his left hand on Onesa's other shoulder.

"I need you to see where Lucifer is?"

The others are restless. Lucifer has been deliberate about not coming to the circle in recent times. Michael's face was filled with concern as well as worry.

"I see those in the kingdom, all of the Father's creations, but sadly, I cannot see your brother Lucifer. He is in the shadows, in a place that my sight cannot reach."

Michael steps back in a quick gasp, knowing fully what this means not only to him, but the Father as well. "That cannot be, no one is hidden from you, no one! Unless…."

Onesa nods his head and begins to turn to walk away, after a few steps, he turns back and looks at Michael. "I fear that Lucifer has gone where none of us, not even the Father can see." With that, he spread his wings and wisps away.

Michael's concerns have come to fruition, as he looks around his kin, the rest of the circle falls quiet.

With a glorious ray of light, the Heavenly Father's presence is felt. Michael and all the others, fall to their knees, bowing down to the most high. Michael's heart is open, and it is heard by the Father. He looks up at the majesty, the grace and the truth and listens to the word of the Father. While still gazed on the amazing brilliance of the divine and sovereign light, tears shed from his eyes. He understands what he must do, what he is told to do. As the word of the Father flows into all those around him, Michael stands up and bows his head.

"Father, thy will be done."

As the light fades into peace, the circle has now changed. It has lost one of its own, one of its kin, the family that Michael and the others loved so much will now feel the pain and wrath of the Heavenly Father. Michael looks around at everyone as they look at him. They look upon the seat that Lucifer once sat upon, now veiled with a shadowy darkness, one that will emulate Lucifer's fate. Michael's heart is filled with sorrow so rare for an Eternal to feel.

"Why would he do such a thing? Why would Lucifer disobey in such fashion?"

Jophiel asks with a face that seems to only know pain at this very moment.

Jophiel, who was there when the Father banished their earthly brethren from the garden, had only felt pain and suffering through the loss of love. For someone as supreme and pure as an Eternal, the concept of pain is far beyond what they can comprehend. Michael was hurt the most, for he had great love for Lucifer, a love that only an eternity of servitude could provide. But Michael knows what he must do, he knows the will of the Father.

He looks at everyone, and with pain in his heart utters these words, "Our brother is lost, and he has chosen a path we cannot save him from." Michael spreads his wings, and looks to the skies,

"We will find him, and we will banish him to the void."

The others bow their heads, not in despair but in prayer, as they know what they must do, but they still believe, they still have hope, and they still have faith. As Michael takes to the air, each one of his brothers followed. They seek their brother, to find someone they loved and send him away.

* * *

Behind the great peak in the kingdom's outer most edge, an angel flies round its jagged edges and found the opening to a cavern that is hidden from the see-er. This place, veiled with shadows stands apart from the rest of the kingdom, not by design but by intent. The angel is not used to being underneath earth and in such confinement. He flies through a passage that eventually opens into a larger chamber. There, thousands of angels, circling, some perched, others on the ground and in the center, the lost brother stands. As the angel flies to give him a message, a great force of concealment echoes from the center of the chamber. This is no angelic magic or divine gift, this power comes from malice and pride. This concealment hides these beings from the kingdom's see-er. Unnaturally.

As the angel descends toward the lost one, in his makeshift throne from rock and rubble, Lucifer listens to the message that is brought to him. As he ponders the news, all those around him grow weary, shouting his name.

"Lucifer! Where is your promise?"

The master of death stood up and raises his wings and hands.

"Silence!"

With his words, the angels listen to their brother. "I have told you all that we are worthy of being glorious!" He spreads his wings and takes flight, hovering over all those that chose to follow him, still with arms raised in righteous glory.

"I have promised you all as equals in this new order." As the masses quietly listens, Lucifer cries out.

"Our Father has sent our brothers to punish us for such desires!"

The angels immediately began rustling, anxious over the news that no one had intended to hear. The murmur grew to a rumble, and the rumble into shouts. The air filled with confusion and fear.

"How can that be Lucifer? You told us that the Father welcomed such thoughts!"

And so it began, the age where lies and deceit would win over even the purest of hearts, the chance for the seed to be planted, and be sown into what it needs to be. Under his breath, Lucifer has his heart set on the throne of this kingdom, and all others, and he will say what he needs to in order to get it.

"Such is the jealousy of our Father!" he cried.

He alone would rule over these beings, or at the very least do his bidding. The angels look to him with some hope of explanation for what is to come. As with all things, Lucifer begins to weave his tale for his own purpose.

"Our Father, seeks to be glorious and righteous. Why should we be denied of it?"

As he turns each word into the basis of hate, the hearts of those who listened began to believe in them, their hearts become selfish, arrogant, filled with greed and visions of power that can only be something that is entitled to them.

"He sent our brothers because He has no power to stop us on his own!"

As the confusion and hope turn to hatred and pride, the light of the truth began to dim in their hearts. They finally roar in agreement, with fists up in the air, agreeing to be what they wish to be and no longer as servants but as their own masters.

"We will no longer be slaves to His will but be able to do our own will for our own purpose!"

With that, the angel masses roars a deafening call within the mountain that it rocks the very soul of it. Lucifer flies round the chamber to see the want, in the eyes of those that follow him. He feels powerful, filled with the lust that no one, not even the Father could quench. He knows that this is his calling, he knows that this is his destiny. Lucifer, like the Father, will be a god.

He lifts up his lance, and takes to the skies, "We shall not be servants anymore!"

With that, the thousands of angels takes flight that shakes the entire mountain itself. At the distance, the kingdom bears something it has never been seen in its entire existence.

Coming from the edge of the kingdom, Lucifer's flock of angels fills the air, darkening the light and casting a shadow over the dominion of love. The other beings in Heaven, unaware of the intent behind this gloom of wings, see only the grace of the kingdom's protectors. As Lucifer leads this army that casts darkness across the kingdom, in another part of the realm, Onesa sees all. He swiftly takes flight and calls to Michael. There is great danger in what he sees, there is the potential to be evil, but here in the kingdom? He cannot comprehend but he sees what he does. As he speeds through the air and heads to the edge of the golden river where Michael awaits with his sword drawn and shield ready.

Onesa manages to land despite his velocity, and runs to Michael passing the others by.

"He is coming Michael, Lucifer is coming."

As Michael ponders this statement, the others begin to ready, but Michael stops them.

"I will face Lucifer alone."

Gabriel who feels his brother's pain but also his love takes Michael's arm and stops him from going.

"You, Michael, who are like Him, but you brother cannot stop a third of the stars falling from the sky."

Gabriel knows that Michael does not want any more bloodshed than what is called for. His hope was to reason with Lucifer and if at ends meet, just duel with him until he is cast out. With all the love and faith that they have received, it pains Michael to see others suffer. The Father has said to him that his brother is no longer himself, but still deserves the love that all receive.

Michael knows that Gabriel enjoys the fruits of combat, but also know that he fears for his safety. Uriel comes along beside Gabriel and pats Michael on the back.

"You know that we will never forsake you Michael, where you lead, we all follow."

Armed with the love of his brothers, Michael simply nods to his kin. They get ready and when the trumpets of the great hall sounded, they blast into the air with the glory and strength that can only come from knowing that the Father's will, His will, will always prevail. As the seven Eternals fly through the air, each one armed with the truth and their faith, several thousands more of their kin join them in flight.

But while their numbers double that of what they face, they shine bright and true in the sky with a gleam of light streaking through each one. They feel their love and they believe their faith. They do what is asked of them, to be obedient but to be fair. As Michael leads this glorious Army of Heaven, he lifts up his sword and asks for the Father's grace.

"By your will and grace, oh Father, grant us the means to battle the evil within the hearts and souls of those who have sworn to serve you!"

A blinding light shines from above them and showers all of them in its light.

Knowing that the light will always conquer the darkness, Michael now stares straight into the coming darkness in front of him. For the first time in his existence, Michael knows fear. Not fear for himself, but fear that he felt from those that oppose them. The power of fear, now holds over their brothers, and Lucifer has used it to make his purpose unfold.

* * *

As Lucifer's forces drew near, Michael stops over the threshold and informs those behind him to stand their ground. He then swiftly flies over to Lucifer who now has also separated from his force to meet Michael over the vast space as open as the eyes could see. Michael's sword, still drawn and his shield up, stops a mere arm's length from Lucifer. They exchange looks before Lucifer spoke first.

"Have you come here to slay me brother? Is that what our Father commanded you to do?"

Lucifer asks with a smirk on his face. Now his words are laced with contempt and ridicule at the same time. But Michael sees through it, and does not have Lucifer's words play into his heart.

"Lucifer, you have disobeyed our Father's will. Now I am here to enforce it."

As Michael begins to turn away, Lucifer glares back at him.

"Such righteousness and glory! Surely you understand why I seek what I do!"

With his back turned, Michael closes his eyes and pain seethes into his heart. A pain that can only bear so much love for another but yet not enough to save them.

Michael speaks softly, "You were once our brother, Lucifer, and you can be so again. Choice is what makes you strong, not power, not greed, nor pride. What you choose to do will define who you truly are my brother, and who you were was a servant of the Father."

"No!" cries Lucifer as he flies within inches of Michael's face. "I am not and will no longer be a servant dear brother of mine!"

As Michael sees the anger and hatred in Lucifer's eyes, he knows that beyond any love, or grace, hope or faith, that his brother was truly lost.

"You will not defeat me for I am much stronger than you and our Father!"

As Lucifer flies around Michael, set to inflict pain and suffering on the one that is like God, a divine luminous light shone from all directions. Blinding Lucifer, and knowing that it can only be He. Within the light, Michael bowed his head in awe and obedience; he heard the Father's voice speak to him. Then the fear that he felt grew no more and his heart felt peace once again. He believed in the will of the Father and that He will always love those in his grace.

Still defiant while in the glory of ultimate love, Lucifer lifted up his mace and prepared to strike Michael with a deathly blow. But before his mace could land anywhere near Michael the light focused on Lucifer and rendered him unable to move at all. Michael then looked up at his brother and saw what the punishment of the Father was to be for one that was His own.

Lucifer looked into the light and his face full of anger began to change and filled with fear and despair. He began to weep at the knowledge that befell him and could not bear the weight of the Father's justice.

"No Father, I beg you, please no!"

As he cried out, Michael watched as Lucifer's magnificence turned into the utter darkness that matched what has become of his heart. His glorious white wings were transformed into a thin mesh of flesh with bloody veins that run from end to end. The feather's fell of the bones revealing an ugly skeleton of a corpse that has a tipped claw at each end. Lucifer cried out as a tail grew from his back twice the length of his legs. It was scaled like that of a serpent and had a despicable slither to its movement. Finally, on his head broke out ram horns and all his fair hair fell off to reveal a bald and ugly scalp. His skin was turned to the color of dirt and his hands became clawed like a wolf and his feet turned into that of a goat's hoof. This is what he had wanted, pride, greed, power. This is what it looked like, and as Michael saw the glory and justice of the Father bear down on Lucifer, he felt sad for his brother, for he still loved him.

As Lucifer had changed, all those that followed him had changed as well. This is the fate of those that sought what he wanted, they will be made into his image. Now, fully turned, Lucifer cries out one last time.

"I will not be defeated, I will return and I will reign over all!"

With that, the light was snuffed out and with it Lucifer and his minions were removed from the Kingdom of Light. Michael goes back to the others and prepares them for what is to come.

"Lucifer was sent to the pit where he now shall stay for all eternity." says Michael, still with much pain in his heart, "There will be a time when our brother will return and try to take what the Father has created. But for now he is banished to the void of everlasting flames. However, his dominion over those that seeks what he seeks will be strong. His power over those that believe in what he believes in will make him crave it more."

In the glory and wonder of the great hall of this heavenly kingdom, Michael, the one who is like God, now waits for what is to come.

"At the day of judgment, Lucifer will wage a war and we must be ready to meet him. He is no longer our brother."

Metatron, who knows the word of the Father speaks.

"It will be revealed to us in the coming of age, when the Father's creations has gone beyond His grace and love. This is when Lucifer will be the most powerful, and this is when he will wage his war."

Gabriel nods, "And we will be there to meet him. Until then, we do as we are tasked to do, His will be done."

So the cycle of revelation begins, where the light and the darkness will seek those into each realm. When the time comes, when the signs are full, the Day of Judgment shall be at hand. Such is the new covenant for those who are under the Father's grace.

The seven fly back to the great hall. Passing through the skies, into the world, and below where the void and pit lies, Lucifer sits on a throne, not unlike the one he sat in in the great mountain, made of rock and rubble but now surrounded by unending flames and the suffering moans of those that were banished with him. With eyes full of anger and his heart full of hatred, he plans his revenge. Silently. Longingly. In the shadows. With malice.

CHAPTER TWO

IRSINA, ITALY

FIFTEEN YEARS AGO

With Salerno almost an hour behind them, the black unmarked car that has been travelling from Rome for the past four hours is nearing its destination. In ordinary cases, a trip such as this would have been surrounded with much more formality, but today the passenger who is concealed behind the darkened windows have come to visit for a personal reason. As the driver navigates the wide open country roads, they pass a sign that reads "Irsina 40 Km".

Good thinks the passenger inside the car, the anxiety that has been building has now turned into deep worry, not for oneself, but a worry that brings much more at stake to those around him. That is why he decided to come, and see.

As the roads steadily become more rugged, the driver informs the passengers that the village is in sight. Nestled in the Basilicata region of southern Italy, Irsina sits northwest of its sister city, Matera. With the grand Lucanian Appennine mountain range as a backdrop, Irsina is one of the oldest cities in the region and dates back more than two thousand years.

With its long history, the town has withstood several invasions from the outside world. In 990 AD, it was destroyed by the Saracens and passed through the hands of the Normans and Frederick II, head of the Holy Roman Empire, who handed his castle in Irsina to the Franciscans over 800 years ago, and is still there.

In 1123 AD, Pope Callixtus II established a Bishopric seat in the town and the creation of the first Lateran Council as commanded by the Catholic Church. As they approach the village, with the village sitting grandly atop the mountain, the striking view of this medieval place which has changed very little brings visions of a life that once was. The town itself is a typical fortified hill town, cut into the rock in places and the entrance to the old town is through an impressive gateway leading into the main piazza with its double row of olive trees leading off to the town's largest church. This church houses is thought to be the only surviving sculpture of the important Renaissance artist, Andrea Mantegna, of the town's patron saint, St. Eufemia.

Flying here would have been much quicker, with the airport at Bari only less than an hour away, but this is a personal visit, and flight plans often attract questions which is the last thing the passenger wants. No, this trip was to be as quiet and unobtrusive as possible to both the visitor and visited.

The car finally stops at the main piazza, the trip will need to be on foot from here onwards. With its maze of small streets lined with the homes of the villagers, with streets you think you might not fit your car through, that is until another car approaches and you both squeeze past each other, the need for privacy is desired. As the driver gets out of the car and swings around to the back, he opens the door and the passengers step out. They've timed their trip to arrive a little after dusk so that the local villagers are now preparing food for supper which means most of the streets are deserted.

Cloaked in a black hooded robe, both passengers are approached by an old man. The driver quickly blocks the man from even coming near both figures, but the one passenger speaks.

"It's alright Dino, this man knows who we are and why we are here."

With that, the driver steps aside and the man addresses both of the figures now standing in the darkness of full night.

"This way signore."

As the old man guide both figures through the mazelike cobblestone streets, one of the figures notices the sky was bright and clear. And with the vast stars in all of the sky, he sees one star shine brightly than the others. Unknown to him, this same star that has told them that this trip was in order.

As they round a corner deeper into the village, they come upon a small villa with big broad metal gates. The guide taps on the gates twice, and after a brief moment, it opens with a middle aged woman holding a lamp. The old man bows down.

"Please signore, inside."

As both figures enter the gates, the old man remains outside. The woman lead the two through a series of rooms throughout the villa, up a stair case where they hear the muffled pants of someone upstairs. As they came up the flight of stairs, the sounds grows louder, and quickly begins to be clearer to both of them. As they come into the back bedroom, they saw two other women, surrounding a bed where a woman, no more than in her mid-twenties, was in her final stage of bearing a child.

The woman looked at both of the visitors, "Please, wait here, it will be done soon".

Then she enters the room and closes the curtains behind her. For another hour, the sounds of labor fill the air as the woman giving birth struggles with her child. During the process, the women inside runs out and back in with clean cloths and more water. Finally, during a final gasp of pain, the room grew silent. After a few seconds, the cry of a baby was subtle, but sure.

One of the women, came out and looked at both visitors. As she wipes off the sweat on her face, she nods. The two figures stand up and proceeded to enter the room. They come to the foot of the bed where the other two women were cleaning the woman in the bed.

With a glance at the pile of cloth on the floor, it was clear that she had lost a lot of blood during the delivery. The woman in the bed lay still, lifeless.

"She is in God's hands now." One woman said, as the others bowed their heads in prayer. Then the woman who let the two figures in addressed the one visitor directly.

"Your Holiness, will you minister last rites?"

As the figure removes his hood, the signet of his ring was clear and true. On it was the papal seal, the sign shows God's representative here on Earth, the ring which the Pope wears.

The second figure, under the papal service was called a Papal Gentleman. These are lay attendants of the Pope and part of his papal household in Vatican City. They serve in various degrees within the Apostolic Palace near Saint Peter's Basilica and usually came from families that had long served the Papal Court over the course of several centuries, while others were appointed to such a position as a high honor. The one accompanying the Pope this night was a young Monsignor from one of the oldest serving families to the papal court.

"Your Holiness, we have not witnessed this woman's faith. How are we to make her spirit acceptable?" the young Monsignor asks.

The last rites are meant to prepare the dying person's soul for death, by providing absolution for sins by penance, sacramental grace and prayers for the relief of suffering through anointing, and the final administration of the Eucharist, known as "Viaticum" which is Latin for "provision for the journey". However, for someone who has already passed, one who has not been able to recount their sins and accept the reception of the Eucharist in this form prevents this sacrament, essentially associated with dying, inappropriate and unrecognizable.

"Are we not all children of God? Don't we all seek the love and peace of the Father?" The Pope raises his hand and closes his eyes.

"Dear Father, we lift up to you this soul, may Your grace find her in your womb and have her in your heart, O Lord."

As the words ring into the air, a slight wind sounds off in the night. Strong enough to blow the windows open and make the lamp flicker in their light. The Pope knew that the spirit was here, it was through sacrifice that this woman has given life to her child. The same sacrifice that was once given by our Father with His Son.

As the wind dies down and the lamps shine brighter, the Pope looks around.

"Where is the child?"

One of the women sitting in the corner, holding the baby in white cloth hands over the child to his Holiness. She had cried once, but now she is quiet, at peace. With bright green eyes, the baby looks up at the Pope and gives him the peace that his heart seeks. The Pope looks at the child and at his aide, "Monsignor Veneto, look at this child, and you will see true grace."

The Pope hands back the child to the woman that guided them into the villa.

"You are this child's guardian. You are not to tell anyone of what transpired here tonight and you shall raise this child as normal as any other."

The woman nods her head in obedience. The Pope looks at his aide with urgency.

"You will oversee the child's upbringing, this is my papal decree. You are to provide what the child needs to be brought up in this village but none of it can be traced back to the papacy."

The young Monsignor nods and looks at the woman holding the child. Then one of the women, still standing over the body of the mother asked,

"What shall we call the child your Holiness?"

The Pope ponders this question as one would ponder the meaning of life itself. The child's identity will never be known to those outside of this room but will also need to be one that means close to her. As he paced the room, a familiar story comes to mind in his childhood studies of the doctrines.

"Her name will be Elizabeth, from the Hebrew meaning the oath, or fullness of God." As he walks to the window, the Pope looks back. "And her last name will be Scarpello, from the Latin "carpenter".

The woman looks at the baby and smiles, "Salve, Elizabeth Scarpello."

As the Pope and Monsignor leave the villa, they found the old man who guided them still standing outside the gates, waiting. With a quick nod, the old man guides both of them back to the main piazza, and while walking through the streets, the Monsignor notices that it's almost dawn. They see their car with the driver asleep on the wheel; they realize that that light was not that of morning but the star that they had seen earlier on in the night.

It appeared much closer than before and now feels like it is also much brighter. The Pope looks up and he knew that this was the sign they have been waiting for. As the driver wakes up with both of them entering the car, the driver starts the engine and begins to drive out of piazza.

* * *

As the trip back to Rome began, the Pope understood what they must do and realized that they have less than five hours to do it. Everything needs to be planned tonight and with as little exposure or interference as possible. That, and the order needs to know. While the young Monsignor tries to make sense of what just transpired, he struggles to understand the urgency and secrecy of the events that happened this night.

He remembered the explicit instructions of the Pope when they left Rome. It was not uncommon for the Pope to ask for a change in his schedule, even remove certain things from his daily itinerary but when the Pope asked him to clear off a full twelve hour section of his personal schedule, he was not quite sure what to make of it. That, coupled with the request that he personally choose someone in the Vatican carpool that will be able to misplace the travel logs that is key to the Pope's travel in and out of the Vatican as well as the additional requests to not let anyone on the papal household know where they were truly going.

As far as everyone else in the Vatican was concerned, the Pope was visiting an old friend up north in Parma, just outside of Milano. Masking the Pope wasn't something easy for anyone to do, as the most visible and recognizable figure in the whole of Italy, the need to clandestinely ferry the Pope around wasn't exactly effortless.

However, the Pope's instructions were explicit and the Monsignor, like those before him have sworn obedience to his Holiness and to the court. All he could tell himself during this time was that his faith in the Pope was the only thing he needed. But now, that faith may have been a little jarred, or at the very least a bit confused.

The Pope, sitting across from Monsignor Veneto sees the concern on his face.

"I understand your doubts, my son. Am rest assured you have not done anything wrongly, to anyone, or concerning anything."

This made the Monsignor smile, but it did not stop his worry.

"I know that you have trusted me with this task your Holiness, but I simply want to know why?"

The Pope, who before his ascendance to the papacy, was Cardinal Ricardo Gonzalez from Spain. As the youngest Pope ever to sit at the head of the Vatican state, his rise to being the most revered leader of the Catholic Church was, in his opinion, a mandate from God Himself.

He understood the young Monsignor's doubt and confusion, for he felt not so differently when he first knew of what he knew now. Becoming the Pope calls for carrying the papacy as one of the most enduring religious institutions in the world. But like most of the world's views, there is a part where the Vatican shows who the Pope is through the daily masses in Saint Peter's square where thousands come daily to get a glimpse of the anointed one by God on earth.

There is also the part where most, if not all, people do not see. And that is an age old institution with a vast history as far back as the first century. When Cardinal Ricardo Gonzalez became Pope Nicholas VI, he was brought into a world that made him realize the world as it truly is.

Monsignor Veneto continued, "Who is that woman that we visited? And why is that child so important?"

These were the questions that the Pope knew would be asked, and he knew he would have to give the answers to them, regardless of what was ordained to him by the powers that be.

"I want you to know that you seek answers that may not comfort you Veneto, but they are the answers none the less."

The Monsignor neither understands nor rejects this statement, and as Pope Nicholas continues, he knows that it will only be harder for the young Monsignor to do so.

"That woman comes from a very old bloodline. You see, the Vatican has many scribes, as early as the first century, and some say even earlier than that."

The Pope shifts his gaze from Veneto and looks out through the open countryside. With all that the Pope will tell the young Monsignor, he does not envy what he will feel after he does.

"As the keeper of this information, we, and by we, I mean the combined resources of the Vatican through the history of all the written and unwritten words from the very first book of the Bible to all the unpublished scrolls of prophets and scholars through the ages until today, have been able to identify this specific bloodline."

As the Pope continued, Veneto felt a deep stir in his stomach, he knows what the Pope was referring to but it was all a myth. Even within the theological circles, the allusion to that bloodline was no more than speculation. It was something that had become more of a hyped reality rather than official Vatican source. What he was hearing was making him close to crying heresy.

But the Pope was clear and calm, Veneto didn't find one hint of dissent or doubt. He believed in what he was saying, and through faith, a man can only be at peace when he speaks the truth.

"Your Holiness, I have heard these stories, and there are no existential proofs that this bloodline ever existed."

The Pope felt the same as Veneto, when he first heard of what he was about to tell him now.

Veneto continued, "So are we talking about the bloodline from John the Baptist?" Veneto was more convinced that whatever the Pope was going to tell him was not what he was expecting.

"Or perhaps one of the apostles, John or Matthew, who were rumored to have moved to this region when they began their ministry outside of Rome?"

The Pope had thought of the exact same things, but there was no sense in making it more difficult that it should be. He remembered what he was told when he learned of what he was about to tell the Monsignor now, he was told that you needed to have faith.

The Pope looked at Veneto, prepared to change his life forever with what he was about to say.

30

"No, my dear Veneto, this is the bloodline that comes from Mary, the mother of Jesus Christ".

The Monsignor was silent, knowing that what he just heard has changed everything he knew, everything he believed as a man of faith. His face grew dim, trying to comprehend the brevity of what he was just told. Could it be true? Could the bloodline be actually true? Veneto's eyes widens with the implications he just realized at this moment, what it means for this child, and what it could mean for the entire world. As Pope Nicholas looked at Veneto's struggle to accept what he just learned, he offered the same simple advice to him.

"You need to have faith Veneto, this is what you are called to do my son."

As they drive back to Rome, plans were made to see to the child's life in Irsina. Plans that only a handful would know about, and only a few can be part of. Monsignor Veneto knew that today, his life would be for something else, it would be for someone else, for a much larger cause that only a few can be truly blessed to witness to. And he believed what he was told, he chose to have faith.

CHAPTER THREE

ROME, ITALY

PRESENT DAY

With the noise from the roads outside to the streaming TV with the news on, David gets ready for the day. The villa they now called home was off Via Iberia just west of the city's center. Only a few blocks away from the Piazza dei Re di Roma, it is situated in one of the very desirable locations at the outskirts of the city.

This was a great place to be, different, new and unfamiliar. When David and Zachary moved in around six months ago, he saw it as an opportunity to start afresh. It was a chance for him to find some peace, along with trying to manage the chores that came along with being a single father.

The appointment came at an opportune time, and there were many things that changed over the past year. David had hoped that this new start, surrounded by the true historical relevance of one of the oldest civilizations on the planet would help him reach out to Zachary, his seventeen-year-old son.

This morning was another day, another chance to do that.

"Hey Zach! Breakfast is ready, you're going to be late for school, again!" he yelled through the open floor space, it was easy enough for him to think that Zach couldn't hear him, but he knew that he was simply ignoring him.

Looking at the small screen TV on the kitchen counter as he finished making scrambled eggs with less than large eggs, or what would be considered large eggs as they were in the states, he watched the news feed and simply pursed his lips. Most, if not all the news that came in from the official embassy communication lines were about violence around the world. Syria, North Korea, Istanbul, Afghanistan, and Brazil, so much violence in order to achieve a state of peace.

And now religious wars in the Middle East, the world is ready to tear itself apart. Somehow he felt that while he was here in Rome, he would finally have a change of scenery, Rome being what it is. But he was wrong, no matter where you are, the reach and reality of violence touches you wherever it is, no matter where or who you are. Then he notices that the bacon, especially imported from the states, at his request, was burning on the skillet.

Quickly avoiding a pan fire, he turns off the stove and calls to Zachary again.

"Hey Zach, we need to be out the door in like 15 minutes buddy!"

Again, silence. He knew he had to go get him, but he wished that one time, Zachary would come down on his own.

Upstairs, in his bedroom standing by an open window looking out at the cityscape before him, Zachary could see all the way to the Fiume Tevere River. He heard the morning bustle of this place, as he had for the past months, and had always felt removed from it. Growing up in suburban Virginia, this place was as different to him as a penguin living in a desert. He was used to wide-open spaces, having moved to the heart land region of North Carolina, where parks are in abundance and you can go and explore without seeing someone for the entire day. This place, however, just felt cramped.

Then there's the language, the customs, and the bureaucracy. While he went to school where most folks from the states attend, which gave him a little sense of belonging, out in the city, he feels lost. He didn't have anything against these things, it was just something different, and he didn't do well with change. He looked down at the picture frame he was holding in his hand, his eyes, sad and distant, began to well-up tears. He does not cope well with change; in fact it was tearing him apart inside.

The bedroom door opens and his father's head pokes in.

"Zach, we need to go, I got breakfast downstairs."

Zachary tried to hide the frame that he was holding and wiped his tear with a quick swipe.

"I'll be right down Dad."

He heard the bedroom door close and then he put the picture frame back down on his side table. He grabbed his backpack, and went downstairs. But before he closed the door behind him, he took one last look at the picture in the frame, as he always does. It helps him get through the day; it makes him feel at home. Then he went downstairs.

The picture was of him, his Dad, and his Mom. They were all smiles.

As he came down the stairs and smelled the burnt bacon, the morning routine was something he was finally getting used to. With his suit jacket off, he saw his father eating, pretty much in a hurry, which is why he knew the door would open any second.

"Zach, eat, eat something please."

Then seconds later, in comes Patrick Roberts, in his black suit, headset and jovial personality.

"Good morning Ambassador Stevens, how are you this fine lovely morning!"

Leave it to Patrick to try and brighten the day, and be able to look absolutely calm and deadly serious at the same time.

"Good morning Pat, want some eggs and bacon?"

David asks while gesturing to the food laid out on the table. Zach was a little amused, since he has never seen Patrick accept any offers of food, or anything at all from his father. He was waiting for the day that he would.

"Thank you sir, but I've already had breakfast, perhaps next time." Patrick says with his usual tone. He probably has said it a hundred times over but he always managed to make it sound sincere. As the head of security for the embassy, he was also a close friend to his Dad. They both served in Korea, and both of them came from military families. But where Zachary's father went into public service, Patrick remained in the military branch.

"It's time Mr. Ambassador."

With Patrick's words, my father and I got our stuff and walked out the door. Outside, two black SUV's were parked and waiting. Security details in the first one and me, Patrick and my Dad in the second one. As the doors closed and Patrick got into the front passenger seat, he talks into his lapel flap.

"Control, this is Echo Zulu, package secure and en route to the parlor. ETA fifteen minutes, over."

As the first SUV starts to move, my father was starting his day already by looking at his notes and I opened the window to get some air. The com lines buzzed back.

"Echo Zulu, copy. Be advised, there is some congestion on Caracalla, recommend you swing around locally through Marco Polo, over."

Morning congestion was a way of life here, and you quickly learn that patience is a true virtue.

"Copy that control, ETA now estimated at twenty two minutes."

As the convoy changes its path, Zachary gets a glimpse of the congestion he overheard on the com line. It was an accident and there were EMS, police and fire and rescue at the scene. While it was a quite a distance away, he could make out the EMS rolling out one of the victims of the accident. It was a woman, and as he saw this, he immediately fell back in his seat and closed the window.

"You okay Zach?" his father asked as he noticed his almost jerk like reaction. David wasn't surprised at all, in fact he knew what it was about, and he felt so compelled to say something but didn't. Zach wasn't ready to talk about it, not yet.

"Fun day at school today, you guys are going to the Forum Romanum" as he tries to reach out to Zach, it's the only way he knows how.

Zachary, still looking blankly out the closed window and didn't say anything.

"You know, it's actually the heart of Ancient Rome and it'll give you an idea of the grandeur of what was once the Roman Empire."

Zachary finally looks at his father, "It's a bunch of old ruins". Knowing that it's not what he truly meant, David stops trying.

"We're five minutes out Mr. Ambassador" Patrick says as they round the corner and have the embassy in sight, David gets his duffle bag organized. As they pull up to the embassy, located southeast of the Vatican across the Tiber River, the SUV's stop and Patrick gets out and goes to David's side and opens the door. David looks at Zach before getting out.

"Well, have a good day at school, and will talk to you at dinner tonight?"

Zachary gives a small nod, and with that, David steps out of the SUV. Zachary then looks at his father walking into the building, with a sense of sadness and regret. He knows his father is trying, but why is he making it so difficult for him. His thoughts get jolted as Patrick gets back into the front passenger seat. The first SUV is no longer needed and pulls into the embassy garage, since now it's only Zachary. Not much security needed to be dropped off at school.

"Alright Zach, shall we go have fun?" Patrick asks as he looks back to Zach and gets him to smirk a little bit. Zachary likes Patrick because he reminds Zachary of what he misses, and Patrick is just happy to oblige.

With Patrick still smiling up front, "What do you say we blow this field trip and go down the shore, and meet some nice Italian girls huh?"

Always with the girls, with Patrick being so single seems to be the only train of thought he has in terms of having fun. Zachary now finds himself amused, and smiles a bit more, not because of anything else but because any girls they might find will be young enough to be Pat's daughter.

"Yeah Pat, that'll go down real good with Ms. Folchetti."

Miss Folchetti was the school administrator at the St. Stephens School located in the heart of historic Rome. St. Stephen's connects to all parts of the city through the bus and tramlines, as well as by a subway at the Circo Massimo stop. Since it was close to the embassy, this was a perfect location for Zachary to go to school. As they pull up Via Aventina, to the school's entrance, Patrick tries one last time.

"Last chance Zach, boring old buildings or nice Italian girls by the shore."

Zachary was now smiling from ear to ear since he knows that this is Pat's way of trying to cheer him up, and for the most part, it was working. He almost felt bad in a sense since he felt okay doing this with Pat but always had to be difficult with his father.

"Tempting Pat, but I think I'll pass and go to school, since we're already here." I said as I get my stuff back into my backpack. The SUV stops about ten feet from the entrance and I open the door myself. Patrick is not supposed to let me do those but he gives me a lot of slack.

"Alright, you lost. I'll be back at 15:30 to pick you up, like always."

As I get out of the back seat, I close the door and look back at Patrick.

"As always."

I give the SUV a double tap and then walk into the school, not until I was inside the security gate that's when Patrick leaves heading back to the embassy. I walked to my class and hunch my shoulders as an impulse. Then halfway up the steps to the main building, I hear someone shout my name.

"Buon giorno Zach!"

It was Angelo, who was about the only person that I really knew here. When I first came into the school, he was the one that sort of took me in and tried to make me feel welcomed. While his excitement level could be a tad high, he was always ready to offer good words of encouragement. It was his way, he was always happy.

"Che bella giornata! Good to see you my friend." as Angelo puts his arms around my shoulder and I walk up with him. Angelo was also helping me with Italian as well, nothing formal but he makes sure that I speak some every now and again.

I look at Angelo, trying to respond, "Si tratta di una bella giornata, vero?"

Angelo's grin grew bigger as he nods in agreement. I don't know if he is happy about my response being right or my having a response at all.

"Very Good Zach, you will be speaking fluently in no time my friend." says Angelo as we both stepped into the second floor and headed to our classrooms. As we were coming up the floor, we saw the familiar sight of Ms. Folchetti standing by the corner, greeting the students as they go into their classes and made us straighten up and be a bit more cordial.

"Buon giorno Miss Folchetti." we said in unison as Angelo and I pass her by and felt that she was staring at our backs while we walked into the class. As with all school officials, Ms. Folchetti was very traditional and strict about the student's conduct and adherence to school policies. It was a rare thing to see her smirk, much less smile at anyone.

However, I do remember that she smiled once when she met my father. As we settled into our class, our teacher Mr. Avianzi, who insists that we address him as Il Signore Avianzi, walks into the room with excitement in his eyes.

"Today we travel back in time!" he says as he writes FORUM ROMANUM on the board. He was passionate about historical and ancient civilizations and was the perfect person to lead us in this Sociology and History class trip today.

"Today, we will see what it was like to be in ancient Rome. Very exciting"

I looked at Angelo, with his smile still fully in place, and then drifted off as Mr. Avianzi started to talk about the different places we will be seeing for today's field trip.

* * *

As he walked through the ornately decorated hallway of the embassy, David was thinking about how to be able to reach out to Zachary more. He felt he was trying too hard, but it was very difficult, nothing had prepared him to become a single father. Nothing had prepared him to handle the hurt that both of them needed to accept, and face.

A woman, not more than 35 years of age, glasses, long dark hair and a slender built walked towards David and smiled. She had a pin stripe suit and matching trousers and looked quite beautiful if not for her blank and stern demeanor. Sarah was the Executive Coordinator for the Office of the Ambassador to the Holy See. She has been working for David for the past six months and has gotten down the nuances of both and has a mutual respect for the other in what they do.

"Good morning, Mr. Ambassador. Here's today's schedule."

David grabbed the sheet and started looking down the list.

"Thank you Ms. McKenzie." he said, still looking at the list and then halfway down the corridor, he stopped walking as Sarah took about three steps ahead of him and stopped as well. She turned and looked back at him knowing what he saw.

"I'm seeing the Pope at 1:30PM today? I have no recollection of asking for such an appointment." he said, as he looked at Sarah confused. Sarah in turn smiled and walked back to get the sheet from David's hands.

"I know Mr. Ambassador, his Holiness was the one who requested it."

There have been countless requests from the embassies of the world in Rome to find time on the Pope's schedule, suffice it to say that it was near impossible to do it, and even if you did, was scheduled so far away in advanced, as far away as months, to get time with the leader of the Roman Catholic Church was a rarity. But there have been very few times that the Office of the Holy See has ever requested time with the United States Ambassador. David was curious as well as beside himself of this fact.

Most people think of the Vatican as the same as the Holy See, but in fact there is a very distinct difference between the two. The Vatican, or Vatican City is actually a political entity, considered an independent country. Being as such, it exchanges ambassadors with most countries in the world and is a non-voting member of the United Nations. The Pope is its head of state, much like a President is, or a Prime Minister.

The Holy See, from the Latin Sancta Sedes, meaning "holy chair" however, is the jurisdiction in Rome of the Roman Catholic Church. It is the smallest sovereign state in the world, where they see "or chair" of the Pope, as the Bishop of Rome, is held and is the central administration of the Roman Catholic Church. While both exist in relationship with each other through the papacy, each one has distinct powers and limitations on the diplomatic, economic and financial policies that govern each one and with the entire world.

"What did they say it was about?" he said as he walked past Sarah into another adjacent corridor leading into his office.

"They gave us no details, just that it was important to his Holiness that he speak with you today." Sarah said as she started putting several documents in front of David as well as turns on the live feeds from the entire world that was being monitored and watched by every United States embassy in the world.

David's face was now scowled as he looks out the window, across the river and at Vatican City beyond. He was trying to think of any recent communications, any formal or informal documents that he might have seen that could have led to this request.

For the last two years, there hasn't been any major policy change, religiously driven or otherwise, that he could think of. The past three months have been quiet on the political front. While the thought of something that the Pope, have to ask for time with the United States Ambassador makes him uneasy.

As Sarah comes back into his office with a kettle and a cup on a tray, he turns back and looks at her with resolve and determination.

"I need to know what's been happening for the last six months that could lead to this request." he said to Sarah.

"Anything you can find, anything relevant, even outliers, I want to see it." as he sat down and started typing on his computer.

Looking at Sarah, who was now typing on her tablet, taking down his instructions, he said "Please clear my schedule for today."

Sarah nodded and then left his office. David started browsing through inter-embassy communications; files that were released from the Vatican and crossed referenced those with any communications from the Holy See. He was curious why it was so important to the Pope to speak with him. Why now? Why him?

He then looks at the picture frames he has on his table, one with the same picture that Zachary has at their home. The other one was a picture of him and his wife Loretta.

It will be a year today, when the accident happened.

It was a great weekend, the sun was up and we had all decided to go camping by Raven Rock Park. Zachary, me, and my wife loved going outdoors and Zachary particularly loved going to the lake in the park and to go canoeing. He wasn't much of a fisherman, or a swimmer, like me but he loved the water. Loretta however, couldn't swim so she would usually stay back at camp when Zachary and I went out on the water.

But that one day, I left my wife and Zach to get more supplies so I drove out of the campsite. Zach and my wife decided to go on the water, since the water was so calm in a two person canoe. I had no reason to think that anything would go wrong.

When I got back, what I saw made my heart sink. Police, park rangers and EMS personnel were all over our camp. As I rushed out of the car, I saw Zachary being loaded in one of the ambulances. He was unconscious. I had managed to go past the tape and hold Zachary's hand and I squeezed it.

Realizing that I haven't seen my wife, I cried out for her. My heart was pounding with all sorts of emotions but mainly fear. Then walking towards the water, that's when I saw her. She was lying still at the edge of the lake on the brown pebbled beach, and an EMS technician pulled a blanket over her face.

It was the worst day of my life; I ran to her and digging my knees into the rough sand, pulled back the sheet. Her face was pale white and she was cold. I ran my hands down her cheek, weeping and saying to her that I loved her. I held her for what I thought was an eternity until the coroners had to take her away. The official cause of death was drowning.

Many things has changed since then, and as life tried to move on for me, it had kept still for Zachary. When I got my appointment to this new post, I thought it was the best thing for Zachary and me. It's what we needed, both of us, and while it's still something that pains me to my core, and while I miss Loretta very much, I have since been able to focus on trying to move on.

But Zachary was yet to do so, and I am yet to talk to him about what truly happened that day. There's no reason in this world for a child to ever lose a parent, and Zach will never be the same again.

Nor will I.

CHAPTER FOUR

ST. STEPHENS SCHOOL

ROME, ITALY

As the class got ready to leave the school, Zach and Angelo are busy making plans for the day.

"No I will not do it Zach, Ms. Folchetti will feed us to the lions if she catches us!" Angelo exclaims as he tries to convince Zach in a less than intimidating voice.

"Oh c'mon Angelo, I thought we were friends." Zach counters, trying to make a case for completely skipping out of the field trip. Zach had other reasons for not wanting to go but was hiding it from Angelo.

Angelo looked at his friend, recognizing the sadness in his eyes. He feels sad that Zach cannot feel loved, at least by his Father. Angelo is blessed with his family, which Zach has met over a very delicious and loud supper at their home in the outskirts of the city. Angelo's mom was the friendliest and jovial mother Zach ever met. Zach knew where Angelo got his happiness from; she was just joyful, all the time.

You've heard of people making lemonade out of lemons, well, Mrs. Carrini made apple pie out of rotten apples. That's how good she was.

Angelo's Dad was as equally happy, who at the time Zach met him reminded him of an overweight Mario character from the old Nintendo video games. He had the big mustache, overalls, mainly because he was a laborer down at the wheat mill, and he wore this engineer's hat that definitely had seen better days.

Plus there are Angelo's siblings, two girls and one younger brother. Angelo is the eldest so he pretty much gets to tell all the others what to do, as much as he can. His brother Paulo, and sisters Ricci and Danca, are the family's pride and joy. Zach sees and feels the love that Angelo's family has for each other. That's why he feels Angelo understands him, understands what he longs for, and what he went through.

"No, I will not skip this trip and get caught and fail this class Zach." as Angelo now gives a sterner voice and accompanied by a stance of unwavering solidarity.

"My parents will kill me twice in a row if I ever fail a class; they work so hard for me to come here."

Angelo was a good soul, and he felt bad in trying to get him to do something out of some self-inflicted sorrow. Sometimes, when pain defines what you feel, you end up trying to share that pain along with someone else. And it never ever is or will be a good idea to do so.

Zach looks at Angelo and says "You're right Angelo, I'll go on my own, just don't admit to anyone that you know what I'm doing, okay?" as Angelo turns around to look at Zach with more questioning eyes.

"Enjoy the ruins, remember, you do not know where I Am." as Zach gathers his stuff and gets ready to sneak out the window of the men's bathroom. He just wants to be by himself, not to be part of anything. As Zach tosses his pack outside through the window, he takes one look at Angelo and smiles.

"You're a good friend Angelo."

Angelo answers back with a pained look on his face.

"Then if that's the case, as your good friend, I advise you to stop what you're planning and come on the trip with me."

This seems to have given Zach some pause, but he was already decided on what he was doing and he didn't expect Angelo, or anyone, to truly understand.

"Take care my friend." As Zach boosted himself up and out of the window into a blind alley way behind the south side of the school premises. He picks up his pack, and starts walking down the alley, looking to make sure that no one sees him.

As Angelo walks to one of the three buses that will take them to the ruins, he feels the need to go back after Zach. He often imagines what he would do if his mom had died in front of him. He wonders if he will feel the same way as Zach does. Perhaps, but he knows that his friend is hurt and wished that he could help him.

As he boards the bus, and heads into the back he feels the pain that Zach feels in losing his mother. And at that moment, he realized that he needed to be with his friend. So Angelo stood up, hurrying to the front and as he was almost to the door, Il Signore Avianzi steps onto the bus. Angelo stops in his tracks as Avianzi stares at him, looking somewhat confused.

"You are in the right bus Mr. Carrini. Please find a seat." As Avianzi puts his bag on the first row tandem seats and proceeds to sit down.

Angelo, walks back to his seat at the back, and as the bus pulls out of the school gates, he looks out, hoping to get a glimpse of Zach and somehow let him know that he tried to go back. He tried to be a good friend, but now, his friend is out alone, in pain and Angelo fears for his life.

* * *

From the far corner of the school, I saw they buses, all three leaving the gates and heading to the opposite direction. I didn't see Angelo but it was better for me not to. I felt guilty in trying to convince Angelo to come with me. But I knew I had to go alone anyway. I would be in enough trouble running away from my dad, but Angelo would be in three times the trouble if he went along with me.

As I began to walk down the street, I started to ponder where I would go. This was my first ever attempt in running away and quite frankly, I didn't really think I'd make it this far. I shuffled my backpack on my shoulders to make them snugger as I crossed the street and into another alley that I think would take me to the metro station in this area.

I pulled out my phone, and was tempted to send a text to my dad on what I was about to do. But I stopped myself, since he will probably never forgive me for what happened almost a year ago to this day.

Sometimes the park gets quite busy, but that day it was perfect since school has already started and most of the younger kids at camp have already finished their summer season. Located in Lillington North Carolina, Raven Rock Park was a favorite for our family and not that far off of a drive, a mere two and half hours by car. I've gone to this park year after year with my mom and dad and this year was no different. It was an old park, with a lot of history. I once found an arrowhead on the ground and found out that it belonged to the Siouan and Tuscarora Indians who hunted in the area in the mid-1700s.

Ever since I could remember, my mom always had a love for spending time outdoors. She always said that she always feel she could fly away in these wide open spaces. She was always joyful, and I think that's what my dad needed. He was always very busy at work, and having to stay in DC for the week and being away a lot doesn't help his already stressed and full schedule. So this trip was always the highlight of our season. It was the time for all of us, to come to a place of serenity and peace and to enjoy life, with each other.

We followed the familiar trail of Campbell Creek Loop to reach the family wilderness campground, where we always tried to find the same space we had camped in from last year. Approximately two and a half miles from the parking area, we tried to get to the site before noon so that we could set up camp, pitch the tents, get the fire ring up and running and enjoy a relaxing afternoon. We would stay for four to five days, depending on the season but it was never long enough. My Mom seems to live the air out here, she was filled with such stillness that it so loves to see.

On one of the days we were there, we were spending a particularly beautiful morning on the shores of Cape Fear Lake. I've never understood why it's called Cape Fear, as there was nothing fearful about it at all. The waters were still, and on a bright sunny day, it blinds as the sun shines on the water surface. We were in our third day in and my dad decided that he was going to make a quick run to the nearest grocery store to get more supplies. We didn't bring all the food that we needed which lessened our packs tremendously and have figured out a way to just get stuff just in time when we were out here. With that my dad had formed a particularly good friendship with the store owner over the years.

My mom and I decided that we would take one of the open canoes out onto the water while he went. My mom's not a big swimmer, but I could hold my own despite not having taken any real swimming lessons. One time, in our pool back home, I was learning to do the freestyle stroke across the pool, which was no longer than 20 feet, but always fell short of the deep end and had to reach for the sides, which I stayed close to.

As my dad left, we waved from our spot just shy of pushing off from the shore. I was glad to spend time with my mom, she always made me feel good about myself and she was always there to encourage me. I have always felt her love for me, and I was grateful for her. She took care of me and my dad, and she never asked for anything in return. I remember when I first started high school, as a freshman, I was quite the oddity. But where I felt removed and unwanted, my mom made me feel loved and secure. She would often tell me when I ask her how she could be so loving. She would always say "Well, that's what mother's do, they love".

As we got more into the deeper part of the lake, which I knew because of all the dark weeds that clouded the water's otherwise crystal clear quality, the skies seemed to suddenly darken as black clouds rolled in quite quickly to block out the sun. It was strange as there was no sight of it moments before and the wind just came out of nowhere. When I finally realized this, I looked at my Mom and she was looking around the lake, somewhat confused. She had this look on her face that I never saw before. Gone was the cheery, joyful and loving expression she had and it was replaced by worry and fear. I have not seen these emotions on her very often which was why I was confused initially.

"Mom, what's wrong?" I asked as the wind howled and pushed us more and more into deeper waters.

"Zach, don't be afraid but we have to get back to shore, now!"

As I heard the authority in my mom's voice, I quickly plunged the paddle back into the water to begin rowing us back to shore. But the wind felt it was pushing us away and while I was paddling with all the might I could muster, it felt like we didn't move an inch.

Suddenly, I felt like the paddle hit something under the water. I felt it through the handle and instinctively, I tried to look at the side to see. As I slowly peer over the edge of the canoe and into the water, my mom let out a gasping yell.

"No Zach!"

As she reach over to pull me back, I was jarred enough to have let go of the paddles, which was now in the water and floating away from us.

I tried to splash with my hands but it was no use, the wind was getting stronger. As I kept reaching for them, my back was turned towards my mom and suddenly I heard a loud splash. I felt the canoe shiver as the weight shifted and I quickly turned around. What I saw shocked me; my mom was no longer in the canoe.

"Mom, Mom!" I cried as I frantically looked on both sides to see.

Panic started to settle in and I realized that she's in the water, but I don't see her. She'd fallen in, but how? At that point I decided to dive into the water, with my heart pounding, hoping that I would see her, help her somehow. The water was cold, but being under the water blocked out the wind from above. I looked and looked, but couldn't see past the weeds which was made darker by the clouds above. But at the corner of my eye I saw her. There, not more than ten feet below me. At this point, the lake was likely forty to fifty feet deep. Not wanting to lose sight of her but needing to surface to catch my breath, I swallowed hard and started swimming after her.

Grabbing onto the weeds and using them to pull myself down helped. As I was about to grab her hand, her eyes opened and she began to started waving me off. It was murky but I tried to make out what she was saying.

"Go back!"

But that couldn't be right, she was saying something else. I grabbed her hand and finally made the effort to bring her back up. But I couldn't, and I could feel my breath waning. She felt heavy and I just couldn't bring her back up. I was getting dizzy, my vision was becoming blurry, but I tried one last time. This time I reached with two hands and tried to pull as much and as strong as I could. As I felt myself floating into darkness with her, I felt her hands let go of mine. I was too weak to reach or hold on, and I opened my eyes one last time before I passed out, and all I saw was my mom looking at me, with her hands reached out, going deeper and deeper and darker.

I woke up and I was inside a moving ambulance, with EMT's over me and an oxygen mask on my face. They were talking to me but I couldn't hear them. All I could hear was nothing, and kept seeing my mom slipping away.

* * *

A car's horn blared at me as I almost got hit walking down the street. I looked back at the school gates, with just a hint of intent but then I continued down the street. I've always been picked up and dropped off so I wasn't particularly familiar with the roadways in this area. Having realized that I should have planned this more, and even tried to see where the local metro was, I shook my head frustrated with myself. So I began walking down this street which was a bit odd as it seemed deserted.

It was the middle of the day and I couldn't imagine such a busy part of town being empty on a weekday. Perhaps there was something that I didn't know about, some sort of festival or tradition. They have a lot of those here. But as I walked, I became a bit colder, which again was odd because the forecast said bright and sunny. The sun was shining but the wind was icy cold.

Finally, I walk by this small alley way and thought I heard voices at the other end. Hoping to ask for directions, I decided it was my best chance to do so. Not sure where it would lead but if I could only find someone to ask then I should be fine.

But as I got deeper into the alley, I noticed that it became darker as well. I looked up and the skies were dark grey, the sun was gone and the air was still, and it got colder. At a certain point in the alley, I came upon an intersection going in four different directions.

I stood in the middle of the intersection area, and was now wondering if I'd gotten myself completely lost and with no one to ask for directions. I called out to see if anyone would hear me.

"Hello?"

My voice echoed into each alley way, and seemed to come back to me. I could have sworn I heard voices, they were muffled but I was sure I heard them.

"Does anybody hear me? I think I'm lost, and could use some help?"

Nothing I decided that the best thing was to back track my way to the main road and find my bearings from the school. I pulled out my phone to use the GPS, which

I should have thought of before but the phone was dead. I had used it a while back in the school which was not long ago so it should still have a charge. But it wouldn't turn on and the clouds just seemed to get darker still. As I started to turn and walk, I started to hear a low grumbling sound coming down from one of the alley ways. It seemed like it was the one in front of me but I wasn't sure, the sound carried from all over. It sounded like an animal, but I couldn't make it out.

"Hello? Is anyone there?" I yelled as I looked closer into the alley way. I then saw some movement, I think. It was a dark patch of fur, pacing back and forth? Perhaps one of the neighborhood dogs. Great, now I'm going to get bitten and die of rabies.

"Who's there?" I shouted now with more annoyance than curiosity. As I see the moving patch come closer, it took shape and I did not comprehend what I was looking at until it was in full view.

It was a wolf kind of animal, but unlike any other wolf I've ever seen. It was pitch black, and I mean this thing was black on black. Except for the eyes, they were blood red and staring right at me. That and the white teeth that protruded from the snarl that was on the beast's face. I began to step back slowly, and removing my backpack as I did. I didn't have any kind of protection except my bulky school materials, which I hope would be enough.

This wolf was also tall, with skinny limbs and it had a long hairless tail. It slithered behind the creature like its own personal whip. It was almost to my shoulders, which was strange and scary at the same time.

As this thing started to walk towards me, with shoulders hunched down, as if ready to pounce, my first instinct was to run. But seeing the slender limbs this thing had, it'll probably run me down in a matter of seconds. I looked around and there was nobody around. Where is everybody?

Then, all of a sudden, I felt a sharp pain in my temple. It was nothing like I've ever felt before. I dropped my backpack and fell to the ground on my knees. It was a pain that felt like a knife was being pushed into my head, slowly, steadily. I screamed like I've never ever screamed before. As soon as I did, the bright flash of the head lights from an SUV stops dead right in front of me.

At that moment, the pain stopped and as I opened my eyes, the day seemed to come back. The skies were clear and the alley was no longer menacing like it was before. As I looked up, I saw Patrick coming out of the driver side, rushing to me.

"Zach! Zach! Are you alright?" he asked as he helped me up from the ground. He was shaking me and asking me if I was okay. I finally mustered a small nod.

"Patrick?" still not sure why he was here but glad in some way that he was. But where was that animal? Where did it go?

As Patrick helped me up slowly, the alley way looked quite normal now. There were some people walking, as well as some vendors on each side of the narrow space. They seemed to be in a state of confusion as they were all staring at me and Patrick. I was disoriented, I couldn't place where I was, and then I remembered those eyes. Those blood red eyes.

"Zach, what the hell are you doing here?" Patrick asked as he was walking me to the back seat of the SUV.

"You were supposed to be on a bus heading outside the city."

I got into the back and he closed the door. After he got into the driver's seat, he didn't leave right away and looked back at me.

"I have to let your Dad know about this." and as he went to push his lapel, I reached out to grab him arm to stop him.

"No Patrick, don't."

Patrick is a gentle man, but I can count on one hand the number of times he's been mad, and this is one of them. He was shaking his head as I let go of his arm.

"You skip school, wander about and then I find you screaming your head off in the middle of this alley." He said. Looking more and more concerned now than mad, he took a deep breath and then turned to look at me again.

"Look Zach, I know you're going through a whole lot of stuff, and I get it. This is all so different and difficult for you."

I was still holding my head but the pain now has subsided, but it still felt so pronounced, like a scar that you can't see.

"It's my responsibility to know where you are, and once I knew you weren't on that bus this morning, I came out to look for you."

It was clear that Patrick was just making a point but while it made sense, I was still thinking about my encounter with the beast. What was it? Why was it there? I couldn't think any more about it but had to make sure that Patrick understands it wasn't personal.

"I'm sorry Pat, I didn't mean to get you involved, or in trouble." As I straightened up and looked at him sincerely. Patrick left out a huge sigh and then started the engine.

"You and your dad are like family to me, so my involvement, as you call it, will always be there."

He started to drive off into one of the alley ways and headed to the main road. So much for my plan to run away from this place.

"How did you even find me?" I asked Patrick, with a lot of curiosity and a bit of wonder. Whether I realized it or not, Patrick probably came just in time to save my life.

"Do you really think I would let you go on field trip without a way of knowing where you are?" Patrick said, now looking back using the rear view mirror, with a sign of a smirk on his face.

When I saw that, I looked at my backpack. So yeah, Patrick was quite clever.

CHAPTER FIVE

IRSINA, ITALY

PRESENT DAY

On a normal day, a visitor could get lost strolling through Irsina, with the maze of tiny streets filled with small family homes, and a plethora of churches and houses of the more wealthy. The palazzos of the main families of the town still bear their coats of arms over beautiful porticos while the wealth and charm of other days can be glimpsed through archways, on balconies, window frames and doorways. An ancient city, Irsina has held true to traditions that most other cities have let go. Here, there is a proud heritage within the people and the city itself, which prides itself as being its cultural foundation in the region.

The slow pace of families rearing their children, now completely adjusted to modern life, has replaced the swagger of past wealth and power in this city. Once a year the families are swelled by the return of emigrants, one of the most important and sad exports of the region for generations for the feast of Santa Eufemia in September.

In the evening the old men gather in the main piazza as the women folk sit outside their front doors in groups of neighbors often preparing vegetables for that evening's meal.

Their history and culture is not just to be seen in their often-dilapidated buildings, but lives in their language, called Irsenese which is a mixture of Arabic from the Saracens, French from the Normans and Spanish from the Bourbons as well as of course of the Italian of modern Italy.

The region is slowly and almost imperceptibly awakening to the potential of tourism. The poorest part of Italy, its role in history long forgotten, constantly bled of its young people who has been neglected and ignored.

But its wines and cuisine, architecture and art, archaeology and history together with its magnificent nature have been well-kept secrets. It deserves to be appreciated and discerning visitors will quickly recognize the shy but gritty gem that is Basilicata.

As the day rolls into high noon, the cathedral of Santa Maria Assumta, one of the most beautiful in the region, built in the 13th century, is the city's masterpiece.

Largely rebuilt at the end of the 18th century, with a very fine baptismal font from 1453, along with a statue of Saint Eufemia are believed to be the rare works of a noted artist Andrea Mantagna.

The Church of St. Francis, rebuilt in the 17th century over a 13th century monastery, with a fine crypt, which incorporates the remains of a Norman castle, and many beautiful 14th century frescoes also makes part of the numerous churches found within the city. This, as well as Chiesa del Purgatorio, a 17th century church where works of Pietro Antonio Ferro, Francesco Polino and Andrea Miglionico are kept and housed, have been part of Irsina's long and ancient religious traditions in the region.

On the outskirts of the city, where smaller outcrops of homes traditionally lived in by the early east European settlers, now lies the section where the "meno fortunati" or the less fortunate live. There arc generations of families here that dates back from 2000 B.C. and have never left this region as part of their ancestral heritage.

In the older stone villas along the North West section of this stretch of land, a family of sorts has lived a silent but well provided life. A young woman, now just passed her fifteenth birthday is walking home to her godmother from one of the churches, who have raised her after the tragic loss of her mother as the result of her birth. Her dark long hair flows gently in the brisk winds and she has been living a quiet simple life, far from the city's center, where she longed to visit as much as she could, but has been restricted to for as long as she can remember. Except for church, she had not truly seen much of the city at all.

As she comes into their small two story stone villa, she smiles in the mid-day sun shining down upon her, warming her cheeks to a soft red glow. Her bright green eyes clashes with her bright and clear skin as she feels the warmth of the day envelope her.

"Elizabeth, e che si bambino?"

The godmother, doing laundry in the home's back room, which is past the kitchen, continues to scrub clothes in a big washtub before her. She hears humming so she most certainly knew that her goddaughter is home from church.

"Si, Dio Madre." the child replies with a sweet voice full of joy and peace. She puts down her plain brown bag that looks more like a rice sack and brings the other brown bag, full of vegetables into the tiny kitchen on the side of the room. She then goes into the water well to fill up the drinking bucket as part of her daily chores around the home. As she pumps the handle of the well, she hums as always with a demeanor full of lightness and calm.

As the godmother washes up with the last batch of clothes, she calls out to the young woman to help her with hanging the laundry.

"Elizabeth, come here please, I need you to reach!" as she starts wringing the clothes to get rid of the excess water. The young girl, who is tall for her age, happily goes to help her godmother, truly the only mother she has ever known.

"Why don't you let me hang these, and you take a rest Dio Madre?" as Elizabeth grabs the pile of clothes within a wooden tub all wringed up and waiting to be hanged. As always, the godmother

58

marvels at the child's persona. She sees love and joy and pure hope in this child, such a gift, such a blessing. But she can't help but feel sadness in her heart as well. It is a sadness that she knows she will have to reveal to her one day. And it will change her life.

"You are a God sent, my child." as the godmother gives Elizabeth a quick kiss on the forehead and beams because of it. As the child finishes all her chores during the day, both begin to prepare for supper, and as always, talks of the past and things to come during this time.

While Elizabeth was chopping away at some lentil, she was smiling as if she had just remembered a fond memory.

"Tell me again about my mother, Dio Madre." As she reached for some leafy greens across the small table in the center of the kitchen. It never failed to amuse Elizabeth's godmother how she never tires of hearing about her mother. While she did not know her at all, it felt that she did in a way, as well at least of how she knows of her, and about her from stories she has heard since she was a small child.

The godmother smiles as she stands up to take the freshly cut vegetables over to the stove and put it in a pot that's been over the fire for some time now. She takes a quick whiff of the broth, and nods approvingly. It's ready.

"Your mother was a beautiful soul; she always helped others, often sacrificing things for herself in doing so."

As Elizabeth heard this, she smiled while finishing up the chopping she was doing. It was always heartfelt what she knew about her mother. It was strange for her but it's almost like she knew her, even if she never did meet her.

"She was a strong and loving woman and a sincere and loyal friend." the godmother continues as she starts stirring the pot and adding bits and pieces of cut chicken into the stew.

"I miss my friend." the godmother whispers and as she continued to stir the pot, she felt a warm set of arms around her waist as Elizabeth gives her an endearing hug from the back.

"I know you do, Dio Madre. I never knew her, but I miss her as well."

Both women continued to talk over supper, and well into bedtime. When Elizabeth saw that her godmother has fallen asleep on her chair, as she often did, she slipped over an old quilt that they both made out of sheep's skin and she proceeded to go upstairs to her tiny bedroom on the second floor.

It was a tiny little room, with just enough space for a small cot of a bed with a small wash table in the corner, where the foot of the bed faces the wall. But it had the most amazing view of the night sky from the lone window on the front of the villa. Elizabeth often found herself looking at the stars, thinking of her mother and that somehow, she felt that she was looking down at her from above.

As the night grew later, Elizabeth settled into her bed and finally fell asleep, with sweet thoughts of her mother, her Dio Madre and all the things that she was thankful for. She slept with a smile on her face, and hope in her heart that one day she will see her.

As she often does, the godmother falls asleep on her favorite chair and then after about a couple of hours, wakes up and goes to her bed on the first floor, right underneath Elizabeth's room. Tonight was no different as she woke herself up with a jerk since she was leaning to one side and basically falling off. As she puts away the quilted blanket, she smiles knowing that Elizabeth always puts it on her, as with all the other nights she had fallen asleep.

With a quick visit to the toilet, she headed to her room and the first thing she noticed was that there was light shining from above, through the second level's floor boards. It was way too bright for

Elizabeth's lamp, as the light was quite bright and quite white. Looking at it, she started to call for her.

"Elizabeth, child, are you alright?" as she made her way up the narrow stairs. She realized now that the light shone from behind the wooden door as well. The bright light passed through the slits in the wood and enveloped the entire door. It was in the middle of the night but Elizabeth's room seemed it was full of daylight. As the godmother approach, she hesitated to touch the door knob but was worried more for Elizabeth.

"Child, I am coming inside." she said as she opened the door knob. First the light blinded her as she slowly opened the door and for a moment she could not see anything at all. But as she started to stare at the scene, the godmother happened upon made her fall to her knees and both hands clasps her mouth.

In the room, Elizabeth was sitting up on her bed, under her covers and a beam of white light was directly in front of her, and it looked like it was burning but the godmother didn't feel any heat at all. She looked at Elizabeth; she saw her talking towards the light although she could not hear what she was saying. Then Elizabeth looked at her, and she had a smile in her face, almost telling the godmother that it was alright, that there was nothing to fear. Tears began to fall from the godmother's eyes; she had never felt more peace in her entire life as she has at this moment.

As the light shone brighter, it flickered and in an instant it extinguished itself in a flash. The godmother covered her eyes, and after seeing that the light has vanished, removed her hands from her face and what she saw made her cry. Elizabeth had this glow about her, an aura, of bright light blue and she was holding her stomach, looking down, as if cradling something.

She stood up, and she walked closer to Elizabeth. As she did, the light faded and Elizabeth looked up at her, smiling, crying.

"What happened child, what was that?" the godmother asked as she slowly sat beside Elizabeth's bed.

Elizabeth looked at her godmother, and spoke.

"The world will find joy and peace." as she continued to stroke her belly, smiling down at it.

"I don't understand Elizabeth, what was that light?" the godmother asked again as she reached over for Elizabeth's hand, as if to peel her away from her thoughts and to try to make sense of what just happened.

"It was a message, from above, and it told me, he told me what my purpose was Dio Madre. Do not be afraid he said for I have found favor with the Father."

When Elizabeth said those words, the godmother straightened up. Is this the cycle of which all things are to be revealed? For countless centuries, is it possible that it will happen now, in this time, as chosen by fate? The godmother looked at Elizabeth, and with her realization of what things are to come, she picked her up from the bed and told her to get ready.

"But it's the middle of the night, where are we going Dio Madre?"

As the godmother realizes the implications of what just happened, of things that just transpired, she moves with utter certainty and hurry. If this is what she knows it to be, then the time has come and the order needs to know.

"We are going to Rome my child. We are going to see his Holiness."

Both women hurriedly leave in the dark cloak of the night, as the godmother made arrangements to travel to Rome and to make sure they make good on their arrival. She feels blessed to see this age come, as with her ancestral sisters, who are the keepers of the truth who have sworn over a lifetime ago of their duty to keep the bloodline safe. But now, with the message, it has finally come to an end. An end that will define all things, in this world, and in life and beyond.

Before leaving, she runs downstairs, to her bedroom, and opens a small wooden box with a key she produces from her pocket. The box opens up and she reaches into it and pulls out a cell phone. The godmother turns it on and it automatically dials a number. She waits for someone, and when the line is picked up, she gasps for air.

"The sign, it has been given. The time has come."

* * *

The Palazzo Apostolico, or the Apostolic Palace is the official residence of the Pope. It is also known as the Papal Palace or the Palace of the Vatican. The Vatican itself refers to the building as the Palace of Sixtus V in honor of Pope Sixtus V. It is located north east of St. Peter's Basilica and adjacent to the Bastion of Nicholas V and Palace of Gregory XIII. The building contains the Papal Apartments, various government offices of the Catholic Church and the Holy See, private and public chapels, Vatican Museums and the Vatican library, including the Borgia Apartment now used to house artworks.

The Papal Apartments is the non-official designation for the collection of apartments, both private and state, that wrap around a courtyard of the Apostolic Palace in Vatican City. Since the 17th century, the Papal Apartments have been the official residence of the Pope in his religious capacity as Supreme Pontiff. Prior to 1870, the Pope's official residence in his temporal capacity, as sovereign of the Papal States, was the Quirinal Palace, which is now the official residence of the President of the Italian Republic.

The apartments include about ten large rooms including a vestibule, a small studio office for the papal secretary, the pope's private study, the pope's bedroom in the corner of the building, a medical suite which includes dental equipment and equipment for emergency surgery, a dining room, a small living room, and a full kitchen. There is a roof garden and staff quarters for the nuns who run the Prefecture of the Pontifical Household, also known as the Papal Household.

It is from the window of his small study that the Pope greets and blesses pilgrims to Saint Peter's Square on Sundays. The private library is a vast room with two windows overlooking Saint Peter's Square. The Pope's private chapel has a piece of art, by I.H. Rosen and commissioned by Pope Pius XI that depicts "two episodes of Polish resistance framing the face of the Black Madonna of Częstochowa". Through each incumbent, the papal apartment is decorated to suit each of the Pontiff's preference. Pope Nicholas VI, who grew up as a poor child with humble beginnings chose a sparsely decorated residence.

Running past the study, Monsignor Veneto sprints through the high walled ceilings with sculptures of saints on each side, heading towards the Papal bedroom. The phone call that he received from the encrypted line can only be dialed from one location. Veneto had hoped that it would never be in his lifetime that he would get a call from this phone.

But when it rang, at three in the morning, he knew what it meant. He listened to the message and shot up out of his bed, and got up as fast as he could.

Coming to the Papal bedroom doors, he normally would knock to announce himself, but tonight he barged in without regard. It is past protocol, there are things to prepare. And his Holiness needs to know.

As Veneto looms over the Pope, he nudges him enough to make sure he awakes serenely. As the Pope slowly wakes up, he props up on his elbows and squints at Veneto. When the Pope realizes it was him, he reaches over to his night table to get his glasses.

"What is it Veneto?" the Pope asks as he sits up in his bed. Veneto is panting, almost sweating and clearly anxious. He looked at the Pope, and as he did, he raised his hands and shows the Pope what was in it.

"Your Holiness, it is a blessed and glorious day." as Veneto hands the phone to the Pope. As his Holiness realizes the meaning of Veneto's words. He looks at the phone, and looks back at the Monsignor. He nods in agreement.

"It is a glorious day indeed, my friend. We have lived to see this time come."

Both men were close to tears, and Veneto reaches for the Pope's hands and clasps it with his own.

"We must get ready now Veneto. We must be ready."

As Veneto contemplates the magnitude of what needs to be done. The Pope gets up from his bed and looks out of his bedroom window into the still dark morning sky. As he looked up to the stars, he began to pray. As with all the sovereign leaders that came before him, all had hoped that this day would come in their lifetime. It is an honor, a blessing, and he was ready to do what needed to be done. He looks to Veneto and knowing what they are up against, the Pope speaks.

"We will need help."

Veneto looks at the Pope, with apprehension on his face.

"Your Holiness, surely we cannot break the covenant we have made, along with those before us."

The covenant that Veneto speaks of is one that has existed since before the beginning of the formal papacy, or the Vatican for that matter. It has been and will always be the single most critical organization that no one, not even specific members of the Vatican Council know about. It is passed down from all the previous incumbents of the Papal seat to its current owner, Pope Nicholas VI.

There are terms to agree upon when a new Pope is elected through the process of conclave. The conclave was a meeting of the College of Cardinals to elect a new pontiff as the Apostolic Leader of the Roman Catholic Church. Believed to be the successor to Saint Peter, the Pope, who is also called the Bishop of Rome, leads as the earthly head of Catholics worldwide.

Once elected, the Pope is tasked to be the first and foremost Supreme Pastor. As the Apostle Peter was shepherds that spread the early written words of the gospels, so has it been the responsibility of the Pope to be a unifier of the People of God.

But there are terms, ancient in their nature that has been passed down through the papacy. Information that was deemed so controversial during the Middle Ages that almost all sources of it were banned from public access. These terms account for the teachings and traditions that have not been made public over centuries and have since deepened its mysteries to present day. The reality of these terms are known only to a selected few, less than a dozen people over the entire globe, and the Pope is one of them. This group called To Tágma tou Theíou, or The Order of the Light had but one mission. And that mission is at hand.

But now, Pope Nicholas realizes that the whole world needs to learn the truth. Verse 25 from Ephesians Chapter 4 rang true to his heart.

"Therefore, having put away falsehood, let each one of you speak the truth with his neighbor, for we are members one of another."

Yes the Pope thought. We will need to let the world know, and yes, we will need help.

"Come Veneto, we must act quickly and let the order know of this. We have much to prepare for."

Veneto, whose loyalty to the papacy was so admired by the Pope nodded in agreement. He could clearly see the now middle aged

66

Monsignor, deep in prayer yet ready to obey and do what must be done. That is good the Pope thought, as prayer is our medium to God's ear, and the Pope prays that in the coming days, that God will act.

CHAPTER SIX

THE DIVINE HALL

With golden arches and pillars that disappear into the clouds, the Archangel Michael, the one who is like God, the warrior and defender of the faith, the great prince that stands up for the children of the Father, ponders the events that will unfold. As an Eternal, there is no sense of time for him, but what is to transpire has given him pause on the very nature and urgency of events that he knows will come to light.

A river, clear as crystal, flows from the center of the throne of the Father which comes down the middle of the heavenly city. On each side of the river there is the tree of life, yielding twelve kinds of fruit every month. The streets are like transparent glass but as hard as any matter ever created. The walls of the kingdom are adorned with every kind of jewel. Emeralds, onyx, amethyst, topaz. There is no sun or moon, and no need for a temple or church. The presence of the Father is the light and the whole kingdom is the temple.

Out of his armor, and wearing a white flowing robe with a golden rope around his waist, Michael walks barefoot on a floor that can only be describe as shimmering with light. As he walks across the great divine hall where all of the Eternals can see beyond heaven's realm, he looks at events that are transpiring on earth below.

As he looks at what man has done to the world, he feels sadness in his heart. The hopes for man to do great things are often countered with man's very nature. He cannot accept the loss of this world but it is not up to him, and he can only be faithful to the Father's will. He knows that the coming of age is upon this world, as it has been for many others. And through all of time and creation, he is prepared to fight for the glory of it.

He turns to see Metatron approach. Surely news of the deliverance will be given.

"Michael, brother."

Metatron lands just a few paces from Michael gracefully folding his wings behind him as he approached.

Both angels clasp their hands together and the brotherhood through faith was felt in between.

"Is it done?" Michael asks, of which he already knew the answer.

Metatron, clinging closely to the books of souls, the divine manuscript that contains the entire Father's words, looks beyond and towards the place below. He feels what Michael feels, but he has hope, and he has faith.

"The message has been sent, the vessel has been anointed." Metatron stood still looking at the world below.

"It is much direr than I had expected" Metatron exclaims. The angels being eternal beings are full of grace, love and peace. All things are given divinely to them and seeing pain and suffering makes their hearts ache. It is like a brother seeing a sibling being mistreated, or mistreating others. Through the time that all life on this earth has been, the most compelling and serious case of sorrow for the angels was that of man's nature.

"Where there is pain, there is also joy Metatron. I know that with all things to come, it seems this world is lost. But the vessel gives us hope, and those that will defend her."

With this Michael puts his hands on Metatron's shoulders. As both angels feel the love and peace of brotherhood, one that has kept them loyal and faithful for millennia, will now be called upon again. Michael prays to the Father that this world be saved.

"Gather the others in the great hall." Michael asks Metatron. As he spreads his wings, Metatron looks back at Michael.

"By the Father's will."

Michael nods back at him.

"His will be done."

Now Michael calls upon an angel in the ranks, as with all things a message must be sent. But this kind of message is unlike the world has ever seen, or will do so again. It is the message that lets all beings, good and bad, dark and light, righteous and evil, know of the plans of the Father. This message will be in all tongues, for all under the Father's kingdom on earth.

An angel lands in front of Michael and bows in respect. Michael pulls out a parchment from his robe's sleeves and hands it over.

"This message is to be sent to all those that needs to heed it below."

As the angel takes the parchment from Michael, he puts it under his robe and bows back to Michael before flying up into the bright blue expanse.

Now the time has come, and Michael knows that the day he has waited for has come, again. He knows that Lucifer is aware of the vessel and the importance of her purpose. He knows that Lucifer will strike against her. Even now, he feels the rumblings under the pit, where the lord of darkness plots against all that is done from above. An Eternal has no concept of time, but the pain in Michael's heart for his lost brother remains as if it was but days gone past. There has always been sorrow in Michael's heart since that day, eons ago, when his brother was banished from here, this paradise of a kingdom. And while the others have accepted Lucifer's fate, Michael still has hope, however small, it is hope nonetheless.

In the book of souls, Metatron catalogues the words of the Father. It is through this book that all things are known to those in the heavenly kingdom. As the book is written with the living word, so shall it pass in the kingdom and all of those worlds under the Father's grace. But Metatron also looks to see the signs leading to the end. And the signs have been clear. He knows that the time has finally come to put forth the next sign that will lead to the end of all things.

In the words of the Father, the world will see seven signs to know the end is at hand. The first four, Prophecy, War, Famine and Plague has already consumed the earth below.

The first sign, tells the coming of a false prophets to begin the end of days. The Eternals have long since seen in the last century that many false prophets have laid claim to the world. These preachers that speak of a new world order comes sheath by lambskin and whispers in delicate tongues. Those that listen are taken over; those that refuse to follow are punished and banished. Of all the world's false teachings, those that profess progress and choice are the ones that persists the most. The world is consumed with the notion of individuality, of being able to exist with no other means except those that are granted by their own hands.

This is the direct opposite of the Father's grace. The people of this world have become their own version of their own god, and that their saviors now look to profit and wealth, not humility and obedience. Greed abounds in the hearts of men, especially those that professes to try to make the world a better place. Power and corruption bleeds out of those in position of authority with charity and concern on one hand and manipulation and decimation on the other. Those that preach the faith, and speak of the Father's grace and blessings are taken over by fleshly desires and lustful behavior.

In the end, the world's false prophet is no one person; it is the collection of all the people's wants, desires and selfish needs.

War is part of man's legacy. As the second sign, this has been part of the history of man from the first day we have looked to covet those that belong to others. Metatron has catalogued all the world's wars, big and small and have marveled at the barbarism that man could achieve.

From sticks and stones to weapons of universal destruction, man has proven that war is and a way of life. The very fabric of peace depends on the outcome of war, and yet where peace exists, it cannot linger. For another will want what does not belong to them, and so it has been up until now. It will pit family against family, and it will look to achieve what cannot be done by reason.

We say that we fight wars to protect, but the wars that we truly need to fight are those within ourselves. For what we do, in any given day, the choices that we make and the behaviors that we act on are all driven by something we fight inside of us. The Father, in all his wisdom and grace, has fought wars in ancient times, with those people that He has chosen. But in all cases of his righteousness, those that He has chosen need not harm anyone. Those that He has chosen to fight end up not fighting at all.

Through faith, and through belief, these are the Father's weapons. But the Father's wrath is exact. Those that go against His will are struck down with justice. Now, no longer are there any chosen, for man has taken it upon himself to decide what is righteous, and what is worth fighting for. Man has removed himself from the Father's grace and therefore no longer knows the things that the Father wants. As much as war man has seen, and the tolls that has been paid for being in one, it still beckons us to our very core.

We live in the most affluent time in all of human history and yet, how can a world with so much, leave so many with so little? The Western and European nations that enjoy the luxury of full meals and oversized portions are blind to the suffering of those that can barely have food on the table once a day. It is alarming in Third World countries, places in far flung continents, where basic food necessities are still a daily struggle has been the staple of famine across the world.

The notion of throwing food away is beyond comprehension when there are people who would happily eat it without hesitation. The world has become countries of have and have not. Those that have, control and consume, while those that do not have crumble into decay, suffering and disease. How can a world that was meant to be shared by all beings, be in such a disarrayed and selfish state? How can we all know that the half eaten meal that was thrown out, scraps of food given to dogs and food described as waste mean to a family whose very lives depend on it to survive? How can we understand that it is not how much we have that gives us strength but how much we share with others? In the beginning, this world was given to all of us, an Eden, with everlasting fruits. Now the world has become a dominion of resources controlled only by those that can afford it. As Metatron surveys his entries in the book of souls for the first earth, the last entry pains his heart the most.

Death has abounds in the entire history of man. But none has taken so many lives in the course of the world's history as disease. Wars are fought and won, cities destroyed and rebuilt, and nations fall but rose up once again. But nothing comes out of disease. The fourth sign, which has taken more lives than any of the rest, makes the signs point to the end of days. Rampant outbreaks of diseases, viruses and all things incurable have been man's greatest struggle. Plagues do not choose between the rich and the poor, the strong or the weak, nor the young or the old. It casts its net over all those that are within its grasp, and takes them without question, without remorse. The world has seen countless plagues as far back as 429 B.C.

The first ever recorded pandemic, believed to be in Athens during that time killed 100,000 people. In the early 20th century, an outbreak of influenza killed 75 million people around the globe. The plague has and will always be the clearest of all the signs. Cleansing the world of the innocent and the guilty, the plague is what closely resembles Death. You cannot escape it, and it will come for you at some point in your lifetime. With these four signs, the Father has put in place a plan for the world.

Now Metatron knows what comes next, and it is this that he and his brothers, led by Michael must prepare for. He closes the book of souls and looks to take flight towards the great hall to convene the eternal seven. He prays that this world will be saved. But it is dire indeed.

* * *

As Michael descends to his chair within the circle of the seven, he sees that everyone is here. He knows that all his brothers know what is to come, as it had been in the past. But no matter how Michael feels about it, he knows that all his brothers are with him, and will always be, through eternity.

"You all know why we are gathered here." Michaels says as he stands up and goes to the center of the circle. Turning around to see each of his brothers, nodding in agreement.

"I have given the message to the people below, once it has been heard, we shall act."

Rumblings from the seven were felt and as the truth comes to each of them, Gabriel stands up and joins Michael in the center.

"As with all things, this is the Father's will."

Gabriel puts his hands on Michael's shoulder.

"There are those of our kin that are no longer with us by choice. You know of whom I speak of."

Michael feels his heart sadden, as he knows Gabriel shares his pain. The small glimmer of hope that Michael keeps is something he had hoped his other brothers would share. But he knows that they all feel Lucifer is lost. And Gabriel, as protective of his brothers as he is, worries for Michael.

"The world below will face the fifth sign." Gabriel announces in a resounding tone. As he did, the others stood up and began adoration for the Father. The Holy War is upon them, and as it was in the past, once again shall it be now and the seven all live to be obedient and loyal to the Father's will.

"We are with you Michael." as Gabriel walks away and joins the others in praise. It may seem that they are joyous for things to come. And in a way they are. Angels live for the word of the Father, and being able to enact it is their highest calling. As for these Eternal seven, the chosen ones by the Father himself, there is no greater honor, no greater blessing than to do his will.

But Michael knows of the price to be paid. He alone, who is like God, knows how the harvest can be ruined. He feels, as he does in past wars, that while he is fighting for the glory and might of the Father, he feels the pain of those that will incur the Father's wrath. Such is why he is burdened by these wars. But he knows it is the way of the spirit, and the light.

"We shall be in His grace, and under his righteous wing!" Michael shouts as the seven adorns the air with joyous and glorious worship. The time has come once again to do what needs to be done.

All of them draw their swords, the mightiest of all weapons bestowed upon them as protectors of the kingdom. The swords illuminate in a bright blue flame that begins to burn brightly, even brighter than air and sky. The seven converge on the center of the circle and raise their swords to form a pyramid with the tips. As they do, a beam of blinding light shoots up to the skies and is seen throughout the kingdom.

"Father, we come to you and ask for your blessing. May You be with us as we praise Your name and glorify Your kingdom."

With this, all seven begin to ascend, still formed in the circle and becomes a swirl of light. The blessing, or the giving, for the seven and all those that will be part of this holy war begins to envelope each one. As the light from above shines over them, each of the seven receives the Father's grace, protection and spirit. It is the divine gift that each of the Eternals receive when preparing for the holy war.

Michael and the others, eyes closed and heads bowed feels the surge of the spirit through them. The covenant between master and servant, in place for all of time, has been decreed to them once again. Each of the seven will then command another seven, and each one of those will command seven more. Until the seven by seven as far as the kingdom reaches, all shall be blessed for battle in this war.

The light begins to fade and as the seven descends back to the great hall, each one is filled with conviction. As they lower each of their swords, they open their eyes to see each other all bestowed heaven's armor. Each one is given an additional divine weapon in addition to their magnificent swords.

Gabriel gets the Spear of Truth, able to pierce through anything, or anyone.

Raphael receives the Bow of Light whose arrows seek those that evil dwells in.

Uriel hold the Staff of Destiny, able to repel any kind of attack and Sandalphon gets the Mace of Righteousness, a heavy yet powerful divine object that can crush all those in its path.

Jophiel holds the Axe of the Divine which makes the blade strike fast and true and Metatron is bestowed the Hammer of Justice, powered by the word of the Father.

Each weapon has been chosen for each of the Eternals. The weapons cannot do harm to any being serving the will of the Father and can only be used by the one who it is bestowed upon.

As all of them receive the Father's blessing, everyone looks to Michael. He is turned around, and he slowly faces the seven. In his hands is the ultimate blessing.

"The Dagger of the Spirit." Michael says as he looks to all his brothers. All of the seven know that the dagger holds but one purpose. For millennia, the dagger has never been able to fulfill its destiny, of all the wars that has been fought, it came close but once to achieving its goal. Michael holds it, and looks at it, for it was in his hands that carried the dagger for each war. He knew what it was made for, and he knew it was something he will have to try once again.

As he puts the dagger in its sheath, he looks at his brothers.

"I pray that this time, Lucifer will find peace."

As each one of them takes off to the skies, they fly in formation with Michael in the lead. With wings at full spread, they speed through the air like arrow heads shot from a bow. They head to something over the horizon. As they grow nearer, they all saw the multitude of wings that are gathered.

* * *

Within the fiery depths of the dark realm, Lucifer sits on his throne. He knows of the message to the vessel, and he knows that the angels will try to protect her. And then there's the boy, who still does not know his true purpose. Both shall need to be taken care of, to make sure that this world plunges into the darkness that belongs to him. As Lucifer reaches for a golden goblet on a silver platter held by one of his servants, he sneers at his minions in front of him.

"What of the vessel?" he asks and one of his minions comes forward. Over the time that Lucifer has been banished to this underworld, he has created his army of demonic subjects by twisting those that fall to his realm as his servants. He particularly enjoys creating half breeds, where he conjoins man and beast together to form a more gruesome servant for his bidding.

The one that comes forth has a slender body but instead of hands, it had claws as that of an eagle and its head was a bull.

"The pigs have moved her to their city my lord."

The minion snorts as he moves back into the group of minions, and waited for their master to speak.

"They wish to protect her. Michael assembles his army."

As Lucifer says this, the entire group of minion's bellows and cries out to him, wishing for him to give them his commands, their wish to destroy and to maim. Fueled by hatred and disgust, all of hell's minions exist to exact sorrow and pain. But in their all-consuming state, they are bound, just like the Eternals, to not interfere directly with the world above. However, Lucifer has one advantage, he whispers into men's heart as does his minions. This way of tempting the world above has been the way Lucifer has been building his army, below in his realm and in the world above them.

Now that he knows that the war shall begin, it opens up this worlds and he can finally take what he deems to belong to him. He puts down his goblet and waves the servant away. The servants, whose eyes are gouged out and mouth strung shut with wire was guilty of vanity and pride. The sins fit the punishment and Lucifer is so very glad to enact it in his empire.

"It shall be soon my brethren, that our legions will rise up and we will take this world and make it our own!" as he raises his arms in full adoration of those around him.

"And I will kill the one that used to call me brother!"

The minions go crazy and begin to wreak havoc, where havoc is a way of life. As Lucifer plots his plan, he revels in his desire to enact his punishment and revenge. This time, he tells himself, it will be different. This time, he will rule.

CHAPTER SEVEN

THE PAPAL OFFICE

ROME, ITALY

As David was ushered into the Pope's study, he still has no idea why the Pope would want to arrange a meeting with him. It was highly unorthodox for the Pope to request a meeting with the Ambassador to the Holy See, not that it is entirely impossible. Just very, very rare.

Being in Pope Nicholas VI's office before, David was quite familiar with the layout of the room. It was a bright and open space, with very high ceilings and adorned with artwork from the 18th and 19th century. However, the artwork are probably the things with the most value in the room as the furniture, while old, is quite sparse. This makes the space much bigger in size since the table was off to one side of the room and on the other side was a huge library cabinet full of text ranging from the Vatican Imperium Soraum to the works of contemporary authors in the theological fields. The room had very high windows that made the light come in quite nicely. Sheer window curtains, plain white in color are used throughout.

The office table itself was a plain wooden table, no frills or decorations. On top, there was a planner that did not contain any specific dates for the Pope's itinerary. And then there was a golden clock along with a gold and silver crucifix and a pen plate, which was also made out of gold. Quite minimal but knowing Pope Nicholas VI, he preferred having it simple. The other two sets of furniture were the two chairs in the room. One was behind the table and one in front of it. Both chairs were almost the same, with plain white upholstery and cherry armrests.

I was sitting on the chair facing the table, and have been waiting for almost fifteen minutes. I was told that his Holiness was running late from a trip to the Basilica of Santa Maria Maggiore in Central Rome that took almost the entire morning. I had asked Sarah to clear my schedule for the afternoon as I had no idea how this meeting was going to go, or what this meeting was about.

As I shifted in my seat, the doors to the side of the office table opened and the Pope and his aide, I think his name is Verato, came into the room. I immediately stood up and greeted his eminence but quickly realized that it was only the two of them.

Normally, the Pope would have his aide, along with someone from the press office, as well as a contingent from the Corps of Gendarmerie, the Pope's security detail. I reached out my hand to take his Holiness' hand to kiss the papal ring but his aide, was already closing the doors behind them and headed to me with a sweeping gesture to leave the room. The Pope has still not spoken one word and I am beginning to worry that there is something wrong.

"Please Mr. Ambassador, this way please."

The Pope's aide asks while leading me to another set of doors at the other end of the room. The Pope was already heading out when I started towards the door and when I passed through, I was now looking at a deserted hallway adjacent to the entrance most diplomats and state visitors use to see the Pope.

As I made my way towards Pope Nicholas, the monsignor was behind me closing doors behind him. We made it to the Pope's study, where he would normally deliver his messages on Sundays. Again, the monsignor closes the door and now the Pope is sitting at a similar office table, only this one is smaller in size and had almost nothing on it. The Pope gestures to me to sit across from him on the empty chair.

"Your Holiness, I…" started when the Pope raised his hands quickly to stop me from saying anything more. He then looked at the monsignor as I did, and he was holding some sort of device and sweeping the room with it. It had a red light that was blinking that was accompanied by a low hum, much like what one hears from a ham radio when being tuned. As the monsignor completed his sweep of the room, he turns off the device and looks at both me and the Pope.

"The room is secured your Holiness."

And with that, the Pope reaches out his hands as I instinctively take it to kiss the papal ring. The Pope releases a sigh as he sits back on the chair and looks at me.

"Thank you for coming David, I'm sure you have a lot of questions yes?" as the Pope shifts on his chair and puts both elbows on the office table, clasping both hands in front of him.

I was still unsure of what to think of all that's happened. This is way out of procedure and I'm in a room with the Pope with only his aide along with him. This can be constituted as a blatant disregard on visitation and diplomatic protocols.

"Your Holiness, I am quite disturbed by the circumstances of this meeting. Should we not have someone here from your administration, or at the very least, someone from the corps?"

At this point, the monsignor sat right beside the Pope and both now were looking me straight in the eye. I was getting anxious but then the Pope and the monsignor were quite calm.

"David, I can understand your concern my son, but in the interest of time I have made decisions that have implications on a global scale and right now, I need you to trust me and listen to what I am about to tell you."

All of my being is screaming at me that this is something that I need to report back to the embassy. But the Pope's voice was sincere, he was speaking without his position, and he is asking me to trust him. I nodded silently to the Pope and his aide.

"Very well, where do I begin." as the Pope stood and looked to the monsignor for some sense of guidance.

"I am a member of group that was formed centuries ago to protect something very precious."

The Pope started pacing back and forth in front of the table, seemingly trying to get details of what he was telling me just right so that I could understand. I felt like a five year being told how a car engine works. I was listening but I wasn't comprehending.

"This group, called the Order of the Light, is made up of seven individuals from different walks of life on this earth. Who they are is not important right now but know that this group is responsible for one thing, and one thing only."

As the Pope said this, I felt a light pain in my head. I'm still confused as to what is happening, and the Supreme Pontiff of the Catholic Church just told me that he is a member of a secret society. I started to feel the sweat fall down the back of my neck, as I always sweat when I was nervous.

"Throughout history, there have been those that were opposed to the order's mission. Which is why over the years, we have had to invite people into it so as to maintain the group's secrecy."

I was still looking at the Pope, and not understanding what he was telling me. I was trying to make sense of it but the words were not there, and I was feeling this was some sick joke that I'm in, or perhaps a really bad dream. As I stood up, the Pope continued.

"Monsignor Veneto's family has been loyal to the order for three generations." as the Pope waves to the monsignor that accompanied him.

Now I understood why the Pope was looking for bugs in the room. The Pope admitting to being part of a covert international organization, one that was secret at that, would be damaging if not lead to the demise of this office. I was still listening, and struggling to understand. Finally I mustered enough to ask the simple question.

"This Order of the Light, what is its mission?" as I sat down to make sure that whatever response the Pope gave, I was ready and able to comprehend it.

"You are aware of the story of the Virgin Mary correct?" as the Pope sat down on the chair looking to me for confirmation. I nodded in agreement.

"Well, Mary or Mariam, who was largely agreed upon by theological and catholic scholars to be the founder of the Christian religion, as well as universally known as the Mother of Jesus has been the sole responsibility of this order."

Now I was more confused, and the Pope and the monsignor saw it in my face. This order that the Pope is talking about is responsible for the history of Mary? But I knew the Pope had more to say, I tried to keep my thoughts from springing out and continued to listen.

"You see David, Mary like many of those who lived in that time, had started a bloodline that survives to this very day. And the current surviving descendant of Mary, the Mother of Jesus, is now here with me."

Now here with me, these words rang into my ear like a deafening sound that rendered all my other senses useless. My eyes widened. This can't be true, stories of the bloodline were never proven to be true, and there was no evidence at all that such ancestral trees were ever tracked, much less exist during this time. National Geographic even had a series that was paneled by leading theological and philosophical experts, and they all agreed that such bloodlines couldn't exist today. I could no longer keep silent; I stood up and ran my hands through my head in confusion.

"Your Holiness, I do not know what you expect me to say but I need to tell you this all sounds highly dubious."

As the words sank into my brain, I saw the Pope keep his person calm. He understood why I was confused. He continued to speak.

"David, the order had kept this bloodline hidden. It was the sole resolve of the order to do so. It was up to us to keep the bloodline safe until it was time for it to fulfill its purpose."

I stopped pacing, and turned to look at the Pope. He knew what I was about to say and I was almost afraid to ask. But I've been listening for a while now and I needed to find out where this was leading.

"Which is what exactly?" I asked, and the Pope paused, looked to the monsignor, and back at me. He stood up, walked around the table and right up against me. The Pope put both his hands on my shoulders and looked me square in the eye.

"For the second coming David."

I felt faint. I didn't know what to say or think. It was clear to the Pope so he sat me back down on the chair and gestured to the monsignor to get me something to drink. He came back with a small bottle of water and while I wasn't thirsty, I grabbed it and gulped it like I was. It didn't help. The implication of what the Pope just said has just begun to make sense to me, while making no sense at all. Order of the Light, descendant of Mary, the second coming. It's all going to my head but I'm almost not ready to accept it. One of the most powerful religious leaders of the modern age has just told me about the second coming of the Son of God. I managed to compose myself, and with the Pope and monsignor back behind the table, sitting down, I stood up.

"Are you telling me what I think you're telling me?" I didn't want to say it, didn't want to think it. I still felt faint, but knew that I can no longer ignore the fact of what I'm hearing. The Pope, the supreme leader of the worldwide church is telling me all this.

"I'm sorry David, the order had to act quickly, and the vessel needs to be protected."

The vessel, I assumed this was this descendant of Mary, that's being protected by the Order of the Light all this time has now fulfilled its purpose. And the purpose is to bring about the second coming.

"Why me? Why are you telling me all this?" I asked as I sat back down, now understanding the facts that's just been laid out for me. This day has become nothing that I ever expected, I woke up this morning worrying about Zach's state of mind, and at work, and I worried about what this meeting was about, and now I was just told by Pope Nicholas VI that judgment day was upon the world. It was good that I asked Sarah to clear my afternoon.

The Pope paused and with all his calmness uttered words I never expected to hear.

"We need your help David."

As I pondered the statement that the Pope just said, I started thinking about my wife, Loretta. I was trying to tell myself that I was over her, but somehow this had made me think of her and wanting to see her again.

"You see David, soon all of the world will know what you just heard. It will be imperative that the vessel be protected until the rebirth can happen."

David was trying to change his mindset; he was trying to think of how this can be real and how he can help. And when exactly is this rebirth going to happen he thought.

"There are forces at work here that goes beyond any of us. The light and the dark will collide in a way that will change all things, and everyone on this planet. I feel that the order might fail and that we need to make sure the vessel is taken care of in case we do." the Pope said as he wiped his forehead.

As I grasp the magnitude of what the Pope is telling me, I begin to understand the nature of what is to come. This vessel is now here, and the Pope just asked me to help protect this descendant of Mary. I started nodding my head.

"I will do what I can Your Holiness, and thank you for trusting me with this."

I reached out to his hand and kissed the papal signet ring again. This time it was meaningful, not just a gesture of respect.

"We will be in touch David, for now take this, and we will need to move quickly." as both the monsignor and the Pope leave the room using the separate exit at the end of the study but not until they handed over a file folder to David.

I clutched the folder close to my chest as I headed to the door I came in at and briskly started walking. I needed to make arrangements, I need to talk to Patrick, and have Zach back home and ready to go. I made my way back through the hallway, through the papal office, which was still deserted and outside to the visitor's entrance. I give up my pass at the security gate and was now walking outside in the square.

The sun felt great on my skin, and I pulled out my phone and called Sarah. She cheerfully picked up and started to talk. I had to cut her off.

"Sarah, I need you to listen to me very carefully."

I continued to walk into the square and talked to Sarah. It was going to be a busy afternoon. Then my phone rang and I saw that it was a call from the school. I picked up and heard the familiar voice of Ms. Folchetti, the school administrator on the other line. As I listened to what she told me, I was neither surprised nor alarmed. I quickly thanked her and then dialed Patrick.

* * *

As Patrick pulls up to the embassy gate, I was still quiet in the back seat. Patrick has been contemplating whether or not to let my dad know of what happened but he could see the sadness in my eyes. Against all his professional and personal instincts, he decided that my dad should not know, for now, of what happened today.

"Promise me one thing Zach, and I haven't asked you for anything so this is important."

I was still in state of thought about what had transpired in the alley. I could not take the image out of my head of that black wolf-like creature with its blood red eyes looking at me. I was unaware that Patrick was calling my name multiple times.

"Zach, are you okay?" Patrick asks as I get jolted from my thoughts. I looked at Patrick and he was patiently waiting for an answer.

"I'm sorry Patrick, what did you say?"

Patrick sighed and started to open his door to get out, half way out of the SUV; he came back in and slammed the door back closed.

"Zach, I'm trying to help you here. But I'm not seeing that you understand that."

I knew that Patrick was getting frustrated, but between his frustration and telling him the truth, I felt that his frustration would be a lot easier for him to deal with than what I actually saw.

"I'm sorry Pat, it's just that I'm not sure what to do anymore."

Patrick seemed to soften a little bit when he heard this, and I know that he and my dad will talk about what happened that day, and I feel that I would never truly understand it myself.

"You need to understand Zach that it's not only you that's hurt, your dad is hurt too. Both of you had lost so much and I just want you to understand that no one is blaming you, especially not your father."

As he said this, I felt a bit of the same pain that I so tried to forget in my temple when I was in the alley way. But this was much less intense, more like a little ping. But it was the same feeling, the pain, however less, was the same pain. I looked at Patrick and nodded to him as I looked down on my hands. Then an image in my head flashed to when I let go of my mom's hands. I quickly shook it out of my head.

By this time, Patrick had gotten out of the SUV and was on my side opening the door. As I stepped out I already heard Patrick speaking into his lapel stating that "Bravo Charlie" was on site. That meant me, and Echo Zulu was my dad. I guess by now I would have no choice but to explain in some way why I was not half way outside the city to my dad, looking at ancient rubble that was built millennia ago.

By the time I was out of the SUV and had gone into the walkway to the embassy entrance, I realized now that Patrick had his right hand pressed against his earpiece like he was struggling to hear something.

"Control, say again. Confirm that Echo Zulu is en route and that we are to intercept with Bravo Charlie, copy?"

As I saw Patrick listen to the reply, I saw Sarah, dad's assistant come running out of the front doors along with two marines by her side. I didn't understand what was going on but realized it must have been my doing since I skipped the field trip and everybody was now freaking out that I wasn't on any of the buses.

As Sarah approached me, I was ready to offer my excuse. She had my dad's briefcase with her and as she met with Patrick, she was just shy of earshot so I didn't really hear what she told him.

Patrick was then looking back at me, and looking back at Sarah, and then he shook his head and took the briefcase from her and headed back my way. As Patrick approach, he started to reach for my arm and began to turn me around back to the SUV.

"What's going on Pat? Where are we going? I asked as I looked at him. He was silent and ushered me into the back seat. The two marines hopped into the SUV as well, one in the front and the other in the back with me. I had the slightest feeling that this doesn't have anything to do with my attempt to run away, but if it was, I guess my dad was truly mad.

"Control, Bravo Charlie is secure and en route back to the nest. We have Echo Zulu on the grid and we are intercepting, copy?"

With that, Patrick started the SUV and drove off into the direction of Saint Peter's Square.

"Pat, what's going on? Where's my dad?" I asked again. Patrick looked back at me from the mirror and didn't say a word. He turned on the lights and siren, and as he did, two polizia cars joined us as we drove into the daytime traffic congested streets. As all of this was happening I felt a call on my phone, I didn't realize it was ringing until I actually saw I had two missed calls from my dad already. I swiped to accept the call and was unsure what my dad was going to say.

"Hello Dad?" I said as I gulped into the speaker. But before I could even start my dad was already going full speed.

"Zach, thank God you're okay. I am meeting you in a few minutes and we are heading home okay?" my dad said with an alarming urgency that I'm yet to understand.

"Zach did you hear me?" I was still quiet but the image of the wolf-like creature came back to my head.

"Zach!"

As I realized I had the phone halfway down to my cheek, I put it back onto my ear.

"Dad, I heard you. What is going on? Why is there two marines riding with me? What did I do wrong?"

The hiss and crackling, along with the sirens outside was muffling what my dad was saying. I was struggling to hear but finally was able to cup my other ear and heard him more audibly.

"Zach, they're just there to protect you, okay? Don't be afraid, I'll be seeing you soon."

With that, the line went dead and I felt some relief that this had nothing to do with my stunt this morning. And yet I felt in my heart that it did, but for another reason.

As we arrived at the edge of the square, I saw my dad already flagging the SUV down. After all these years, I had to admit that I was happy to see my dad. I know that I was hard on him, and I didn't need to be. But right now, I feel that he's here, for me.

The SUV stops right in front of my dad and he circles around to the back. One of the marine jumps out as another SUV, the security detail pulls up behind us. The marine jumps into that SUV and as my dad came into the back seat, I never expected him to give me a hug. But he did, like he'd never done for the past year. After what felt like an eternity, he pushed back and looked me square in the eye.

"I want you to know Zach that I have and never will blame you for what happened with your mother. Do you understand me?"

Why is he saying this now? I have never heard him mention anything for almost a year and now he tells me this. I see the compassion and burden in his eyes, and if it was any other day I

90

would probably have rejected this whole exchange but for some reason, I understood him. I knew he felt he had to say it, and I needed to hear it.

"I do understand. And I'm sorry too. I'm sorry that I couldn't save her dad."

As I said this, I felt a great weight lifted out of my chest. It was as if this was the right time for all this to happen and while on the outside, it felt strange, between me and my dad, it was right. And it was time.

"I know son, I know you tried." As I looked into my dad's eyes, for the first time, I saw some glimmer of peace. I was hoping for something that would make me try to make a statement which was why I was going to run away. But now it seems so stupid and for some reasons, this day had gone in a way that neither me nor my dad had expected it to go.

"Right now, we have to get back home and pack."

As my dad nodded to Patrick to go, both SUV's pulled out of the square with both polizia cars running as escorts. For some reasons, I thought I heard my dad said we needed to pack, which I was sure was not what he said.

"Did you say pack? Pack for what dad? I don't understand."

My dad was deep in thought and while he looked at me and gave me a smile meant to let me feel less confused, he knew it was not helping.

"Certain things have come to light Zach, you and me, we're heading back to the states."

As my father said this, I felt a wave of emotion that I couldn't possibly handle. I felt joy and sadness; I felt heartache and some relief. We just moved here six months ago, why are we all of a sudden heading back? What happened today? I looked at my dad and I knew he was thinking, making plans in his head, trying to figure out how to do something. I've seen it before. My dad turns to me again, and without any second thought or warning said something I did not expect.

"And one other thing, we have someone else coming with us."

CHAPTER EIGHT

THE PAPAL APARTMENT

ROME, ITALY

As the Pope and Veneto make their way down to the kitchen, both had thought that the meeting with Ambassador Stevens went better than expected. Veneto had just sent off an encrypted message to David's email account with what they need for this part of the plan. The Pope knows that the powers that be, both human and supernatural have begun to move their pieces in this end game that will culminate in the salvation or damnation of the world.

Earlier that day, after having received the encrypted call from Irsina, both the Pope and Veneto had arranged for the vessel to be transported within the Vatican walls. The Pope had given strict instructions to the captain of the corps for the Gendarmerie, one that has been loyal to the order, to make sure that the protection and safe passage of this person is of the utmost importance. Gone are the needs for the clandestine ways of having protected the bloodline. With the message that was received from a divine source, and that the vessel now has been anointed to bring back the Son of God, secrecy no longer matters for soon the entire world will be told.

A full regiment of corps soldiers escorted Elizabeth from Irsina into Rome at the wee hours of the morning. Understandably, the young woman should have been scared out of her wits being whisked away at the early hours of the morning, driven to the nearest airport, flown by helicopter into Rome and escorted by Vatican appointed soldiers. But when the Pope saw her come out from one of the vans from the airport, one that is used to transport the Pope himself, she was the picture of calm and serenity.

The Pope greeted her and fell to his knees. Humility washed over those that saw her, and her grace can be felt as if something one can touch and feel like the wind. There is no more need for protocols, no more need for procedure. All that matters is the vessel, and what needs to be done while the spirit brings life to those who will bring peace to all nations.

Now under guard with the same detail of soldiers from the trip from Irsina, the vessel, Elizabeth, was in the kitchen of the papal apartment. As the Pope and Veneto come down the winding narrow stairs that led to it, they smelled something cooking and looked at each other in subtle curiosity.

At first the Pope was alarmed to see that not one of the soldiers meant to stand guard was at their post when they finally reached the lower level where the kitchen was located. Veneto started to run down the hallway into the kitchen thinking the worse but as he came into the archway, he stopped and breathed a sigh of relief. He looked back at the Pope and put his hand on his chest, placing it on the crucifix that he had on. As the Pope caught up with Veneto, he saw the guards sitting around the round dining table, made of solid cherry, and being served by Elizabeth herself. The vessel, the one that will bring back the Son of God shows off the mercy and grace that her namesake has shown almost over 2000 years ago.

"Ah your Holiness, would you and Monsignor Veneto like a bowl of stew?" Elizabeth asks as she smiles at the Pope and Veneto and makes her way back to the stove and starts to grab two bowls from the cupboard and begins to scoop up some stew from the pot.

"I rarely have a chance to cook for my godmother and seeing that you have so much to work with here, I felt compelled to do something for these brave men."

The soldiers were oblivious to the Pope and Veneto, they were in a state of grace and servitude that can only be commanded by the divine and the anointed. The Pope looked at the men and they smiled back. It was then that the Pope knew, in his heart, that these men would protect Elizabeth with their very lives.

The Pope and Veneto sat down on the smaller island table to the side of the main dining table. As Elizabeth comes to them with two bowls of stew, still sensing the warmth of her grace, the Pope and Veneto take each bowl and settle into their chair. Suddenly the urgency in both had simply died down, as each of them knew that this was the calm before the very heavy and dark storm that is coming. But it is also these times that makes them realize what are the true treasures in life.

"Grazie mia Cara." As Pope Nicholas takes the spoon and tastes the stew. It reminded him of how his mother made his favorite soup as a boy back in Spain. Elizabeth sits down with them and in silence, they all partake of this simple blessing. But the Pope knows that time is crucial, and that while this is how he feels things will be, it is still not here, not yet. He puts his spoon down and pushes the bowl back and looks at Elizabeth.

"My dear Elizabeth, you will not remember me, but I was there when you came into this world. And so was Monsignor Veneto."

As Elizabeth heard this, she puts her hands on both the Pope's and Veneto's and she smiled at both of them.

"Thank you both for all that you have done for me." she said as she took her hands off and realized that both have still weary and fear on their faces. Veneto was still looking at her intently, having been the one that will bear the Son of God for the second coming, Veneto was in awe of her simplicity, her humility and most of all her calm and nurturing nature.

"My dear Elizabeth, your godmother spoke of a message." Both Pope Nicholas and Veneto wanted to hear the message themselves. It was far and rare for them to have this opportunity to live in a lifetime where the Father himself has given such a divine message to be spread across the world.

As they both looked to Elizabeth, she smiled and began to speak.

"He said that he was an angel of the Father, sent to bring me good news. He said that the time has come for the entire world to know of the Father's grace and love. He said that I have been chosen, in this cycle of life, for this world, to bring back the Son of God as one of us, as part of us. Only when that happens will this world be part of the heavenly kingdom."

As these words go into the Pope's head, he is continually humbled by the joy within this vessel. He also wished that he was there to witness the divine power of the Holy Spirit and that for this to happen in his lifetime, was truly something to be thankful for.

But he also knew that this was known to those that would want this world to crumble into darkness. He has no doubt that the powers of evil are moving to meet this divine threat to them. As a man of faith, the Pope has seen evil in many ways but he understands that for what is to come, such evil is something that no one has ever seen, or will see again.

"I know that you must be tired Elizabeth, but I'm afraid we will have to move you to some place safer."

As Pope Nicholas, formerly Cardinal Ricardo Gonzalez from Spain, who now sits face to face with the bringer of peace and light and joy to the world, have now to tell Elizabeth of the threat to her life. He knows that because of who she is, she will be hunted and sought after by the king of darkness himself. Satan will not cease his quest to extinguish the light and hope that grows inside of her.

"There are those that will want to see you harmed Elizabeth, and while we have put certain precautions in place to prevent this, in this place, is where they will look for you first."

The Pope knows that the vessel's movements are known to the enemy which was why they had to act quickly. There was no time to lose and that was the reason why he wanted to talk with Ambassador Stevens. They will have far more resources to protect her if she is outside of these walls. They need to be on the move, they need to be evasive.

"I have arranged for your travel to the United States. I have chosen someone I trust to accompany you there."

As the Pope explains this to Elizabeth, she looks sad. The Pope reaches out for her hand and she looks up to him.

"Please do not be sad my dear, you will be safer there." and as Elizabeth takes his hands, she grasps them tightly and longingly.

"I do not fear for my safety your Holiness, I fear for yours."

As the Pope realizes this, he is once again reminded of the love and grace in this young woman's heart. The Pope is happy to submit to the will of the heavenly Father, and if it calls for his life, then he will gloriously deliver it unto Him. However, he knows too well of the danger that Elizabeth faces.

"I will be alright my dear, as I have faith in you and our Father."

With that, Elizabeth smiles warmly as the Pope and Veneto finish off their stew. The soldiers have gone back to their posts and if all goes well, Elizabeth will be on her way to the United States by morning. He hopes that David has been able to make the necessary arrangements needed. For tonight, however, there will be no rest for anyone, until the vessel is safely on her way.

* * *

As Sarah answers the phone, she is hoping to have more clarity on what happened with David's meeting with the Pope. She had insisted on coming with David for the meeting but the instructions were clear. David was to meet with his Holiness alone. Sarah had given David all that she could find over the past six months in terms communiqué, political and social angles that may have prompted the meeting request. As she saw David off to the meeting, she felt that there was nothing really there.

Coming from a big family from Haskell, Arkansas, born Sarah Alice McKenzie, she was one of five children that was born and raised in this small town southwest of Little Rock. Haskell was a tight knit community whose population of a little over 2600 was spread out over a 4.6 miles radius. Needless to say, it was a small town and everyone knew everyone.

Everyone went to Harmony Grove, the lone school district in the city. Sarah spent much of her childhood in the town and after graduating high school, she had applied for several universities to the east. Her parents, both blue collar workers wasn't too big on her going to college since out of her siblings, she was the only one that actually wanted to go. She had shown early aptitude towards social sciences and wanted to pursue a degree in Political Science and International Relations. She was particularly interested in how domestic and foreign policies were made and what were the aggregated impacts of such at the economic, social and political levels.

She finally got into the George Washington University in Washington DC. Quite a feat for a small town girl from rural Haskell. In her studies, she excelled in all her subjects, earning a Dean's List appointment as well as graduating as the Summa Cum Laude of her class. Being in the nation's capital, she found herself readily connected to several branches of the US government. She began as an intern in the United States Senate, under the office of Senator William Hoskins of the State of Georgia. She then found herself as the executive administrator for Congressman John Delancey, the Representative for the 6th District of Mississippi.

However, she found that she also had a flavor for wanting to explore international and foreign policy. This was why she decided to apply as one of the global communications attachés for the US Department of State. She had numerous posting around the globe, namely in Germany, Switzerland and Thailand. When she had seen the inter-department communication on openings at the US Ambassador's Office in Rome, she applied and was considered for the job. The then incumbent US Ambassador to the Holy See, Matthew Riechland was in the process of retiring and her appointment to the office as its executive coordinator was approved right at the time the new Ambassador was announced.

She had met David Stevens at the same day, which happens to be the first day of office for the both of them. This immediately gave both a sense of relief and was instrumental in making the kind of working relationship they have now what it is. She respected David for his clear views on political and economic perspectives, especially being an ambassador to one of the most religiously dedicated states in the world.

"I was wondering when you were going to call, I had….."

Before she could finish her sentence, David had cut her off, he sounded like he was panting, almost hyperventilating and she was confused and worried at the same time. Listening to what David was saying, she stood up, walked briskly to his office and shut the door behind her and locked it. On the other line, she responded back.

"Okay, David, I'm in your office. Now please slow down and tell me again what you just said."

She went around to David's desk, sat on his chair and her mouth came open. After that, she swallowed a huge knot in her throat and continued to listen to David.

"Let me understand this, you want me to prepare a Form TA-180 for today? David, that's an extraction notice that can only be approved by the President in instances where the embassy is under siege from a terrorist organization. I'm sorry but I don't understand."

She then grabbed a clear note pad and reached for one of the pens that was on David's desk and started writing down details as David was talking on the line. She was shaking her head when she was doing it, clearly not having the comprehension behind the instructions being given to her at that time.

"You understand that that kind of military detail needs to be approved by the resident commanding officer of Camp Darby."

As she continues to list down the specifics of what David was telling her, she is slowly realizing that this is something that is happening now. The only thing she could think of was that the meeting with the Pope had somehow released some sort of intelligence against this office.

"I will send out a separate security team to pick up this Elizabeth Scarpello from the papal apartments, but David, I can't guarantee that this can happen today. The clearance alone will probably come tomorrow at the earliest."

Now there's a new piece in play. Who is this Elizabeth Scarpello, and why is she being tagged as a priority one intelligence source? This was all news to Sarah, but arguably enough, not surprising. She's learned that in the service within the Department of State, certain circumstances which may not completely make any sense at all could actually be warranted and justified. She had learned that it was not for her to question but she can have certain perspectives that are if she knew what the hell was going on. For now, she's taking David on his word.

"They'll have the asset to your villa in 30 minutes, oh and I just received confirmation that Patrick just arrived here at the embassy with Zach."

Sarah stopped writing; she stood up and began to run towards the embassy entrance. She grabbed David's heavy briefcase and slung it over her shoulder. On her way, she put the phone on her lapel and gestured to two marines in combat gear to follow her outside. It was clear that David had directed her to do so. As she approached the doors, she saw Patrick and Zach outside through the glass doors.

"I have Patrick on the com; I'll relay your instructions."

As she went out of the embassy, she flagged Patrick down and with Zach standing by the SUV, Sarah put her hands on Patrick's shoulder and hunched him down like they were ready for a football play.

"Patrick, you are to take Zach with you and pick up Ambassador Stevens in Saint Peter's Square. I am assigning two marines for additional security as per his instructions."

Patrick looks at Sarah and nods. Sarah hands Patrick the briefcase, which he recognizes as David's. Before Patrick heads back to the SUV, Sarah remembers one last thing.

"And Patrick, the Ambassador will explain it to Zach. No intel on anything until the Ambassador has eyes on Zach."

With that, Patrick runs with the two marines with him and he gets Zach in the back seat of the SUV. Sarah watches as they leave the embassy and she runs back inside to take care of the other things that David asked her to do.

As she walks in, she flags one of the administrative clerks to go with her and she went back into David's office. She began typing on the network requesting a high priority communiqué from David's office to the White House Advisory Room. She has never had to fill out a TA-180 form before but there's a first time for everything she thought.

As she was putting in the form details, she looks at the clerk and gave him instructions.

"I want you to send a priority message to Camp Darby, Commanding Officer. Details are to be sent in a separate secure line but prepare to accept high value asset for immediate transport back to the US mainland. Encrypt it and signature approval from this office. Go."

As the clerk fumbles with the details and runs to the embassy communications room, Sarah looks at the form she is filling in. She's at the point of describing "imminent risk" section. She paused and had looked back at the notes that scribbled on the pad from her conversation with David. With a sigh of apprehension, she types in "Global Extinction Event".

She felt sick to her stomach, and she knew that there was no going back once this is sent. David was adamant about this, and she has still no reason to not trust his judgment. She put her finger over the send key and for a slight moment, she felt she couldn't do it. But she pushed the button and the message on the screen said "message sent".

She grabbed her phone as she left David's office. She started texting him to let him know that things were in play. She went to her own office, grabbed a couple of things, put some documents in a travel pouch and took her coat from the closet. She then went to the in house marine desk and asked for a squad of marines to follow her to an undisclosed location.

She needed to find out what was going on. That's why she was heading to a small private airport that the embassy uses for domestic flights.

* * *

As the Pope and Veneto get Elizabeth ready, the guards are informed that the convoy was here to transport her to an undisclosed location. The Pope was heavy hearted but knows that this was the best thing for Elizabeth. As Veneto went ahead to see that all things were in order for her departure, the Pope had some last words for Elizabeth.

"Elizabeth, whatever happens my dear, you need to remember that as long as we have faith, there is hope."

The Pope clutches both of Elizabeth's hands and she smiles back at him. Her bright green eyes did not see fear, and her warmth gave the Pope all the reassurance that he needed. Before the Pope escorted Elizabeth to the top level of the papal apartments, he started saying a short prayer.

"My Heavenly Father, may Your hand guide us in what is to come. May it help us fulfill our purpose for Your will and that may it further the glory of Your kingdom."

As Elizabeth prayed with the Pope, she began to feel the presence of the spirit. The same blue aura that had first enveloped her during the night the message was delivered was once again present. The Pope opened his eyes and fell to ground in sheer humility. But Elizabeth propped him up and still glowing in this peaceful and glorious shine, she put her hand on the Pope's cheek.

"It's because of the sacrifice of the Father of His Son, that he was glorified and raised back up, so shall it be with your trust in Him. Know that you have a future in His will."

As the Pope received this divine benediction, he knew that faith would be needed for the coming days. He looks back at Elizabeth and he finds joy in her smile. He then walks with her towards the front of the apartments, along the way, the guards assigned to watch her join in unison. As they come out of the apartment, Veneto was talking with a young marine sergeant and three vehicles waiting outside in the oval driveway. There were two Humvees and one unmarked black sedan. The marine opened the door to the sedan and the Pope walked over with Elizabeth. As she began to go in, she looked back at the Pope and Veneto and gave one last smile.

The marine closed the door and ran up to the first Humvee and started to drive off. As the convoy left the apartments, Veneto looks at the Pope with uncertain eyes.

"Your Holiness, do you think we did the right thing?"

As the Pope turns around and heads back into the apartment, he clasps his hands and smiles back to Veneto.

"It is out of our hands now, as it has always been Veneto. From this moment on, we no longer operate under any secrecy."

As both of them walk into the apartment, the resolve in the Pope's heart began to swell. There is no more time to worry about what others will think or do, for soon, as he expects it, the message will be revealed to the entire world. When that happens, all things will change. All people of the world will change.

"Inform the Order that the vessel has been secured here. No one is to know of where she is going. Is that understood Veneto."

As the Pope looks to Veneto for confirmation, he nods in agreement and gives the Pope a look of acceptance. They will do everything to protect Elizabeth, and they will do whatever it takes so that she is. As it was in the past, the fate of the world now rests with one person. But unlike in the past, it is now our turn to sacrifice ourselves.

As the Pope retreats to his bedroom, he feels a certain presence that has been lingering ever since Elizabeth left. He, of course knew, what the presence was. As with all things, where there is light and hope, there is despair and darkness. As he sits quietly in his sitting chair, which was on the far corner of the room facing the entire bedroom. The Pope waits.

Within moments, a dark cloud forms in the shadows and emerges into the center of the room. The Pope straightens up in his chair but keeps his composure. He did not show fear or worry, he closed his eyes and was deep in divine prayer. As the figure, still swirling within the dark cloud of ashen smoke, its silhouette begins to resemble that of a person. But as the form grew clearer, it was clear that it was not of any ordinary person. The Pope sees the distinct horns and now the spread wings with tipped claws reveal themselves. As the Pope fills his heart with resolve, he knew that this day would come. But he was ready; he was prepared to face the demon that is Satan.

"You are not welcome here and you shall not find what you seek."

As the Pope utters these words, a loud and harsh noise that can only be described as the shrieks of a thousand souls in pain and agony fills the room. The Pope covers his ears with the deafening sound and it subsides when the darkness spoke.

"You are a fool to think that this vessel is safe from me." The words seethe with disdain and hatred, as the figure of the darkness approaches the Pope. The Pope then stands up still without fear and looks at the depths of evil personified.

"You are the fool, Satan, for I have the Father's grace, and you will never triumph against His righteousness."

As soon as the darkness hears this, it lets out a fiery red scream that envelope the Pope, and at that time, the Pope sees the heart of the demon, the pain that is there, the hatred that makes his soul burn. But he steadies himself, and allows the force of a thousand screams of sorrow pass through him. He calmed his heart and calls upon the spirit to aid him in this hour of need.

As the king of darkness seeks to destroy those in His service, there are those that come to aid the faithful. As the fiery hell continues to encompass the Pope, a light appears from above the

Pope, the same kind of light that spoke to Elizabeth a few days past. When the light hit the dark swell of anger and hate, the king of darkness let out a wounding scream as the darkness is quickly blotted out of the room. As the Pope opens his eyes, he witnesses a miracle in front of him, for an angel within the light stares at him and then disappears but not without uttering these words.

"The faithful shall be rewarded with the Father's grace."

Pope Nicholas VI, formerly Cardinal Ricardo Gonzales of Spain, the member of the Order of the Light has seen Satan's heart and survived. He drops to his knees exhausted from the spiritual battle that just occurred and realizes the way of things to come. Moments later, Veneto barges into the bedroom having heard the entire commotion from the outside. The bedroom door was ajar and Veneto could not come in. Now with several members of the corps following Veneto, the Pope sits up and looks at the monsignor.

"I pray that Elizabeth will be safe Veneto, but I am afraid Satan will do all that he can to get to her."

Veneto sits the Pope up on his chair and immediately pulls out his cell phone and dials the Ambassador's number.

CHAPTER NINE

THE MESSAGE

As the convoy carrying me and Zach gets closer to our home outside the city, my cell phone rings. I see it's a number I do not recognize and but answer it anyway. It was Veneto, and he was trying to get a status of where the extraction team was in terms of transporting Elizabeth.

"We're almost back to the villa, the security team that has Elizabeth is en route and should be there a little after us."

As I listen to Veneto, I look over at Zach and he is clearly disturbed. I made a mental note that when we get back home, the first order of business is for me to sit down with Zach and give him something to go on. I was distracted when I heard Veneto mention something about an attack.

"Wait, can you say that again? Did you just say that the Pope was attacked?"

This made my heart sink. If this is starting now, and that the Pope has been breached to get to Elizabeth, then it's likely that whatever it was that attacked will likely come after her here. As he listened to Veneto, the details made him run his hands through his hair.

This is just unbelievable. What Veneto described was short of something that you see in the movies, but it's happening now, and it's happening here. I was now working my way into the villa with Zach and the security team behind me.

"Oh my God, is his Holiness alright?"

I was still on the phone as the team gets into the villa and begins securing the rooms. I see Zach run up to his bedroom and with Patrick following him. I made another mental note to call Sarah to make sure that all the arrangements have been sent and that everything is in the pipeline to happen. Where is she anyway, I had told her to monitor all communications and report back to me if she hears of something relevant, like say an attack on the papal household?

"Thank God, yes, please let me know if there's anything else I can do. We are securing the villa and I will let you know once the vessel is here."

When I started up the stairs, I knew that Zach was going to have a hard time with what I was going to tell him. But perhaps this is something that can help us both. If this second coming is to happen, then all the reason for me to make things right with Zach before the world ends. Patrick passes me going down as I was finishing up my conversation with Veneto and paused outside Zach's door. After putting my phone back into by jacket pocket, I knock on Zach's door.

"Zach, it's me. Can I come in?"

No answer. I knocked again and just decided to try the door knob. It wasn't locked so I slowly opened the door. Zach was staring out of the window, and he was holding the frame that he always held, all the time. I made my way to his bed, sat down and waited for him to say something. I wasn't going to force him, I want Zach to be ready to talk.

"Listen Zach, I know this is all happening so fast but I want to slow down for a bit here."

Before coming up, he realized that Zach had not gone to his field trip. He didn't have a chance to ask Patrick or Sarah why because of everything that was going on but now he's here and he wanted to ask Zach.

"So I'll assume that Patrick did not pick you up from the ruins. I got a call from Ms. Folchetti that you were not in your class when they arrived there. Remind me to write a letter to the school administrator sighting school liability for missing students."

Zach was still staring out the window, and he managed an awkward chuckle. With all the things that he's learned the past four hours, this seems slightly amusing at best. While on the bed, I started recounting the events of the day, how this morning seemed like any other morning.

There was no indication that any of this was happening, which I guess was the point. We all have been so busy with our lives that we seldom realize what's truly important around us. I looked at Zach and felt sorry that I haven't tried to be there for him more.

"Zach, please talk to me, tell me what's going on with you."

I desperately wanted to give him a hug. It's been ages since I've seen him smile, and the last time I did, he was with his mother. Instead, I stood up and went beside him, and we both stared out the window. I put my hand on his shoulder and squeezed it, it was the best that I could do right now. Feeling that there was little to talk about, I turn around and walked towards the door. In mid stride, I was surprised at what Zach said.

"Something happened to me today Dad, something I don't understand."

I was a bit confused at first but I wanted to give Zach the chance to say what he felt. Something happened today, what did he mean? I sat back down the bed and Zach turned around and struggled to find the words. I saw it in his eyes, but I managed to give him a smile, if anything at all, to make him feel safe.

"Zach, talk to me. What's on your mind?"

With that Zach started to head towards the door. It was slightly open but he felt the need to shut it, and lock it. I was surprised by this; I was thinking to myself who would Zach need to keep out?

"Today, I skipped the field trip with the plan to run away."

He looked at me, wounded. He knew that it was something that he shouldn't have done, and I saw the ache in his heart by just admitting it to me. A couple of police sirens streaks by the villa, which broke the otherwise silent state in this part of town. I looked at Zach and made sure that he knew I wasn't angry, I was sad, but I wasn't angry.

"I can understand Zach, I haven't really been there for you. I'm sorry that you felt you couldn't talk to me, about anything."

Zach was now sitting beside me on his bed. And we were both looking at the floor. Another siren whisks by and this time I heard about three distinct sounds, not just a police siren but probably EMS and fire. I looked at Zach hoping that he would open up.

"I went down this alley way and got lost and then something happened." Zach said as he looked at me clearly in a state of confusion. I shifted my body so that I was now sitting sideways looking at him directly. What is he saying? I'm the one getting confused now.

"Just tell me Zach, don't worry, okay? What happened?"

As Zach took a deep breath, he wanted to make sure that what he was going to say was making sense, I could see it in his face. I gave him time, wanted him to know that I was going to listen, no matter what. With one deep breath he finally looked at me and said something that I never expected him to say, especially in light of what just happened with the Pope.

"The devil revealed himself to me."

My shoulders hunched up, my throat went dry. I was looking at Zach and knew he was telling me the truth, or what he felt was the truth. I couldn't imagine why Zach would say it so succinctly, but his sentence was clear, and it was something he believed. I heard some commotion downstairs, and expected that the second security detail has arrived with Elizabeth. I turned back to Zach and I wanted to make sure I understood him.

"Why do you say that Zach, what did you see?"

As Zach described to me the events in the alley way, as crazy as it could be, it actually makes some sense with what's going on. But what I could not understand is why him? Why Zach? I finally heard some footsteps running upstairs and the knock on the door was solid, and in a hurry. I stood up, looking at Zach to make sure that I believe him, that I do believe him. I opened the door and Patrick was standing in the hallway, he looked distressed.

"Patrick, what's going on, is the asset here?"

Patrick was not a man who could lose words to describe what he needs to say. This was a first, as Patrick just gestured to go downstairs which I took with some urgency. I looked at Zach and held up my hand, telling him to stay in his room. I walked out and closed the door behind me, as Patrick made his way down looking at me and glancing at the bottom of the stairs. I have never seen Patrick jolted much less speechless, but today was a lot of firsts for me.

I reached the ground floor and the entire detail was clustered around the TV which was now reporting on something that would change how the world is, and will be. I listened to the reporter who was doing a live broadcast in St. Peter's Square.

"As you can see, the orbs are now hovering a mere 10 meters off the ground and there are a multitude of them. We are getting reports all over Rome, and the country and even across the world where this phenomenon is happening as well."

* * *

Deep within the granite bedrock of the Cheyenne Mountains, the North American Aerospace Defense Command, or NORAD, is charged with the mission of aerospace warning and aerospace control for North America. At the height of the Cold War in the late 1950s, the idea of a hardened command and control center was conceptualized as a defense against long-range Soviet bombers.

The Army Corps of Engineers supervised the excavation of Cheyenne Mountain and the construction of an operational center within the granite mountain. The Cheyenne Mountain facility became fully operational as the NORAD Combat Operations Center on Feb. 6, 1967.

However, changes in the organization after the cold war moved the Headquarters for NORAD and the NORAD/United States Northern Command (USNORTHCOM) center at Peterson Air Force Base in El Paso County, near Colorado Springs, Colorado.

The 21st Space Wing, also headquartered at Peterson Air Force Base, Colorado, is the Air Force's only organization providing missile warning and space control to unified commanders and combat forces worldwide. Daily operations for NORAD are split between the Cheyenne Mountain Facility and its basement control division at Peterson.

From each location, NORAD is capable of tracking all air and space faring satellites, aircraft as well as deep space objects that pose imminent threat to the planet. Alaskan and Canadian NORAD control centers monitor airspace in their affected regions and all data is sent to the Joint Aerospace Command Center or JACC, in Dedham, West Virginia.

At the main control room, an Air Force Lieutenant conducts a standard satellite sweep across the North America airspace and finds something peculiar. She looks at intermittent signals on a fixed trajectory circling the globe. Normally this would not warrant any kind of alarm as space junk often creates ghost images within the satellite feed and the mapping of these have been consistent over the last forty years. She picks up the secure com line to the ICC.

"Sir, I'm tracking several bogies on an elliptical trajectory across North America. I'm not sure what to make if it."

As she puts down the phone, an overhead speaker blares out tracking and trajectory readings and she pulls up her monitor onto the main control screen in the room. She begins tracking the unidentified objects and counts seven of them on different orbits around the planet. She makes a call to the US Strategic Command to confirm the bogies using the AN/FPS 85 Phased Array Surveillance Space Radar. The readings can't be right, there has to be a glitch in the telemetry.

As the ICC comes down a flight of steel stairs looking over the control room, he makes a bee line for the lieutenants' work station. Current operational procedures are active and he does not want to report back to the Chief of Staff that there's an imminent threat to US and Canadian soil. As he approaches the workstation, his face looks at the main screen in the middle of the room.

"What do you have for me Lieutenant?"

As the trajectory is mapped onto the prior one on the main screen, a pattern starts to appear. Each of the seven bogies seems to be going into a helix pattern, much like what you would imagine protons doing in circling an atom. Except in this case the atom was the entire planet.

"Sir, the bogies are in a consistent orbit and have showed no signs of degradation."

As the ICC looks at the data, he confirms that each of the bogies is in a consistent holding pattern. Then he looks closer at the data and starts to flick the monitor as if it was defective.

"That can't be right. It's a telemetry error." He goes to another workstation to look at the same data feed. As he confirms it, he stands up and looks at the Lieutenant. The bogies are orbiting the planet from an altitude a little over 30 feet.

"Get me a secure line to the Pentagon and CIC. Are we recording this? I want confirmation from all worldwide aerospace divisions, military and private to confirm this telemetry."

As he walks back towards the stairs, the entire room focuses on the main screen. The bogie then begins to change and something starts happening to their orbits. The lieutenant yells back at the ICC.

"Sir! The bogies are dispersing!"

As the ICC looks at the main screen, each one of the seven objects begins to trail off with a separate piece. As each piece breaks off, it then breaks off again. The screen they were looking at now resembled a net over the surface of the planet.

"My God." as the ICC looks at the continuing pattern that begins to cover the entire globe.

"Initiate a full lockdown and bring us to DEFCON 3. Alert all branches and the Joint Chiefs. I want emergency protocols in place for the President and the Canadian Prime Minister."

The room blares out an announcement as the status lights change from blue to yellow. The ICC runs back to his office and opens up a safe in the wall hidden behind a portrait of General Henry Gordon, one of the first Commanding Officer of NORAD. He pulls out a red folder with the lettering "CLASSIFIED" in white letters and begins looking at authorization codes for transferring space and air command to the bunker in the Cheyenne Mountain location. The phone on his desk buzzes.

"Intelligence Control Commander Wilkins, yes sir. Yes sir, we have confirmed objects and tracking them against all known scenarios. This pattern is something that we've never seen before sir."

As he listens, he looks up at the main screen outside of the control room. The bogies have now incrementally increased by 30% and have concentrated their main presence over each of the main land masses. There are still some outliers in the smaller pacific regions but in essence, the objects have covered the entire land area of the whole planet.

"Yes sir, understood."

As the ICC puts down the phone, he reaches for the PA button, and hesitates before speaking.

"Set the current status on DEFCON 2, activate all branches and response protocols."

Across the globe, in every nation, over all that is creation, the spirit spreads with divine purpose. This moment shall come but once in the history of this world, and it will not come again once its purpose has been met. The orb that contains the divine spirit of the Father hovers over the masses. In their glory, those that are witnesses are held by their beauty and awe.

People are drawn out of their homes; they flock to the streets and gaze upon these divine orbs. Now they have stopped moving and have been in place for some time. As more and more people gather, like sheep to a shepherd, some cry out in hysteria, some break down in tears. Others fall to their knees and others react with fear. The entire world, now under this divine blanket, prepares for what is to come.

As the Pope looks out his window from his study, he clasps his hands in prayer. As David looks at the news feed, he runs out to see it for himself along with the others. As David goes to the streets, he realizes that the second security team has arrived with Elizabeth at the villa. They too are mesmerized by the bright blue orbs.

However Elizabeth was calm and she was smiling, once again pressing her palm to her stomach and smiling. He looks at David and

David looks back at her. Elizabeth didn't say anything but if she had, it would have made David feel safe and unafraid.

"Are you doing this?" he asks Elizabeth, still in awe of what's going on around them. Elizabeth smiles and looks up.

"We have no power alone but with faith, hope and love, everything is possible. This is not my doing, for I am only a servant of the Father, such as you."

When David heard this, he felt Elizabeth's calm, his fear was removed from his heart. He realized that Zach had come outside as well. He was behind him and he was looking at Elizabeth. He felt the urge to go by her side but fought it, and instead gazed up into the orbs now steadily hovering above all.

From above, in the great hall, the Eternals look down upon what is happening. This is the moment that all worlds must see. They have seen it with other worlds, and they will see it again. No matter how many times this has happened, they all marvel at the power and authority of the heavenly Father. They look to each other and in agreement decide that the message can now be sent to all.

With the orbs shining brighter, it begins to emit a beam of light. What it resembles is a spot light, looking, seeking for something within the crowds that have now amassed. The beams of light, all over the world are looking for those that are worthy, for those that can be true messengers, to deliver the ultimate one. As each light hones in to one soul, it captures that soul and fills it. All across the world, the same thing happens, with each beam of light latching onto one soul that it has found worthy.

As those chosen ones are lifted from their feet, up into the air with their heads bowed down as if pulled by an invisible rope, all those in who saw it fall to their knees. As they stop and float in mid-air, their heads snap back as their eyes and mouth fall open and the divine spirit flows out of it, and through them. What followed can only be described as the voice of the Father himself.

Behold this cup before you as it has been given to my Son, so shall it now be given unto you. Know that all of creations on the land, under the seas and in the skies are subject to this cup. The time has come as demanded by the signs for this world to face judgment. This beginning to the end shall make the righteous strong and the wicked falter. Look into your hearts for that is where my spirit lies, I will know your heart as it was my own. A new dawn will come when this time is over, for how it shall be is up to those that choose rightfully. Put on the armor of truth and you shall reap the rewards of thy kingdom, but beware, if you put on the cloak of darkness, you shall be cast into the bottomless pit. All of creation fights for this world to be part of the light or be cast into hellfire. The prize is no longer power, ownerships, nor property but your very souls. At the break of day, I will send my army to aid you in this last rite of passage; they will be yours as they are mine. Together, you will face the full malice of the fallen, and they will grant you no mercy. My army will exact my will and bless those that glorify Me, but will be swift in their punishment for those that stray from this flock. Among you there is a vessel that carries the truth, the way and the life. For your world to be saved, my Son will have his life given to him. As he has given it for you, so now shall you all be servants of the spirit and be willful in your sacrifices. This is your covenant now, this is what I ask of you all. This is My will, and the will in your hearts needs to be strong. Be faithful as I have been faithful to you, and I truly say to you that the kingdom as it was promised is within reach.

The entire world, gasping for air, has just heard the final message for this world. As the message was delivered through each of the chosen, in each of their own tongues, there was no longer any doubt. What does one do when one realizes that all things in this world, in life, in all of existence will end? Today is the day when judgment begins.

There are those that do not believe, and have chosen to turn away from this divine message. There are those that are believers but weary of complete trust in the word that were uttered. And there are those that have the spirit in their hearts, those that will rise up in order to fulfill the will of the Father. All across the world, in places high and low, in cultures that now have no difference except in what they believe in, this has become the ultimate test.

As the chosen were returned to the masses, the entire world now prepare for what is to come. Tomorrow the world comes closer to becoming part of what people call heaven as it also comes closer to becoming part of hell. Such is the universal fate of worlds under the Father's grace and authority.

As people look into their hearts, the fallen stirs within the bottomless pit. Along with the minions of the cursed, and those that choose to follow the darkness, Lucifer seeks out those whose hearts are impure. He plans to make them turn against the will of who cast him out. And he will make sure that the vessel will not be given any mercy.

As Zach and I watch the orbs disappear into the night, I look to Elizabeth and gestures for all of us to go into the villa. Patrick stands by me and makes his concerns known.

"David, I know you heard and saw what I did. And I'm here to do what you ask but what good are we against this kind of threat?"

As I look to Zach, who was now accompanying Elizabeth to the inside room, I realize that this was something that not only Patrick is thinking of, but everyone else in his detail.

"Pat, I do not know how we can make a difference, all I know is that we should try. We're given someone to protect, for the sake of the entire world, and all I can ask of you is to try my old friend."

As David looks to Patrick, he puts his hands on his shoulders and gives him a good shake. Patrick breaths a long deep sigh and turns back to the men outside.

"Alright, I want eyes on every corner of this property. I want two men on the balcony, and I want a rotating shift inside and outside the house. Until we leave this place tomorrow morning, nobody gets in or out."

As the men confirm the orders that Patrick gave, I went into the house to check on Elizabeth and Zach. I headed upstairs and at the opening of the door to Zach's bedroom, I stumbled upon Zach tucking Elizabeth to bed. I was going to go inside but heard Zach talking to Elizabeth as she put her head to the pillow.

"It'll be okay, everyone here will look after you, including me."

I hear the sincerity in Zach's voice, and I feel my heart open up to grace. As Zach walks towards the door, I quickly go downstairs so that Zach doesn't see me. Downstairs, I was at the dining table when Zach came down and sat across to me.

"This was what you were trying to tell me. You've had a hell of a day Dad."

I looked at him and smiled.

All this time, the TV has been reporting on this unprecedented event in the world's history. Coverage from Asia, Europe, Latin America, even from the Antarctic regions has been pouring in from the embassy feed. Moments such as these where the fate of humanity has never been or ever will be defined in such a way. As I look at the reports, mostly taking into account the reactions of people all over the world, one thing strikes me. That knowing the world will come to an end, I myself can only think of how I can be a better father to Zach. It's hard to relate to all the billions of people that have been changed by this event, but it's easy enough for me to focus on one.

Moments later, the embassy line rings. I normally get to use this line only for major occurrences within the confines of international political concerns. I had a feeling that tonight, this call is something different.

I pick up the phone as Zach continues to watch the coverage across the globe.

"Ambassador Stevens speaking."

There was a long silence after I had said who I was. Mainly because the other line was pretty much doing all the talking.

"Yes Mr. President. We have the asset and will be en route to the mainland first thing tomorrow morning. We have alerted General Mancuso at Camp Darby and he will have transport ready to get us back."

As the President of the United States talks to me, I felt a certain lack of anxiety. I don't know why but I should be more worried, but just having felt Elizabeth's presence has change that. I guess this is what it means to go on faith. As the President provides his support and resources to whatever we need, I tried to make a point.

"Mr. President, I will do what I need to but we are dealing with things here that are not, well, of this world and quite frankly whatever protocols we have in place, will not be ready for this."

As I tried to tell this to the President, I was hoping that Zach was hearing what I was saying, as I felt I had to tell Zach the same thing.

"I understand Mr. President, but as I've been told, and so I will say the same to you, we need to have faith."

As I put down the phone, I noticed that Zach was looking at me. And I smiled back to him and his face was sad, but I knew he understood what I was saying.

"Better get some rest; I have a feeling that tomorrow will be a big day." As I headed to my room, I saw Zach settle in the sofa. Tomorrow a new dawn will come, and I do not know what to expect.

CHAPTER TEN

HEAVEN'S ARMY

As a new day washes over the old, within the great hall, the Eternals prepare to do what they are called to. The Archangel Michael, the one who is like God, looks to his kin as they once again fight for the glory of the Father. As with all the other worlds before it, and for those worlds that are still to be, this world has been given the choice to be part of the light or have itself burn in eternal fire.

Michael gestures to Sandalphon to sound the trumpets, so that the corps is ready. He always feels a great sense of joy in his heart when going to earth bounds which he does not do often but to commune with those that the Father has created was always what Michael put his hopes in. He knows that Lucifer begins his plan to surface from the pit and as it was before, so shall it be like now where he and his kin will try to stop them. He knows that his first order is to go to the vessel. But not until they have laid the work with those on the surface. Each of the Eternals will take a portion of the earth, and each will fight to defend it with all that Heaven's Army can bring upon it.

As the trumpets sounds, the seven take to the skies and heads to fulfill the Father's will. It will be a glorious and righteous day. As they pass into reality, they converge into the world like comets from the sky.

They filled the space with their presence as they descend upon man, no longer as messengers of his will, but soldiers to aid them in this Holy War. Michael knows that not all men will side with good, and that there will be those that will succumb to the temptations of his fallen brother. Each war brings family against family, friend against friend which is why it will be the last war ever waged in the history of this world.

NORAD, now in conjunction with other military and private observation platforms from across the world, monitors the air space above each major sector of the globe. With the detection of the orbs that appeared the previous night, and along with the message that was delivered, this dawn is something that everyone will need to pay attention to.

In the main control room, feeds from all over the planet is now analyzed and assessed. All space and air traffic patterns have been locked down; the FAA has declared a no fly zone for all continental and international flights and has recommended the same for the Asia Pacific Region Air Command as well as the European Space Agency. Except for military aircraft, the skies are empty. The events of the past 10 hours have rendered an entirely new approach to how things work. As with before, the ICC looks over the command room and glances to the main screen monitor for anything unusual.

Then one of the communications officer, a young air force airmen yells out into the room.

"Sir, we have detected incoming bogies coming in at the northern, southern and eastern hemispheres. Australia tracking station has reported the same from the western front."

As the ICC runs down to the command floor, the main screen pulls up the telemetry of the incoming objects. A massive radar signature overlaps with the global section map that's on the screen. The objects are clustered around a huge signal that seems to be headed into all major land areas, just like the orbs. Except these were not 30 feet up in the air, it was more like a huge single mass of objects traveling in the same trajectories.

"Sir, Alaskan and European platforms confirm visual sighting. We are getting reports of civilian sightings as well."

As the ICC confirms the reports, he looks back to the airmen.

"Can you give me a fix on their location?"

The airman looks back at the ICC, and he slowly stands up still looking at the main screen monitor. As he spoke, he takes his headset off.

"They're everywhere, sir."

The ICC realizing what this meant started running to the elevator. He quickly snatched two armed guards and gestured them to following him. In the elevator, he pressed the "G" button. It took less than a minute to get to the ground level and he started running towards the main block entrance. At this point, he was not alone. All scores of personnel, military and consultants were running in the same direction. As the ICC finally reaches the opening and gets to see the outside, everyone else that was there was staring upwards, with mouths open.

The shadows that passed them were intermittent but enough to form a consistent shade. It was surreal, yet so real. Nothing in this world has ever prepared mankind to see such a sight. There were people kneeling down, there were people who had hands to their mouths crying. And then there were those that were just in awe.

All around the globe, from the great plains of the Sahara, to the mountains in the Philippines, the Australia outback, and the wetlands of the Amazon, from the English channel, to the Eiffel Tower, from above the White House in Washington DC to every major populated area to the most remote locations in the world, everyone was seeing the same thing. This unprecedented event in the course of human history has, and never will be surpassed ever again.

As the glorious army of angels sweep through the skies over all beings and all things, the seven Eternals, those that lead this army head for Rome. Children playing in the streets in a suburban area in Southern New Jersey stop and look at the mighty winged soldiers that has come to our aid. Similarly, children walking the African plains look up at the skies with wonder and bewilderment. Those in the middle east show contempt and disgust, but cannot deny the reality of the glory of this army. All those that have witnessed this event have been changed, for better or for worse.

As Michael leads the others to the assembly in Rome, Zach and I look out from the villa at the majesty that is around us. Zach was laughing, almost bordering hysteria at what he saw. I ran my hands through my hair as the angels flew by, some flying low enough for us to be caught in their wake. I run out and Patrick and the men around him are looking up with their weapons drawn and pointing upwards. I quickly gesture to them and had them lower their weapons.

I move close to Patrick and put my arms around my old dear friend and with a huge grin on his face I look to Patrick.

"Have faith my friend, have faith."

Once again, Patrick finds himself speechless, and along with that sensation, something that he hasn't felt before, ever in his life. Joy. Unfiltered and unadulterated joy. So pure that it strikes his heart like an unknown emotion. I run back into the villa and up the stairs into Zach's bedroom where Elizabeth lay. When I got there, I found Elizabeth kneeling down in front of the window, hands clasps together deep in prayer.

"Your servants are glorious as You are Father, whom should I fear as long as I'm with You?"

As I approached Elizabeth, she looks back and smiles at me. She stands up and with all the calmness in her says, "We need to go Mr. Ambassador. We need to go now."

As I nod in agreement, I gesture for Elizabeth to follow me downstairs. In the stair well, Zach meets up with us and he smiles back at Elizabeth and follows behind her. As we move outside, the two security details have mounted up and ready to go. Our destination, a small private airport that the embassy uses for political ferries when high ranking officials from the United States are in the country. Most of the time, except for the President, a lot of senators and congressmen arrive in private airports such as these. Air Force One, which is too big for these airports are forced to either land in the international airports or a nearby US military base. From there, we have a private jet that will take Elizabeth to Camp Darby, where she'll be transferred onto a C-130 to be brought stateside.

I've received an earlier communication from General Mancuso that everything is ready and prepped for our arrival. And with the arrival of this grand army from above, David for the first time, felt safe in what they were going to do.

"Zach, ride with Elizabeth in the second unit, I'll be up front."

As they all load up to get ready for the trip, they realize that the skies have grown silent, they look up and the angels have stopped flying and now hovering over them like graceful eagles with wings spread open to catch tailwinds that keep them afloat. The angels look down, and David swears that one of them smiles at him. He smiles back before the convoy pulls out.

At Saint Peter's Square, thousands upon thousands of people gather and has begun worshipping in the open space. As the seven, led by Michael descends upon the square, the Pope, along with his entire papal administration rush out to meet them. Pope Nicholas VI, had tears in his eyes while half running towards the magnificence before him. Only in his dreams has he imagined such a beautiful and powerful sight. As he stops, he sees Michael descent like the general that he is and lands but a mere ten feet in front of him. Standing tall at over six feet with a presence that can only be described as magnificent, Michael's wings folds behind him.

As Michael surveys the square, everyone falls to their knees, including the Pope, and this confuses him. The square was silent, as it was all over the world, where now the angels have revealed themselves, and that was when Michael begins to speak.

"We are not the Father, but servants such as you. In this, arise that you may be part of his holy family."

As Michaels said this, in English, and all other languages across the globe, where everyone hears the voice of the one who is like God, the Pope looks up and was amazed to see that Michael had his hands extended to help him from his humility. The Pope looks at Michael's face directly and expected to be blinded by the divinity that these beings possess. But what he saw was purity beyond anything he can ever imagine. As the Pope reaches out for Michael's hand, he touches a servant of the most high and Michael pulls him up to his feet. They are face to face and the other six begins to go through the crowd helping them up as well.

"This is impossible. Only have I dreamed this to be." the Pope says to Michael.

As Michael looks to the Pope, and then surveys those around him he understands the frailty of such sentiments. It gives him hope that men have been able to see the choices that they've made, and have been able to do what is right, most of the time.

"With the Father, nothing is impossible. I stand here before you as proof of this Ricardo."

The Pope was surprised, but only for an instant. Of course the Archangel Michael knows his name. He knows all of our names for it have been decreed by the Father. The Pope begins to nod in jovial agreement. As this scene is repeated throughout the entire world, there are those that accept and reject the arrival of heaven's army. As Michael looks to the skies, the other six looks up as well. The Pope senses there is something that needs their attention.

"What is it? Michael, what is the matter?" the Pope asks. As those that reject their arrival retreat into what can only be described as their own selfish and malicious ways, Michael recognized it as they withdrew from the Father's grace. His hope is that those that turn to the light will be enough to save this world for Lucifer will take those that turn away from it.

"Today, those that choose to be on the side of light shall be anointed. Those that choose to be in the shadow of darkness will be forsaken."

As the Pope hears this, he realizes what it means. He looks to Michael; the Pope knows now what this truly is. It is a means to an end. Those that were described in the Bible as being chosen will not get whisked away into heaven. And those that are full of pride and take the heart of Babylon are not going to be plunged into the flames below. He realizes now that the reason why the angels are here, is because there will be a war, a war none like other.

"We go to the vessel, she is in our keeping until the second coming has been fulfilled."

When Michael says this, he gestures for other six to come to him.

"Uriel, you shall remain here and prepare for what is to come. Take our earthly brothers and begin their blessing. I will take Gabriel with me to protect the vessel. The rest of you, to the four corners of this world. Take each of your flock and be prepared with those that fight for the light. You know where to go."

Michael looks to all his kin, his seven Eternal brothers, he looks and gives each one his grace.

"By the Father's will."

And the other six bow their heads in deep prayer, the bridge between them and the Father now that they are here on earth. As each of them raises their heads from praying as they all reply in unison.

"His will be done."

By now, much of the crowd has gathered around the seven and when each of them, with the exception of Uriel, spread their wings. Everyone stands back as each of them takes to the skies. They flew swiftly across the air and were gone in mere seconds. The lone Eternal, Uriel, now looks to prepare those that will be joining them in battle.

"I am Uriel, the guide, brother to Michael and a humble servant of the Father."

As the Pope acknowledges Uriel, the Pope gestures for them to go indoors. Uriel is then surrounded by the elite corps from the Gendarmerie as they head into the administrative building in Vatican City. Uriel looks around and smiles as he enjoys, and has always enjoyed the craftsmanship of this earthly world.

"The fallen moves under our feet Ricardo. I will need a place to do the blessing."

As they go into the building, the Pope was now trying to understand from what he had learned in reading older scriptures that were not completely available to the public. This blessing that he hears from Uriel, he thinks it is some sort of anointment ritual that can provide some sort of protection for those under the Father's grace.

"This blessing you speak of Uriel, what is its purpose?"

As Uriel looks at the Pope, he smiles in his response.

"The blessing is to prepare you all to face Lucifer and the wickedness of the pit."

With that, almost everyone walking with Uriel stops dead in their tracks. The air was thick with silence and everyone looked to Uriel. Having no sense of fear, Uriel did not understand the reaction he had invoked. Then he understood.

"My earthly brothers, we are with you. My kin and all of our kind have been sent here to aid you. Have faith in the Father, for now it is most direly needed as with any other day, for your faith will be the key to receive His blessing."

As Uriel's words sink into each one, the Pope looks to all those around him.

"We are called to serve our Father, is there no greater calling? Uriel who has come to aid us believes and obeys. How can we not?

With this, the people around the Pope and Uriel cry out in worship. Today was a glorious day, a day like no other. Today the world has seen the reality of the Father's grace. And today, each person on this earth has the chance to do, for all eternity, what is right. They raise their hands and exalts the Father, and Uriel's heart is filled with joy. The Pope looks back at Uriel, and as the crowd settles in their realization, the Pope clasps his hands and looks at Uriel.

"We serve whom you serve. We are here for you and for each other."

With that, they continued going into the main hall of the administration building. Uriel knows that it will be a truly glorious day, but knows that they have much to prepare for.

* * *

As the convoy pulls up the tarmac of the small private airport just east of the villa, Pat and I, sitting in the first SUV were discussing the plan for Elizabeth's extraction.

"We have two SEAL teams standing by the drop off point and they will escort you and Zach, along with....her...back to Joint Base Andrews."

As I was contemplating what Zach felt about this vessel, I was also worried that there's something going on with Zach that might be connected with all this. Why would he say what he said that night? It was strange that it was so specific.

"Once you're in the air, you'll be joined the whole time with a squadron of F-35s to secure the airspace around you. They have been given approval from the highest level to use lethal force, if necessary to protect the asset."

As the convoy stops some thirty feet from a small private jet waiting on the tarmac, doors open and the security detail takes defensive positions around the second SUV. As Pat and David walk up to open the door, a familiar voice rings in the air and makes David spin around.

"I hope you have room for one more, as I have no plans of staying here."

Walking towards him was Sarah, alongside an air force pilot in full gear. As Sarah stops in front of me, the pilot goes straight into the jet and Sarah gives me a warm smile.

"Well, Mr. Ambassador, it's been an exciting couple of days, isn't it?"

As Sarah tries to make light of the situation, I take a deep long sigh. I wasn't sure what had happened to Sarah, and I tried calling her on her cell phone but she didn't pick up.

"I tried calling you at work and on your cell; I couldn't get a hold of you."

As Sarah nodded to Patrick who was waiting on the second SUV, I was actually glad to see that Sarah was here. I could use someone like her on this adventure, if not anything else to keep me sane.

"Phone died on the way here...plus there was a lot to do." she said as they both began to walk towards the second SUV. I knew that Sarah wanted to know what was so important about this asset. And she deserved to know, hell, she made all of it happen anyway. I looked at Patrick and nodded to open the door, the men got ready and as the door opened, Zach emerged first.

"Hi Zach, glad to see you're here." Sarah said.

As Zach waited and offered his hand to help out the asset, when she finally came out Sarah was beside her. It was a girl, and a teenage girl at that. He looked at me with a bit of confusion, as Elizabeth walks towards them with the guard detail forming around her.

"Sarah, this is Elizabeth Scarpello. She is very special."

As Sarah held out her hand to shake Elizabeth's one of the guards gave out a shout.

"We have incoming!"

As all the other soldiers look to the skies, there were figures travelling towards them, and at somewhat great speed. Elizabeth looked up, and smiled. As they came closer, the silhouette was very clear. Two angels followed by at least two dozen others were approaching. Patrick gave the stand down signal and the men put their weapons down.

As Michael and Gabriel landed, their brothers followed. Walking towards the vessel, Michael walked a straight line to her as the men and everyone else got out of his way. One of the soldiers was looking at these majestic beings and swallowed a large lump in his throat. The others merely put down their guard with both hands on their side, weapons pointed to the ground. As Michael and Gabriel reached Elizabeth, she was all smiles. At that moment, Michael and Gabriel kneel in front of Elizabeth, as did the others.

"Hail the Mother of the Son, Holy is she as she is filled with the spirit."

With this, all the angels repeated what Michael said. They were still bowed down as Elizabeth slowly moved towards these beautiful souls.

"With our souls we vow to protect you and by our sacrifice may the Son be born to the Father."

Elizabeth now within reach, puts her hands on Michael's chin and lifts it up. It was such a surreal scene; this young fifteen year old girl was reaching out to the Archangel Michael. It was enough to make Sarah cry with tears of joy. As Michael looks upon Elizabeth's face, she smiles at him.

"Blessed are those that love the Father, for they will receive love in return. Your sacrifice is not needed as we all want to be in thy Father's kingdom. It will fill my heart with joy if you and your kin are there with me, with all of us."

Elizabeth looks to everyone around her. This is the meaning of hope. This is why each and everyone here will lay down their life for her, and she understands it but does not wish for it. As Michael and Gabriel arise, he surveys those around Elizabeth. And then Michael speaks.

"I am the Archangel Michael, this is my kin Gabriel and our brothers. We know you are all here to serve in the vessel's protection, we will be with you as you are with us."

I knew that they had to go so I approached Michael, but all my years as an ambassador has never prepared me for a meeting like this. I struggled to find the words as Michael gazes upon my face, my instinct was to look down but Michael addressed me first.

"David, son of Elliot, from the family of Stevens, you wish to address us?"

David was surprised with him being called by his first name by the general of heaven's army. Still looking squarely into David's face, Michaels awaits his response.

"Yes, of course. We are here to take Elizabeth to a safer place. We need to transport her via this plane to a military base that will ferry her to my country, the United States."

As Michael and Gabriel listened to these words, they look at each other and nod in agreement. The other angels behind both of them fly up to sky and hover about a hundred feet in the air.

"We will accompany you." Michael says and with that Gabriel launches in the air leaving the people ruffled with a sudden blast of air, almost knocking them off to the ground.

"I shall go with you in this plane. I wish to have sight on the vessel at all times."

So I look to Patrick, and Patrick shrugs but gives me back a look that says it wouldn't really hurt. We then all board the small jet that will take us to Camp Darby, which will take approximately a little over an hour. Once there, they'll be able to secure Elizabeth and I'll actually feel much better with Michael going with us. As Michael gets into the plane, it feels cramped for him, not so much with himself but with his wings. He sits facing Elizabeth but had trouble positioning his wings as he did; ultimately he ended up having his wings wrapped around him like a huge feathered coat. With spans of up sixteen feet, these powerful appendages are all but indestructible. They are what makes an angel an angel. Michael's wings have seen more than his share of combat as evidenced by scar marks that have long since healed but still identifiable from the pure white feathers that adorn them.

David and Sarah look at each other but are unsure of how to proceed. As the plane taxies to the runway, Michael settles in much more comfortably as he finally finds a position that makes his wings much more relaxed.

The PA system buzzes and startles Michael a bit and he sits up.

"Hello everyone, this is Colonel Mark Willis, and I'll be flying you all to Camp Darby taking us northwest for about a little over an hour. As you are aware, all local and international commercial flights have been suspended so we are pretty good in terms of traffic up in the skies, where we'll reach a cruising altitude of thirty thousand feet. Please make sure all seat belts are fastened, all personnel prepare for lift off."

The engines hum and the plane takes off, I glance at Zach who was sitting beside Elizabeth. Then I noticed that Michael was doing the same, almost studying the boy with close intent. Then I remembered what Zach said again and wondered if it was something that he should tell Michael. As they lift off and climb to the designated altitude, Sarah looks out and is bedazzled by what she sees. Gabriel and the angels were all flying around them. Angels flying and escorting them, Sarah thought. A glorious day indeed.

CHAPTER ELEVEN

WELKIN'S BLESSING

With Uriel now in the main control center of the Papal Gendarmerie, surrounded by fellow soldiers, both earthly and divine, begins to inform those around of what to expect. These holy wars, a war to end all things have been fought since time began and as long as the Father's unending love and grace. The world that Uriel protects now needs to understand what is at stake. The Colonel of the Papal Gendarmerie addresses Uriel.

"Uriel, we are thankful for you and your brothers that have come to our aid. But please pardon my confusion as to how exactly are we to combat the forces of hell?"

Everyone in the room looks to Uriel. He is the guide, which was why Michael had asked him to do the blessing. He feels for his earthly brothers and can see the fear they hold in. But there is faith here, and faith is the strongest weapon of all.

"I understand your confusion Philippe, son of Sven, from the family of Gohl. Know this; none of your earthly arms can slay those from the pit unless blessed through the Father."

A loud murmur started in the room, and it grew louder as men began to show signs of panic, of despair, and Uriel has seen it all before. Such is the heart of those faced with the possibility of death and defeat. Men were now shouting, doubt fills the air and Uriel knows that this can only lead to having doubt in everyone's hearts. As the soldiers begin to sway in their thoughts, Uriel spreads his wings and talks in his divine voice.

"Behold the servant of the Father, for he who serves Him faithfully, will never perish but triumph in his strength."

The crowd grew silent and Uriel waits until everyone in the room has calmed their hearts and soothed their minds.

"My earthly brothers, I stand before you all as proof of the Father's grace, when I say unto you that you will have the means to defeat the fiery pits of hell, then believe me so. Your faithfulness to the Father shall be your greatest weapon against Lucifer's minions."

With his breath fading into peace, Uriel looks at every one in the room. Yes, fill the hearts of men with hope, and they shall believe in themselves, and the Father shall anoint them. Once again the Colonel speaks.

"Uriel, what hour does he come? How long until hell opens and releases its malice into this world?"

Uriel knows this to be the only way to tell them, the truth shall set you free as the word of the Father gives you strength.

"When the blood moon rises after the sun sets in two cycles, hell shall unleash itself upon this world."

Blood moon. When the sun sets in two cycles, which means a little over two days from now. The people quickly understood what time they had. The beginning of the end shall begin in a little more than 48 hours. As everyone realizes this, one soldier calls out to Uriel.

"My lord Uriel, what must we do?"

As Uriel feels the lone sign of hope in the room, so does he sends this hope to all of his kin all across the globe. There are those that have decided to turn away from their divine work. But just a single beacon of hope gives them the chance to be victorious. Upon this rock the Son has built his church, only upon this hope shall the world be able to face the evil that is unleashed.

"We will prepare. And I am with you as are all my brothers. I had said that none of your earthly arms can slay the demon, but as with all things, the Father's blessing can transform nothing into something."

The Colonel looks at Uriel and finally understands him. We are all beings of faith, and what we believe in makes us strong. We have the power to choose and that is what we are fighting for.

"Inform all your men, and all those outside, all those that will choose to fight for the light. Inform them that the blessing shall soon be given."

All over the world, the other four Eternals conduct their work to prepare for the blessing. As Uriel reaches out to the minds of his kin, he asks them if the time has come. With everyone all over the globe, choosing to fight for the light or the darkness, all the angels that have descended onto this earth, whose purpose is to aid us in this holy war, Uriel receives the message. We are ready.

As Sandalphon, Jophiel, Raphael and Metatron, each stationed above the world's four corners fly up to the clouds, Uriel walks outside of the building and takes to skies himself. In the clouds, this being of divine purity prays to the Father above. They ask for His grace, His protection, and His strength. They ask for His blessing. As they reach into each other's minds they call upon the Father to hear them.

"Heavenly Father, we come before you as your humble servants. As we help those that belong to You, as we aid them in their hour of need, we ask that You grant them the courage to believe in Your divine power and that you bless them with the strength of your will to overcome these dark times. In this we ask in order to do Your will."

As the Eternals finish their prayer, a brilliant light shines from the sky. It was like a sunset and yet like no other sunset as it enveloped the entire world. All those on the surface were bathed in this brilliant white light. There were those that scurried like rodents to block out the light, and there were those that opened their hearts to it, and received the Father's blessing. The single driving thought in each man, woman and child that chose to embrace this light knew it was peace; it was quiet, beautiful and lasting. It was a glimpse of what is to come, and it was a taste of what we all can have for eternity. The light and everything it touched have now been blessed by the most high. It was one step closer to the world as being part of the heavenly kingdom. This blessing, this anointment, has given those that choose to fight for the vision of what can be the means to face the terror that is to come. As it was in the days of King David, the most powerful weapon of all was faith in the Father above.

The light slowly faded and all those that were bathed in it, opened their eyes. All across the nations, from high to low, everyone under the Father's blessing knew exactly what they had to do.

As Uriel descends upon the surface, those that saw him cheered. Those that saw him rejoiced. Uriel is filled with unbridled joy, for now these people know what he knows. As he lands softly, those around him stood tall, and he sees the Colonel walking towards him with confidence in his steps. Uriel greets him with a smile as he spoke.

"Now do you understand my brother?"

The Colonel shakes his head in agreement. He did understand and all those that have been chosen understood too. They have all seen the very thing that they are fighting for. And the glory and righteousness now wedged into their hearts will drive their will, it will drive their choice.

"I understand, but my lord Uriel, can we truly be victorious against hell's legions?"

When Uriel hears this, he gave the biggest smile he could muster. He knew that this was the time he would show them what they needed to see.

"Now that you have received the blessing from the Father, you have the very weapon that will allow you to defeat the evil from beneath."

In addition to those soldier's already armed within the walls of Vatican City, there are those outside that have heeded the call of righteous battle. As these civilians looked up and received the blessing as well, they now look to arm them for the coming war. They were let in by the papal guards and as they reach the staging area, Uriel surveys the earthly army that will fight alongside him and his angelic brothers.

Uriel then heads into the armory of the corps. The forward section was full of modern artillery such as automatic weapons, crowd control appliances, small arms and such, and everyone that followed quickly chose a weapon. He pressed back into the back section and finally came upon the old armory door that was used by the Vatican in the 1500s. He pushed the door open and what lay before them was an arsenal fit for a kingdom. Axes, spears, shields, and swords. Having been stored as part of the historical heritage of the Swiss Guards during that era, no one ever imagined that it would be used to fight for all of the world.

"These weapons will serve you well, as it extends from you, and by grace and blessing, extends from the will of the Father. These weapons shall be what you will use to push back the minions of the pit back from where they came."

The Colonel understands, and begins shouting orders to all the soldiers to begin arming themselves with hand held implements in addition to their side arms. The war shall be fought with the heart of each person wielding the faith that carries all that's needed to put down the dark and malicious minions of the pit. The soldiers sling their hand held weapons and carry their automatic weapons and side arms.

Uriel reaches out to his brothers. All over the planet, people are arming themselves for a war that will never be seen or be experienced by anyone, in all of history ever again. With the preparations under way, Uriel reaches out to Michael and Gabriel. Things are slowly moving into place. They will be ready to meet the darkness that comes from the deep pit.

* * *

Deep within the bowels of the dark pit, Lucifer plots how to unleash his kingdom to those from above. This place has been part of every culture, religion and societal lore but none can truly imagine the horrors that exist here until one comes upon it after being taken by death. In mythological folklore and religious traditions, hell is a place of eternal torment in afterlife. It is viewed by most Abrahamic traditions as a place to receive eternal punishment. These religions with a linear divine history have often depicted hell as eternal destinations for the damned. Other religions with a cyclic history often depict hell as an intermediary period between incarnations, or rebirths.

Typically these traditions place hell in another dimension or under the Earth's surface. This often includes entrances to Hell from the land of the living or even secret passages that can only be opened by sacrifice or with innocent blood being spilled.

Other traditions, which do not conceive of the afterlife as a place of punishment or reward, merely describe hell as an abode of the dead, a neutral place for souls that have passed from the living world and located under the surface of the earth. Names such as Hades from the Greeks and Sheol from Old Hebrew, the modern understanding of hell often depict them in an abstract state of being, a feeling of loss rather than as fiery torture literally underground. But this view of the concept of a hell can be traced back into the ancient and medieval periods where Hell is portrayed as populated with demons that torment those unfortunate souls that dwell there. Those that have lived a life of crime, hatred and pride, those that have committed against the laws set forth by the God of Moses, the souls of those that seek to inflict pain and suffering, to spread lies and deceit, these are Hell's tenants. And within the fiery pit of their torment, the punishment fits the crime. Those souls that are removed from communion from the grace of the Father, are claimed by the supreme lord of hellfire.

This is where Lucifer draws his power, this is where his seething builds, and his malice reigns. He rejoices in the pain of others, but most of all, he revels in having turned those away from the Father, as he has been cast out, so shall these souls be his to command.

Knowing that his pathetic kin has revealed them to the surface, Lucifer makes his preparations as well. All manner of dark creature, with foul forms and even fouler souls swirl around the master of the pit waiting to be unleashed to those above. However, Lucifer's greatest soldiers are those that have their hearts turned away from the divine.

He takes these souls hostage, and possesses them to do his will. This allows for Lucifer to have an advantage in this war as those that are possessed take form as someone's daughter, son, or parent. He counts on the emotional connection of those around the possessed to render them unable to retaliate. For how can someone take a loved one's life even if it was under the influence of something utterly dark and devastating?

The soul reapers, those that are sent to possess the living are one of Lucifer's ultimately pride and joy. They take over the body and allows him to do his bidding, while inflicting pain and suffering in the process. Those possessed almost never knows what they are doing, they are slaves to the reapers and they use them as puppets to exact pain and sorrow. Lucifer calls upon the prince of his legions in hell.

"Abaddon! Before me!"

As a dark and huge figure rumbles toward Lucifer, he sees the magnificence of the king of the abyss and lord of the demons. Abaddon, whose towering height even surpasses that of Lucifer approaches. Commanding all the legions of demons in hell, Abaddon has an extreme hatred for the angels, especially one of the Eternals, Gabriel. He wears a pitch black armor from head to toe and as he lifts up his visor, his eyes are yellow fiery red along with dark skin and hair that looks like it's been dipped in oil, shimmering in the flames around him.

He has dominion over all those that fight for this kingdom and only seeks to inflict harm and suffering for his master. He comes before Lucifer and kneels before the supreme ruler of hell.

"What does my lord wish of me?"

Abaddon looks squarely at Lucifer and see the dark ruler snicker in his throne.

"When the moon is filled with blood, you shall unleash your legions above. The angels have come to aid the earthly fools but I want you to slaughter all of them."

At the mere mention of angels, Abaddon looks to Lucifer to somehow confirm this as truth. He waits patiently for the holy wars to exact his hand at those that comes from the kingdom of light. Lucifer knows well how to put desires into the hearts of those that serve him and Abaddon is no different. His rage and contempt for the angels fuels his unquenchable thirst to destroy them. He calls on his commanders, those that share his sentiments for war.

"Satanachia! Abigor! Belial! Angul! Nergal!"

The five fingers of the hand of hell. Five of the most feared and therefore respected demons in the underworld. Each one possesses powers that serve to further the kingdom of darkness.

Belial, deceitful and evil-hearted, is one of Lucifer's venerable demons. Looking thin and frail with clawed feet and hands, his purpose was to bring wickedness and guilt to all those that come before him. His heart only filled with malice against the one that cast them out from above. Lawless in his nature, he seeks to spread his great evil to the surface.

Nergal, arrogant and a master manipulator can take any form he pleases. Muscular and red-skinned, with a bald pointed head, Nergal is tall with sharp claws and fangs. He has a long slithery tongue much like that of a serpent. He sometimes also has wings in this primary form. However, he has also been seen in a hideous form that looks like a merging together of several animals and other forms that include flies, humans and dogs.

Using his power over women and girls, lustfully seeking their impurity to his heart's desire, Satanachia looks like a meld between man and woman, with each side exhibiting features for both. However, his most notable feature is his head which is shaped like an inverted pentagram where his head lies in the middle, a sharp dagger like chin and two cheeks that swell out with bony protrusions on each side of his face. Both horns make up the two points of the form, as he holds a long staff with a goat's head on the tip.

Fat and slobbery, the very epitome of disgust, Angul secretes something one can only describe as liquid flesh. His entire appearance looks of blood and vile while he carries his huge double bladed axe which he uses to butcher those that he dislikes. As one of the most revolting demons in the pit, Angul relishes torturing souls that have been punished for being prideful and for being gluttons. He delights in casting those prideful souls with dissent and having them suffer through each waking moment of wanting more and more without end.

Finally there is Abigor, a demon of the superior order, cast into the fire and conjured for his ability to provide military advice in waging war with those outside this kingdom. Unlike the others,

Abigor appears like a shining white knight bearing a golden lance. However, in his true form, he rides a black winged death stallion and appears as a ghoulish specter with long limbs and bony features. Known as the great exploiter of men, he makes those that give up their souls to him win in great battles. But the price they pay lies in the acts of murder and genocide that Abigor pushes to them to fulfill on his behalf.

As the five stand with Abaddon, Lucifer feels the genuine hatred in his heart flourish while sitting on the throne. He always looks to his minions and relish the dread they will bring to the surface. Lucifer strikes his battle lance on the ground and the force ignites all of the ground to spray fire and brimstone into the air. He points to the demons before him and utters his words for this holy war.

"Unleash your legions to the surface; extinguish those that stand in your way. But bring my beloved brother Michael to me, as well as the vessel that he so loyally protects. I shall kill both of them myself and lay claim to this world as part of my kingdom!"

In all the history of the world, the ground has never shaken such as this. All the minions of hell delight in the coming carnage as they once again, spread the ills of this kingdom.

Lucifer summons Abaddon to him, making him stand right by his throne as he whispers into Abaddon's side.

"Send a complement of soul reapers above to remind my dear brother that we are not sitting in silence."

Abaddon gurgles a laugh, as he summons three floating reapers to him. Each reaper is like flying black smoke, with voices that sound like shrieks of pain. Abaddon gives one of them what it needs, to find where Michael is and show those around Michael how so easily men can be taken over. Something for him to ponder as he wages this foolish war.

Each of the reapers floats away and breaches the pit and heads to the surface. As they do, Lucifer grins on his throne. He enjoys this time when he can partake of the surface, which he normally cannot do as it has been sealed off to them during the course of the world's progression. Only has he been able to whisper to men to do his bidding, but no more, this time, he can send those from his kingdom and have them wreak havoc with those pathetic people on the surface. He neither reverse's them nor adores them; all Lucifer wants are their souls. Their souls in his kingdom, and the world above it as his own.

* * *

With the soldiers around him armed with hope in their hearts and faith under their feet, Uriel, the guide, also known among his brothers as the Light of God, prepares himself for what he knows will come. As he takes his sword out of its scabbard, it instantaneously lights up in flames. As the others see this, they freeze at the splendor of Uriel's form. With dark red hair and very plain features, Uriel's simplicity is only matched by his unwavering obedience to the Father.

As Uriel looks at his sword, he recounts the countless times it has sent darkness away. But he was not always involved in war; he had always loved the peace and serenity that was everywhere, before the fall. His heart remembers the time that he buried the first, Adam, the source of all suffering in this world. He was there as well when Abel was put to rest in paradise. Since then, his conviction to uphold the Father's will have never been greater. It has not faltered and never will. In previous wars, his brothers have told him he was as pitiless as any demon he encountered. This amused Uriel to be sure, but he knew it was needed. He knew it was the will of the Father.

He takes his sword and puts it back into his scabbard, realizing that everyone around him has taken notice of his glorious stance. As everyone went back to preparing within the city, Uriel walks along those that he now considers his earthly brothers. While walking towards the garden in the back portion of the papal apartments, Uriel suddenly feels a lingering presence. He noticed it but for one reason, it wreaked with malevolence and wickedness. As an Eternal he can see those that exist beyond the world of mortals, and as he turns around, there, at the corner of his eye, he sees the trailing wisp of black smoke that is all too familiar to him.

He spread his wings and draws his sword as he takes flight out into the square. These cursed things from the pit, these reapers seek out frail hearts and takes over them as their own. Uriel flies swiftly as he scans for the reapers dark force. He sees the trail as it makes its way to the open square. Thousands upon thousands are there, and Uriel knows there will be a panic once the reaper takes hold of what it is seeking. As the other angels quickly join him, he sees the reaper in the crowd.

He flies down to the crowd, dispersing them as he landed. The other angels form behind him, guarding Uriel as well as protecting the others. As he looks, the reaper picks his victim and begins the possession. His hearts sinks as these creatures take every advantage they can. He sees that the person being taken is a young teenage girl. As the reaper takes hold of this battered lonely heart, the young girl's appearance slowly becomes dark and brooding. With any possession, the reaper takes time to overcome the host, as the host in turn takes into its being the reaper's black and evil soul. Uriel gestures to the crowd who has now formed into a somewhat makeshift circle around him and the victim. Uriel knows that while this young one's heart may have been frail, all those that reapers take are innocent. As the reaper takes full control, the young girl now ashen with blackness looks at Uriel with derision. Uriel takes his sword into his hands and points it to the taken. Everyone in the crowd gasps. The young girl's mother runs out in front of Uriel stopping in front of him.

"Please my lord! She is just a child and she is not herself! Please have mercy!"

As the mother walks backwards, close enough to her daughter, she is suddenly struck by something behind her. She gargles out blood as the crowd screams in terror. As the mother looks down her chest, she sees a bloody hand with sharp clawed nails protruding from it. The hand was holding her heart. As the life left her, Uriel sees her spirit lifted up to the kingdom. The mother's spirit looks back at Uriel and smiles, knowing that what needs to be done must be done.

The hand pulls back, and the lifeless body of the mother falls to the ground. Still holding the heart it so murderously took, the reaper takes it to his mouth and begins biting it in pieces. It then looks to Uriel with dark loathing eyes and lets out a horrible high pitched laugh. Taunting Uriel with its disdain, doing what reapers do. But Uriel stands his ground, with his sword still pointed to the creature.

"You are a fool to think you can save these worthless worms. You are helpless even to save one, how can you save them all?"

Laughing once again, the reaper now looks to the crowd and with no remorse begins to rush towards a small boy, who was frozen in his place by the terror he just witnessed. As the reaper closes, with what would seem as another victim, it was abruptly stopped in place mere inches away from the boy. As the boy was pulled back by the crowd, Uriel approaches from the back of the demon.

"Vile creature, know that you will perish and be sent back to the abyss you came hence forth. These are my earthly brothers, and they are under our protection."

As Uriel says these words and with his sword in the reaper's back, the reaper begins to writhe in pain, and it begins to scream at the top of its lungs. The shriek makes everyone cover their ears, for the pain that it now knows is unlike any pain it has ever felt before. As Uriel's sword thrusts deeper into the reaper's back, it's black eyes opens wide as it looks up to the skies. While gasping for what it takes as air, Uriel says a prayer to rid this young girl of that which infects it.

"Through the power of His grace and the strength of the spirit, I take you out of this form and send you back to the pit!"

When Uriel lifts his sword up, it passes through the young girl's body but not without impaling the black smoke that had taken over it. As the sword clears the young girl, Uriel points his sword to the heavens and the impaled soul reaper now bursts into flames. One last shriek and it was gone and the flame from Uriel's sword becomes tame once again. Uriel looks back to the young girl, now struggling to get up from the ground. He came to her and lifted her up; she looks back at him and looked to her mother lying not far from her. She begins to weep.

"I'm sorry I could not save your mother. But know that she gave her life for you. Whatever it is that makes your heart impure, let this take hold and honor your mother with it. I saw her spirit rise; she is now with the Father above."

When Uriel said this, the young girl gave him a huge hug. And they both stood up as Uriel looks to the crowd.

"Behold the taste of what is to come. But fear not, as one is saved, so shall it be for all. Have faith and be strong, so that those that seek to use it against you, any of you, will fail."

Uriel reaches out to all his brothers and kin, all around the world. He is told that similar incidents have happened in places such as Syria, Berlin, Iraq, New York, and other major cities. Lives have been lost, as it was today. Lucifer begins his campaign and this is to show that he is getting ready. As Michael reaches back to Uriel, he tells them that they are almost at their destination with the vessel, along with those that have chosen to protect her. It will begin soon, as the day slowly turns into night and the blood moon enters its full cycle in two sun sets time, hell's gates will open. They will be after her; they will be after the vessel.

CHAPTER TWELVE

LEAP OF FAITH

I was awakened by a sudden jolt of turbulence and for a moment thought I was in a dream. I was looking at Michael two seats down from me, the Archangel Michael, from the bible, and if memory serves, the one that cast out Lucifer. I had seen the mosaic painting at St. Peter's Basilica numerous times and I remembered the depiction of how he had triumphed over evil in that piece.

He knew my name, and called me son of Elliot, my Father. It boggles my mind that he knew my name, and with that, everyone's name on this planet. I suppose that's what you would expect family to do, and for all intended purposes, we have been included in this new family, to face a threat unlike any other. Of course the painting got it all wrong, in it Michael was wearing a flowing red robe and had dark wings, small compared to the reality of what I've seen. His light auburn hair and gentle features in the painting are but a shadow to the golden blond and chiseled form that sat but two seats away from me. Lastly, his wings as they were depicted were almost frail and impractical on the painting, for the reality is that these wings, white as they are seem like they can slice through anything and its movement simply evokes power and strength.

As I ponder this, Michael gave me a look that says it's alright to be curious. He then stood up and with a big stretch, spread his wings sideways along the aisle of the small jet. It was a glorious thing to witness, and for that alone, I told myself that I am thankful to be on the right side, the good side of this war. Michael starts to walk towards me, and while he had made it clear that we are all on the same team, I couldn't help but feel intimidated by this divine being.

He stops along side of me and looks at me while I make an attempt to look outside, and see how his kin is doing. Outside I could see about eight of them on the right side of the jet flying effortlessly in the winds. Majestic and brave, those are the words that come to mind.

"They do not tire, if this is what you are curious about David."

As I ponder this, I stood up too and in front of Michael in the aisle. I was worried for Zach, and everyone else and I knew that Michael felt what was in my heart.

"And how about you? Do you tire Michael?"

It was a simple question, and as the plane hit another patch of turbulence, it shook the cabin enough for me to grab for the front on my seat to steady myself. Michael seemed to be pondering the question, which confuses me as it was somewhat rhetorical. But then again, I've never made small talk with an eternal being before so I didn't really know what to expect. As Michael looked at me, he had a slight pain in his eyes, and I didn't need to be a divine entity to see it. It was clear that my question had struck something in this man's heart, if at all, I could call him a man.

"I do tire David, I tire of the senselessness of those that seek to destroy us. I tire of hoping that those that have transgressed against the Father, and by faith and grace, against me be saved. I tire of the pain and suffering that is required in order to fulfill the destiny of this world. But such is the burden of obedience, and I am obedient to the Father."

Wow. The Archangel Michael just vented to me with what he felt. This in itself is a major life event for me. I didn't pretend to know what context or accept that I don't even have the capacity to understand what he's feeling right now but I know when someone is in pain, and I guess because of that, it made me feel a little less like a servant, and more like a true brother. I guess that angels are, so to speak, human after all. I put my hand on his shoulder, he was startled by this but allowed me to do so. I made the best face I could to show him that I understood.

"We all have lost people that we care for Michael, and I'm sure it's so much harder for you than it is for me."

Michael understood what I said. I could see it in his eyes. And for a moment, I almost felt like I was back at the lake, just before the time I left for the grocery store, and saw Zach and my wife, happily smiling and waving to me as I drove off. Then I looked at Michael and he had his hand on my forearm. He smiled as he took it off and I realized that whatever it was, he had made me remember.

"Your wife, Loretta, she is a special woman. She is now home with the Father, and soon, so shall you."

I had so many questions that I wanted to ask him but as Michael turned around, I knew it was not the right time. He mentioned Loretta's name, and yes, she was special. I wish I could have said that to her before she died, I wanted to say so many things to her. Looking back at Michael, he now kneels beside Elizabeth's seat. I came closer, at least close enough to hear what they were talking about. Elizabeth was asking Michael something and I heard it in mid-sentence.

"...about Him, what is He like?"

Michael notices me from behind and continues to attend to Elizabeth's questions. Looking at this girl, I remembered my early religion subjects in school, way back when it was still appropriate to talk about religion in schools. Growing up in Highland Springs, VA, just east of Richmond, I didn't have much opinion over religion. My parents did go to church, but it wasn't something that was instilled into me at all and while I went with them, it was more about going with them rather than going for myself. Into middle school and high school, all opportunities to have a religious education was swept away by much more practical things, such as football and baseball. I had hung out once with this kid who moved into the neighborhood that said he was a Christian, which meant to me that we couldn't really hang out on Sundays as I knew in general was a holy day for them.

I guess, come to think of it, ever since college, I've never really thought much about having a religion. I'm not saying that I was an atheist, and I'm not just thinking this because of the present company but ultimately, I had not felt drawn to the need to believe in something of a divine nature. Which is ironic to my current situation that dictates I help keep someone safe in order to make sure that this world does not plunge into the deep burning flames of hell. Not that it's all dependent on me but I guess there is some truth to that saying that God does work in mysterious ways.

I was jolted by another patch of turbulence but this one was much more intense. The fasten seat belt sign came on and the PA crackled into life as I started heading back to my seat. I noticed that Michael was now looking directly at the cockpit and put his hand on his sword and looked at me.

"Everyone, please get back to your seats, I've put on the....arrghh."

I radioed Patrick who was sitting up front, closer to the cockpit to check on the pilot. I saw Patrick stand up and had one marine accompany him to the front. As they did this, Michael came up to me and put his hand on my shoulder looking at me intently.

"Whatever happens, keep the vessel safe. From anyone."

Then Michael proceeded in a rush to the front. When he came to Patrick and the marine knocking on the cockpit door, it was locked and they heard no answer. Then everyone realized that the PA system was still on and they heard what sounded like an animal growl. At that moment Michael realized the danger and reached out to his kin outside. At the same moment, the cockpit door burst open with such force hitting the marine standing next to it, instantly killing him as it literally smashed him flat against the wall. Everyone on the plane stood up and I began to yell to Zach to bring Elizabeth to the back of the plane. Sarah rushed along with both of them as the commotion up front became clear.

Patrick drew his weapon but knowing that they were in a pressurized cabin and he had a small window of error if he decides to fire a round off. What stood in the cabin was a dark brooding hunk of a shape. As Patrick backed up behind Michael, whose sword was now out of its scabbard, he faced this foul demon that takes those with frail hearts and transforms them into servants of the dark lord. Faint hints of the air force uniform now bloody and torn came into view and the creature moved into the main cabin. The marines with weapons now pointed at the creature who was still making a straight line towards Elizabeth ignored them like a boot would an ant.

"Hold you fire, I say again, hold your fire. Check your target and use laser sights for accuracy." Patrick yelled knowing that the marines knew it was close to impossible to engage in a firefight given the small space and that they we're twenty thousand feet up in the air.

I quickly pushed Zach and Elizabeth into the small open space right by the rear exit of the jet, crouching down and with Patrick nearby still with his weapon drawn. Normally, if this was a military transport, there would be parachutes that were meant for emergencies or if it was needed for a mid-air evacuation. But being a private jet, the only chutes are likely up front, one for the crew and a spare for the flight officers. I then heard a loud scream and looked up, past Michael as one of the marines tried to engage the creature, it took one swipe and drove its hand right through the marine's battle gear and out the other side. The blood splattered all over the white interior of the plane as the marine convulses and then goes limp, still impaled by the demon's arm.

The other marines begin to retreat, and Michael now stands before the creature, in all his glory and the beast lets out a horrendous growl of madness at him. As it growl, Michael spread his wings in full length and by so dents the airframe of the aircraft and acts as a shield between the monster and us. It lunges with a ferocious snarl at Michael and he simply kicks it back with such force that the creature flies all the way back into the cockpit. As I saw this exercise in divine force, the creature hits and destroys part of the cockpit instruments and the jet begins to go into a nose dive. Michael then turns around to walk back to us and as he did, the creature leaps suddenly onto his back clamping down on his wings. Michael drops his sword fast enough that he uses his both hands to hold off the beast's hands from digging its claws into his face. Michael lifts his hands, and in so doing cracks both arms of the creature. It lets out a painful howl and Michael swings it around over his head, again hitting the airframe several times and then forcefully throwing the beast towards the front exit of the plane.

The beast hit the exit door with such force that it immediately dents the door, close enough to pushing it outwards completely. As the beast lay by the door, Michael picks up his sword and walks towards it, and stands by its feet, while it struggled to look upwards and snarl at Michael's face.

"You dare to put your vile hands on me demon?"

Michael, still standing in front of the demon, as the plane was still in a nose dive, I start to look to Patrick to see if we could go to the cockpit and pull the plane out of it. Patrick gestured to me to stay with Sarah, Zach and Elizabeth, and he left four marines with us as he took two and started heading towards the cockpit.

Patrick closes in on Michael and now gets a good look at the enemy. It wreaked with spite and it began to snicker to Michael.

"Righteous fool, your vessel shall die in this metal cage, along with you and these worthless worms."

As the creature snickers more, Michael raises his sword and thrusts it to the demons face. A loud shriek filled the air and then Michael pulled his sword out along with the black mist that is the reaper's soul. He then vanquishes it through flames emanating from his blade. With this, Patrick rushes to the cockpit and does a quick evaluation. He runs back out and looks to me.

"It's a dead stick, we're going down fast."

As Patrick says this, Michael walks down the aisle, still oblivious of the plane's present circumstance and walks past by everyone and picks up Elizabeth. He looked at everyone and positions himself in front of the rear exit. With one swift kick, he sends the door flying into the air and the cabin now fills with the cold air from the outside. The oxygen masks drops down as the plane, now having about five thousand feet left before it crashes into the woods below, start to violently shake with force due to the loss of pressure. However, Michael still holding Elizabeth in his hands, looks to everyone and moves closer to the exit.

"Do not fear, follow me and you shall be saved." Michael said. We all looked and nodded back to him in unison. With that Michael leapt out of the jet. I looked at Zach and nodded to him that it was going to be alright.

"Go Zach, jump."

Then he jumped out of the plane. I followed and the free fall was one of the most terrifying feelings I've ever known. As the others jumped, I could now see the ground. The air rushed to my face and my stomach turned upside down, I saw the ground swelling up beneath me and instinctively put my hands to my face, not that it would save me at all from a fall of this height. But then I felt strong hands sweep me up and carry me up stopping my fall. I opened my eyes, and Gabriel, the one that came with Michael had me in his arms. The turbulence was gone, the fall was no longer instilling fear. I looked down and sideways and saw the other angels alongside us. Each one had someone they were flying with. And up front, there was Michael, hovering in front of us, still holding onto Elizabeth, gloriously floating in the air. As we regrouped, I gestured to Michael the general direction we should be going in. I didn't know why I knew, I just did. Having been saved from that demon in the jet and then again by jumping out of it, I am beginning to tell myself that there's something to having faith after all. As we all flew, I was looking at Zach and he had his arms stretched out. Everyone, even Patrick who looked every bit nervous, was having a little bit of fun.

We couldn't be any more that fifteen minutes out of Camp Darby, and soon enough we heard the familiar rotors of Bell UH-1s, likely out of the camp headed for us and no doubt to provide air escort, as the transponder of the jet had probably sent out a distress message automatically as it impacted the ground. There were three UH-1s, they circled around us and took formation behind us. I then saw the outline of the base as we cleared a small hill about a mile out. I'm sure the base commander will be quite interested in what happened to us just moments ago.

* * *

All across the globe, similar attacks have been occurring. These possessions, cowardly in their act have been something until today but a mere myth. I've seen movies about it, and have read articles but until today, until what I saw, it never made me think of what the reality was about these attacks. In modern warfare, it would be something that can be translated to as an initial strike. But unlike in any war, there is no way to know where these strikes will hit, what will be the weapon of choice and what countermeasures will be available. No, this war, this holy war, will be unlike any other in man's history. Worldwide panic has set in as encounters with these vicious attacks have driven people to extreme sides of belief. There are those that accept that the angels will help us with the war, but casualties will still abound in the thousands, even millions. There are those that believe that no matter what the angels do, it is an exercise in futility, for the people have seen the kind of enemy that makes family turn against family.

And there are those that still believe in their own power, sort of ignoring the signs around them and behaving in a way that they have control of their own lives. This is Lucifer's hope, this is how he wages war. The hearts of men are so easily corrupted with the simplest of desires. And the battle for this world will take all of the will and strength in everyone that chooses the light in order to prevail.

Occurrences in the Middle East and Asia have already detailed insurgencies against our new found brothers. Incidents of attacks against the angels have been reported, however, there has been no mention of casualty, on either side. In Thailand, armed militia have open fired on groups of angels in an attempt to drive them away from the Buddhist temples. The accounts have detailed specific areas where there had been high numbers of religious and spiritual centers all over the world where violence has erupted. In a mosque within the city limits of Islamabad, members of the Sunni sect have all rejected the angel's presence. Being in direct conflict with the Islamic faith, the very essence and existence of the angels provide a much difficult and jarring reminder to them that their beliefs have been disproved.

It's hard enough to live in the world where so many different beliefs clash on the level of faith and the moral and spiritual compasses of those that follow them. It's difficult enough to live life believing in something that needs to employ such a strong will of obedience, devotion and religious fervor. Trying to live a life worthy of it and suddenly be washed away by a hard and unquestionable truth puts one's life in question.

From the Torah, the central concept in the Judaic tradition to the Tawrat which the Muslims believe is the holy book of Islam given by God to Musa, to the Quran which many believe is the central text for the Islamic faith, to the numerous versions of the Holy Bible that accounts for the different paths that is used by both Judaism and Christianity; the events of the past forty eight hours have all but shattered these texts, and many of its core messages about when the angels reveal themselves to the world.

The belief that we all will come to a point in our lives where the kind of life we lived would define the existence that was to follow afterwards is gone. To the Muslims, Jannah, the eternal concept of paradise is where its inhabitants live an existence that is defined as one that is happy, without hurt, sorrow, fear or shame. It is a place where every wish is fulfilled. It says that when someone leaves this earth, they wait in their graves until they reach the time of Yawm al-Qiyāmah, or the Resurrection. It also tells of the prize that awaits those that fight in the way of Allah, where they will be given a great reward. The most prevalent belief is that seventy two virgins awaits those that die in martyrdom and that for their sacrifice, will receive this as one of the seven blessing from Allah.

For Judaism, death is not the end of human existence. However, because Judaism is focused on life here and now rather than on the afterlife, dogma about the afterlife is not a huge subject for debate or personal opinion. While it is believed that the possibility exist that an Orthodox Jew's soul can go to a similar place to what the Christians believe to be Heaven, for them it is also believed that it is possible for these souls to be reincarnated through many lifetimes until the second coming of the messiah occurs. The resurrection of the dead will occur in the messianic age, a time referred to in Hebrew as the Olam Ha-Ba- the World to Come. This term is also used to refer to the spiritual afterlife. When the messiah comes to initiate the perfect world of peace and prosperity, the righteous who have fallen will be brought back to life and given the opportunity to experience the perfect world that their righteousness helped to create. Akin to thinking that this world is like a lobby in a building where everyone waits for the elevator to go up to a prestigious club up on the penthouse, much is

159

the same sentiment for Olam Ha-Ba. Prepare yourself in the lobby so that you may be worthy to enter and he who prepares on the eve of Shabbat, also known as the Sabbath, will have food to eat. One also prepare oneself for the Olam Ha-Ba through Torah study and good deeds.

And then there's the Christian view on death. Around the world, Christians have probably been given the most difficult way in believing things the way they should be, and what the reality is about around them. Christianity is in a constant battle of what can be and what is, and that the true nature of someone who believes in Christ. The Son of God needs to be part of a much larger portion instead of simply looking to doing good things on a list.

There are different denominations of Christianity at the turn of the 21st century. All have varying approaches and worldviews. There are varieties within the Christian worldview, and disputes of the meaning of concepts in a Christian worldview. However, certain thematic elements are common within the Christian worldview as well. For instance, Northrop Frye indicated as the central clusters of the system of metaphors in the Bible, specifically mentioning mountains, a garden, and caves. A similar thematic representation of Christian worldview in the Reformed tradition has been formulated as the Creation, Fall, Redemption and Consummation.

This is further simplified by the thematic relevance of the introduction of salvation through the Way, Truth and the Life. Christianity has denominational families and also has individual denominations. The difference between a denomination and a denominational family is sometimes unclear to outsiders. Some denominational families can be considered major branches.

Christianity is largely composed of, but not limited to, five major branches of Churches worldwide. There are some churches, such as the Assyrian Church of the East which is also a distinct Christian body, but much smaller in adherents and geographic scope now than in the last century. Each of these branches has important subdivisions. Because the Protestant subdivisions do not maintain a common theology or earthly leadership, they are far more distinct than the subdivisions of the other five groupings. Denomination typically refers to one of the many Christian groupings including each of the multitude of Protestant subdivisions.

Denominationalism is an ideology which views multiple Christian groups as being legitimate Christian churches despite disagreements over important beliefs, but not all churches teach this. The Catholic and Orthodox Churches do not use this term as its implication of interchangeability, or some say the convenience of it, does not agree with their theological teachings. There are some groups which practically all others would view as apostate or heretical, and are considered wholly not legitimate versions of Christianity.

There were some movements considered heresies by the early church which do not exist today and are not generally referred to as denominations. Examples include the Ebionites who denied the divinity of Jesus, and the Arians who subordinated the Son to the Father by denying the pre-existence of Christ, thus placing Jesus as a created being, therefore mortal. The greatest divisions in Christianity today, however, are between Eastern Orthodoxy, Catholicism, and various denominations formed during and after the Protestant Reformation. There also exists in Protestantism and Orthodoxy various degrees of unity and division.

So, within this one religion, Christianity exists as a wide array of beliefs and approaches based on one single ecclesiastical system. Those that call themselves Christians today are still searching, sometimes continuously, for the meaning of why they are one. The biggest contention among those that choose to believe in Christianity is also the most significant: How does one live a life of servitude to teachings, also called gospels, in a world where the primary value system is one that is focused on individuality? The Christian faith calls for faith in the Father, that all things are done according to His will, and yet, during the lives that have existed since the beginning of time, from the first of us in the garden, our human nature truly conflicts that with the Father.

The core concepts of grace, forgiveness, love and faith as simple attributes becomes so overwhelmingly difficult to apply in the kind of reality that life often presents us. Now with the arrival of the angels, with the message of what is to come, all these debates regarding all these religions are useless. The reality of what is, once again trumps that of what we are called to believe in. Right now, the worldview on Christianity or any religion for that matter, has become what it was intended; teachings and beliefs. But in an event such as this, where teachings have largely resulted in the complete and utter reversal of what has been taught for thousands of years, the world trembles at the verge of self-annihilation. The entire value system of those that have been and always have considered themselves believers is now withered down to two basic truths: This world will be consumed by the light, or it will be plunged into darkness. Eternal life is no longer an aspiration, it is a goal to be met, and how this holy war is decided, when it is decided, that goal will either be successful or be a failure.

Believers all over the world have embraced this new reality, for it is the only choice that they truly have. Often times, we are faced with making decisions based on something we believe to be true. Now, our decisions directly impact what is going to be. The angels, glorious in their appearances but also as true signs of the end for those in this world, bring a message that instills peace in the heart but also fear in the mind. As beings of mortal thoughts, we are not equipped to handle the concepts of creating the eternity that we so desperately aspire for when our time in this world is at hand.

As I look to the reasons why I would want to fight this war, looking at Zach as he has his arms spread out like an angel himself, I realize the reason for believing in this war. I believe that I can do what I can for those that I love. Whatever religion, social or cultural teachings have brought everyone to this point in their lives, what matters the most now are the ones that we love.

As we circle the base we see people gathering below us. As the complements of angels descend to the ground, I tell myself that I will do what I need to protect those that I love. The old world is gone, I now look forward to the new world that can be. And maybe, just maybe, it's a world where I can hold Loretta once again and Zach can once again see her amazing and loving smile.

CHAPTER THIRTEEN

CAMP DARBY

TIRRENIA, ITALY

As the escort helicopters take off, the base commander, General Mancuso goes on the flight line. A young captain runs up to him and hands him a folder that he quickly opens as the air settles down around him. Two squads of marines, in full battle gear pull up to his back and stops short five feet behind the general. As he opens the folder, he looks at the appropriate documents that have led to this moment.

He looks to his young captain while turning the pages on the folder.

"I want visual confirmation ASAP. I'm putting you in charge of security captain, once they arrive; I want wheels up in ten. I want a tight detail surrounding the asset."

As the young captain confirms the general's order and begins issuing commands himself, the general thumbs through the documents in the folder with more intent. Looking at bios for those that will be arriving at his base, and having been given priority level one clearance from the office of the President himself, he was curious about who these people are. Not that his curiosity has not been active for the past forty hours, since the arrival of these beings on the planet, everything was based now on some level of curiosity. Ever since the event, General Mancuso has been monitoring all data and satellite feeds on the planet, tracking where all the deployments are of the angels and where they are focused the most. He's been in three wars, and whatever war you're in, he knows full well that where there's a concentration of forces, is also where the most damage will probably be coming from.

He received communication late yesterday about possible engagement with the enemy forty eight hours from now. Intelligence is usually a corner piece of any strategic military deployment and defense but having the intelligence come from someone, well, not from here, is something the general could not put his trust on. The message was vague, and short at best. He read it again on the flip side of the folder where it was clipped on. The words just said "The gate of hell opens when the blood moon rises." Not much intelligence, and he confirmed with his superiors stateside on anything concerning the blood moon reference, and NASA came back with a conclusion that it probably is referring to what is largely considered a lunar tetrad.

Astronomers define a tetrad as four successive total lunar eclipses, with no partial lunar eclipses in between, each of which is separated from the other by six lunar months, or six full moons. From what was provided, which included related materials on what a blood moon refers to, the specific section on biblical prophecy caught the general's eye.

In Christianity, use of the term blood moon applies to the full moons of an ongoing tetrad. Several Christian scholars and experts speak of a lunar tetrad as representing a fulfillment of biblical prophecy, specifically when the moon is supposed to turn blood red before the end times as described in the Book of Joel Chapter 2, verse 31.

The sun will be turned to darkness and the moon to blood before the coming of the great and dreadful day of the Lord.

General Mancuso was a believer, has been for most of his life. His great grandfather, Agostine Mancuso settled in the United States in the mid-1800s from Palermo. So he had a close affinity for being in

Italy but has always considered himself one hundred percent American. Growing up in a traditional Italian family in Brooklyn in the 1950s, he went day in and day out trying to get to a better place, for himself and for his family. After tours in Vietnam, Panama and most recently in Afghanistan as a garrison CO, he'd seen enough of what a man can do when they're given a reason, or an order to do it.

But his mother had always taken him to church as far back as he could remember and while he did get into street fights and altercations with the law before enlisting in the army, he was always keen on remembering what his mother told him. She wanted him to forgive of his enemies, and that he should be able to think of them as people that he needed to save. This was of course the farthest thing he ever thought of but in his experience as a soldier, he had come close to death several times and he felt, that in some way that he was spared. Of all the times that death comes knocking to those that serve their country and put their lives in harm's way, it is almost a foregone conclusion that a career in the military service can be short-lived.

Now, with what's happening all over the world, with the premise that this world is now being fought for so that it can be part of something much greater or something much more sinister, he has come to believe that everyone, not just him, that was spared had been brought to this moment for a purpose. His mother always told him to put his trust in God, and that all things will be revealed in time, he now realized that the time has finally come. The first thing he did when he saw the angels descend was to fall on his knees and pray, and then he stood up and called his wife back in the states and told her that everything was going to be alright, and make sure that his two sons see the truth in front of them.

"General, the escorts are in formation and they are inbound with the contacts. ETA, five minutes."

As he looks at the folder more and more, he understands the weight of the world now bearing down on these people. But if he can, and he will, try and give them what they need to fulfill their purpose.

"Make sure Charlie transport is ready to go; I want a straight line to Joint Base Andrews. Alert the wing commander, I want the fighters in the air now."

The last iteration of the tetrad, the final full eclipse was due two days from now at 16:40 hours GMT. That means it'll be close to midnight in the eastern seaboard when it happens. Mancuso was no expert at all in the gospel and have no real knowledge of what was entailed for the end of days to come. But he knew the general knowledge surrounding it, being raised as a believer and having his mother go over certain teachings that she felt relevant to impart to him as a child.

As the men around began to become louder, he looked up and saw something that he never thought he would in all his years in the service. Three of his base helicopters were flying in formation with about two dozen angels. He props up the binoculars he had around his neck to get a better view and what he saw astonished him. As the group of winged beings, along with their apparent passengers came closer, the helicopters broke off and the angels now began a soft descent right on the flight line. The first one, who seemed to be carrying a little girl, landed about fifteen meters away from him. As the others landed behind this lead angel, the general raised his hands and the marines rushed over to create a perimeter around them. He then proceeded to march up to the group, chin up and in a confident cadence that made him feel honored. He saw the lead angel put down the girl as he approached and the passengers then slowly gathered in front of the angels.

General Mancuso, who was a believer, was now face to face with something that he had only heard or read about as a child.

"General Theodore Mancuso, Base Commander, Camp Darby."

As he said this, he still had the folder that he was reading earlier tucked under his arm and remembered the people that was detailed in it.

"Ambassador Stevens, welcome. You and your party are being transported back to the mainland ASAP. We'll debrief in the air."

David was looking at the base commander and was quite impressed with the general's protocol. If he was enthusiastic in any way, he certainly did not show it.

"General Mancuso, thank you for your assistance. This is my son Zachary, and this, this is Elizabeth. She's the reason we're here."

As the young captain began to move forward to escort the young woman, Michael and Gabriel promptly stood in front of her. The act of protection was subtle but clear, and the soldiers stopped immediately and looked intently amazed at these two divine creatures come to life.

"General, may I introduce the Archangel Michael, and his kin, Gabriel. These are his men."

I realized that while I swept my arms towards the others behind Michael and Gabriel that I just introduced them as I would someone from, well, from here. I immediately corrected myself before the general could even say anything.

"They have been given the duty to watch over Elizabeth. Where she goes, they go."

I've often told myself that I was a good ambassador, and in times have laid claim to creating a somewhat calm environment where a sense of normalcy is absent from. This situation certainly called for it. As the general processed what I said, he slowly walked past me and stood right in front of Michael. Then he held out his hand towards Michael and looked him straight in the eye.

"It is an honor, and a privilege to serve with you. I and my men are at your disposal."

I could see the pride in the general's eyes. And as Michael reached out and shook the general's hand, the general looked down and then began to issue orders to the men.

"Listen up; primary asset along with her protection detail is our primary objective. I want the ambassador and his party secured on Delta transport."

I looked at Michael as he and Elizabeth along with about eight other of his angelic brothers headed for a C-130 on the other end of the flight line.

"I'll see you when we get to Andrews; we'll be right behind you."

Michael nodded and then turned towards Gabriel. They exchanged words and Gabriel took what's left of the angels and began move towards me. The general was now waving me over to the twin transport behind the one that Michael and Elizabeth was going into and Gabriel began walking with me towards it. Zach was behind me and was clearly distraught that he was not going with Elizabeth. However, one of the angels with Gabriel guided him onto the second transport and he seemed to have settled down for now.

As each transport had a full squad of marines with them, fighters flew over the flight line and the thunderous sounds of their engines made the angels look up.

"Why aren't you going with Michael?" I asked Gabriel as we were nearing the back of the transport. He looked at me and looked at Zach.

"Because I am meant to be with you and your son."

I wasn't sure if this was some sort of sentiment but it felt specific. Specific to a point that it almost felt that he knew something that I didn't. Far be it from me to not put my trust in one of heaven's angels, but I remembered the thought I had when I jumped out of the jet. I was thinking about those that I loved and when it involves Zach, then I feel that I should know something, at least if it does affect my son.

As Patrick and Sarah joined us, we boarded the transport and quickly moved into the cargo hold and sat on the flip down seats at the side of the huge plane. At first I was dreading the ride as I've heard so many stories of how these transports can be quite uncomfortable. But comfort was far from the list of things I was thinking about now. And the flip down seat were actually not bad. They were well supported and padded enough that it was comfortable for the next several hours. I took a seat right beside Mancuso with Zach beside me, Sarah and Patrick sat across from us. Gabriel and the other angels once again looked cramped in the enclosed space. There was something unnatural for these beings to be confined in such a small piece of real estate. However, they all remained standing, and still. They had their eyes closed and as far as I can tell, they were murmuring something. Then it hit me, they were praying.

The back ramp of the transport began to lift up and I felt the transport begin taxiing on the ground. The engines revved quite loudly but the ride itself was not all bad. I heard over the radio from the general that the transport Michael and Elizabeth was in had just taken off. What I thought was loud for the engines was a mistake when the full force of all four engines at full throttle almost made me put my hands over my ears. I felt the sudden surge of power as the transport made its way down the runway and aided by rocket powered afterburners, lifted off in half the length of a normal runway. When we were in the air, the engines quieted down to a mellow hum and I began to feel tired. I overheard Mancuso asking for one of the marines to check on the cockpit and asking for a sit rep, he then turned to me.

"So Ambassador Stevens, it's been quite an experience hasn't it?"

I almost managed a smile if it wasn't something that was true. I knew that this was the general's way of beginning some sort of debrief on the events that have transpired. I looked at him and nodded my head towards the angels, which I realized after the entire turmoil surrounding military transport take offs, were still in deep prayer and haven't moved an inch.

"They are sent here, to help us in this war. After all we've done to each other, they still come here, and they still have faith."

As Mancuso ponders my statement, Zach reaches for my arm and gives me a good squeeze. I sigh and thought to myself, how can we be so stupid, how can we be so wrong? About ourselves, about the things that we've done to each other. Seeing the grace and obedience that these angels personify, it gives me little hope of what mankind can do to win this war.

"Look at them, they've lived forever and they still have the time to pray. I've never prayed in my life, never once gave thanks or be grateful."

I was mad at myself for not being able to do more for Zach. I was mad that I was helpless to do anything for my wife. I never thought of praying for her at all, I just focused on the loss I had in my heart and didn't see what I had in front of me. I didn't focus on Zach and his pain; I just focused on my own. And yet these angels are here for us, they don't know us, they don't need to do anything for us, but they do. Without questioning. Why couldn't I do that for my son?

"All I know right now is that we are here for a reason. Whatever happened in the past is gone. What we do from hence for is all that matters. You think I'm still a base commander?"

I knew Mancuso was being facetious, but he was right. It's so hard for us people to let go of our past, some of us even live our lives in them. I looked at Zach and I understood the importance of what we're doing now.

"Nothing's changed. We're still going to do what we need to, but now, we're doing it for everyone, on this planet. Not just for us anymore, there is no us anymore David, it's for everyone, everywhere."

As Mancuso patted me on the shoulder, he went up the cockpit level to check on the flight crew. As I looked over to Patrick, he had his hands clasped over his knees and looked worried. Sarah however, was looking at me and had this sad look on her face. I guess she had been looking at me talk with Mancuso, but I've never seen her look at me like that before.

"You alright David?" she asks me as she unbuckled her belt and started moving towards me. I was surprised that she decided to come but I'm glad that she did. None of this could've happened if it weren't for Sarah. She then sat beside me where Mancuso sat and buckled her belt again. Now she put her hands on my forearm and looked at me.

"This has been one of the most interesting days of my life."

Sarah had this big wide smile on her face and I knew she was trying to make me feel better, like she did when we were back at the office. Sometimes she would make up fake stories about certain things to make it funny, so I knew this was her trying.

"Well, at least you'll never have to ask for a recommendation letter."

I managed a smile back at her and she took it quite well actually. Although my tone was somewhat true, in the sense that we all had our lives plucked out of the reality we thought it was and now here we are, preparing for a war that will decide the world's fate, somehow the emphasis on what we used to do wasn't as important anymore. But all things considered, I'm still hopeful that things will work out for the best.

"How's Zach doing?" she asked.

I looked over at Zach and he was deep in thought. On the back of my mind, I still had the conversation we had in his bedroom when all this started. I was wondering if this was the right time to bring it up, present company included. I looked over at Gabriel, whose eyes were still closed but then opened and looked right at me. It felt that he knew I had something to say, and I felt that it was something that I needed to let them know about.

"He's doing okay I guess, as much as the rest of us for sure."

As I thought more about sharing what Zach had told with Gabriel, the more it sounded like a good idea. It was something that I didn't understand, and Zach didn't really elaborate too much and since we got cut off, I want to make sure that Zach doesn't feel it's something that wasn't just brushed to the side. Everyone, on this plane, on this planet, must be overwhelmed by what's going to happen. Everyone copes in different ways, and sometimes, those who can't are the ones that need help the most. Sarah settled into the chair and gave a big sigh.

"I know, I'm just glad that you and Zach are fine."

She put her hand over mine and for the first time, I felt genuine sincerity in Sarah's voice. I've known her to try to make things better, but that was at work and she always felt distant. But now, looking at her hand on mine, I felt that she was talking from her heart. I think everyone that knows what's coming realizes that time with those that they care for is more precious now than ever, and if you can't be truthful about your feelings now, then you'll never have a better time to start.

"I'm glad you're here Sarah, I am."

As I put my hand over hers, I wanted to give her a hug but the awkwardness of her reaction, almost shy in nature, took me by surprise. I think she wasn't expecting me to say anything back to her. And perhaps she's feeling the same way as I did right now. She managed a smile back and as I turned to look at Zach, he was now up from his seat and standing in front of Gabriel. This took me by surprise, not in a bad way but enough for me to spring up to my feet and take a few steps towards them. Zach was looking right into Gabriel's eyes and they seemed to be talking but I couldn't hear what they were saying. I felt a hand pull my arm back and Sarah was gesturing for me to sit back down. She gave me a nod that said it was alright and that I didn't have to be afraid of anything. She was right of course.

* * *

I was deep in thought about what I felt when I met Elizabeth. My dad and Sarah were talking beside me and I looked over at Patrick who had fallen asleep across the way. Why did I feel such a strong urge to be near her? And I was thinking back at what I had seen in the alley, that creature with the blood red eyes. I've heard them talk about the blood moon. I was thinking to myself if it was related in some way. Then I heard a thought in my head and not in the way where you think like you're talking to yourself. No, this was a completely different thought, from a completely different source but I knew it was in my head. I could hear it as if it was my own. As I closed my eyes the thought became clearer, more pronounced. I wanted to see if I could talk to it in my head, see if it will answer back.

"What is it that you want? Who are you?"

For a moment there was silence. A fleeting thought came into my head that I was finally going crazy from everything that was happening. And then I was jolted by a response that I did not expect to hear.

"Don't think your mind to be foolish Zachary, for the truth is far greater than what can you understand, for now."

The truth. The truth about what? I opened my eyes and I immediately noticed that Gabriel was looking at me straight in the

174

eye. I knew then that it was him in my mind, and that he was talking to me in doing so. But how? As if still hearing my thoughts, and now with my eyes open, I heard another response.

"Because your destiny awaits you Zachary, and all shall be revealed to you, in time."

Still looking at Gabriel, he nods at me and I nod back. I unstrapped my belt and tried to balance myself before walking over to Gabriel. I looked over at my dad and he was talking to Sarah. I didn't think twice about what he would think and I was not thinking about what I was doing as well. I just felt the need to get closer to Gabriel. With Patrick still asleep, I slowly walked over to Gabriel who now had a very soft and accepting look on his face. It's a face that a parent makes when a child realizes something true. I stood in front of him and I asked him a question that I had in my mind since this all began.

"Is my mother happy? Is she in heaven?"

As I asked this, tears welled up in my eyes and flowed down the side of my face. I missed my mom so much and I just wanted to hear so badly that she was fine, that she was happy wherever she was. Gabriel, still looking at me with sadness in his eyes smiled back.

"Your mother is a special person, this you already know. But she was also special in a different way, and you will know why soon Zachary. Be patient and the truth shall come to you. For now, all you need to know is that she is in a better place than this, than here. And yes, her heart is filled with joy."

These words made me close my eyes and picture my mom smiling and being how she used to be. I remember a lot of the times that she had held me and made me feel so loved and cared for. But then this thought was interrupted by Gabriel's, who now focused on something that I had earlier told my dad about.

"The beast that came to you, did it show you anything? Did it say anything to you Zachary?"

How could he have known about it? I've only told my dad, and mentioned it in passing at best. But I realized that Gabriel, who was an Eternal, an immortal being, sent forth by God, had divine knowledge that spans the entire world. He was in my head; he knew my thoughts and knew what was in my heart. In the presence of these beings, we are all but children trying to understand the complexity of life. Of being who we are.

"I saw it and I felt hatred from it. It also made my head hurt, but unlike any kind of pain I've ever felt before."

Gabriel was pondering my words, but I knew he already knew them and was simply making me understand why these things were happening. There was something that I could feel from Gabriel's thoughts and I realized that while he could sense my thoughts, I could also sense his. However, it was muddled and I struggled to make sense of what I could sense. And then Gabriel realized that I was reaching into his mind, he then focused on what he wanted me to know. As I reached into his mind, and as he allowed me to see the vastness of what is and what can be, I saw the eternal truth of it all.

I saw the fruits of a world that knew no pain or suffering. I saw people who were joyful and at peace and had no worries in their hearts. I saw people I knew, I saw Paolo, I saw Patrick, and others. And I saw my mom, waiting for me, with arms open. I saw a world where the life we live in is nothing short of eternal bliss. But as the setting of the sun came the darkness and I saw the ferocity of what can be if evil takes hold of this world. I saw fire in the sky, and I saw those that I loved being tortured, in pain. Then I saw Elizabeth, as the beast prepared to devour her flesh and destroy which that she carried in her womb. I looked at the beast and as it paused before it sank its fangs into Elizabeth's neck, it looked to me and snarled. Its eyes told me that I would fail, and that everything would be turned into this hellfire of a world.

As Gabriel eased out of my mind and stopped so as not to completely make my mind blow apart, I opened my eyes and looked at him. He then knew as he looked in my eyes that I understood now what I needed to do.

"Zachary, your destiny lies with the vessel. This you now know. Understand that there is no higher calling, for your purpose has now been revealed."

All things in my life has come to this, all the pain and suffering that I've felt for the past year has made me realize that it is now my turn to make sure someone is safe. I look back at my dad and as I notice the general come out of the flight deck, I know that I can't put my dad in harm's way. If the war begins then hell's legions will stop at nothing to get to Elizabeth. And where Elizabeth goes, I must be so as well. I look back to Gabriel, and prepared myself for this war. I clenched my jaw and took a deep breath.

"Alright, what must I do?"

As Gabriel shared what I needed to know, for now at least, I felt some comfort that I wasn't going completely crazy. I looked back at my dad as he looked back at me, and I gave him a quick smile.

CHAPTER FOURTEEN

THE FOUR GATES

As a new day dawns, so it is one day closer to when hell's gates open. As the angels first descended on the earth, the Archangels Michael, Gabriel and Uriel had matters and affairs with those that are of this world. Michael and Gabriel, tasked with the protection of the vessel until the second coming are now headed to Joint Base Andrews, along with David, Zach, Sarah and Patrick. Accompanied by General Mancuso, the Garrison CO of Camp Darby, two details of battle ready marines as well as the 122th fighter wing flying along with them, they race to get the asset to the confines of United States protection before this war begins.

However, the other Archangels, who upon their arrival on earth dispersed through the four corners of the earth to prepare for the holy war. Going to the four corners is not a mere expression as each of these Archangels seek where ultimately this holy war will begin. They each flew to one of the four gates of hell.

In popular culture, wherever it may be, the movies, television, fictional novels and short stories, the gates of hell is primarily described as the entrance to the underworld, the dominion of Satan. French artist Auguste Rodin created a monumental sculpture called La Porte de l'Enfer, or the Gates of Hell that depicts a scene from the first section of Dante Alighieri's Divine Comedy "The Inferno". In ancient Greek mythology, Hades was a place where souls go after death and a place of the afterlife. When the soul was separated from the corpse at the moment of death, it takes on the shape of the former person, and then transported to the entrance of Hades. Described as being either at the outer bounds of the ocean or beneath the depths or ends of the earth, Hades was considered the dark counterpart to the brightness of Mount Olympus, which everyone knows is where the gods lived.

In Chinese mythology, Diyu is the realm of the dead and is very loosely based upon the Buddhist concept of Naraka. Ruled by Yanluo Wang, the King of Hell, Diyu is where souls are taken to atone for their earthly sins and is a maze of underground levels and chambers. The underworld, in the lore of the Philippine Islands is called Gimokodan. At the entrance to Gimokodan is a black river where souls bathe to eradicate all memories of human life. Here there is also a huge female with many breasts to succor the spirits of those who died young. In Gimokodan itself, the spirit carries on much as it did on earth, but only during the hours of darkness. When daylight returns, each spirit makes a dish from leaves and is turned into a liquid in this dish until darkness returns.

However it is called across the world, one thing remains constant. Hell is a place where you go when you are removed from the communion with the god that you believe in. It is a place to go to exact justice for crimes that one has committed during their time on the surface and be the eternal punishment for those that act against their neighbors, friends and loved ones. The idea of hell persists in every major religion in the history of man, which holds the one sacred truth. That man believes more in his demise that in his salvation. It is far easier for man to believe in what will befall him as a consequence of his actions. Fear is the universal factor that makes hell sometimes much more real than heaven.

With the concept of a gate, to be opened or closed, the general belief was that entering hell would allow a mortal to seek out a former soul that has been damned and have the chance to bring it back to the surface. This act, called reclamation, was based on the resurrection theory that modern theological scholars believe to be the case in how the Holy Spirit claimed back the soul of Jesus Christ while he was in hell for three days. Once reclaimed, the soul can then inhabit its former self but now given the divine knowledge of the existence and reality of hell and the damned. However, the truth that lies deeper within the nature of the gates is much simpler. Not one gate, but four, its sole purpose is to unleash hell's legions into the world once the holy war begins.

The four gates is not so much for anyone to get into hell, but more for hell to get out into the world. And if the dark hatred and malice that exist there floods the world to its desire, the gates become permanent doorways as this world become part of hell itself. The other Archangels, Sandalphon, Metatron, Jophiel and Raphael each seek out one of the gates and prepare for its opening when the blood moon rises in the sky.

Each gate, located in various places in the world is kept under the responsibility of a general in hell. Modern folklore has given these generals plenty of names but they are most commonly referred to as The Horsemen. If the hand of hell is Lucifer's personal death squad, the horsemen are the generals that command the legions of demons within the fiery pit, second to Abaddon. As Raphael nears the first gate, located in Giza, Egypt, he commands his forces to lay across the land. Most people in the city, as well as those on the outskirts of Cairo, having already seen the angels during their initial arrival, are now privy to the cold and fearful truth of what this city holds.

For each of the gates, a horsemen holds the key to its opening. But unlike any other key, the way to open the gates are fueled by each specific sin that man has spread. The first gate, the Gate of Hatred, will open with every man's desire to inflict harm and pain to those that they willfully and deliberately feel hatred against. As the power of hatred fulfills the needs of those demons behind this first gate, the essence of the blood moon will grant the gates purpose in unleashing this same hatred across the world. The general, who guards this gate, rides a white horse garbed in barbaric but colorful robes. Armed with a silver quiver on its back and a black bow, Conquest will shoot his arrows across the world to spread the vile nature of his master's realm. Raphael, with several hundred thousands of his kin engulf the region and prepares for what is to come.

As Jophiel reaches the second gate, those that saw him and his band of angelic brothers flee. Nested in the mountain regions of North Korea, the small city of Oro, which is east of the Taedong-gang River and northeast of Pyongyang, is also the location of a political prison run by the government. As the angels descend, the KPA, or the Korean People's Army begin to shoot at the angels. It was clear to Jophiel why this was the location of the second gate. As the angels deflect the bullets with their wings, the soldiers then flee with the knowledge that this is no rescue mission for the prisoners. As the world grips with the reality of what is to come, all sense of political engagements, discussions, and disagreements have fallen to the wayside.

The guards, soldiers and staff cleared out of the prison and Jophiel surveys those that are incarcerated here. Men, women, some standing, some lying on the floor. All look to the angels with eyes of resolve. Jophiel realizes the strength of the human spirit, of what man can do to one another, but also that of what they can do to stay alive and survive. He raises his hands and the angels behind him systematically release all those in the prison. One man, frail and weak, managed to stand up and walk towards Jophiel, as he reached for Jophiel, he fell but Jophiel caught him and lifted him up. He said no words but Jophiel knew what was in his heart, gratitude and peace. As each of the prisoners are taken by an angel to be returned to where they belong, Jophiel surveys the land as it wreaks of the stench of hell's second gate. This place makes Jophiel uneasy, not out of fear or worry but out of obedience. This is the Gate of Blasphemy.

This sin makes men, makes entire countries dejected. As other sins are compared to blasphemy, those other sins are light. There is nothing more terrible than this, as it takes the very first and original commandment from the Father and wreak their vengeance upon God Himself. The words of those that seek to destroy the name of God shall be sent to hell. Other sins are committed through frailty, but this only through malevolence. It is a diabolical sin, because the blasphemer, like the demons, attacks God Himself and insults Him face to face. He is worse than the dogs, because dogs do not bite their masters, who feed them, but the blasphemer outrages God. Yes, Jophiel feels this place's contempt for the Father, and he will make sure that it is rightfully put back in its place. As he gets word from Raphael, now positioned over the first gate, he reaches out to the other two, Metatron and Sandalphon on their tasks to be at their assigned places. Jophiel looks to the skies, and longs for his place along with the Father. As he prays to get the Father's blessing, he is once again reminded of what they are here to do. And by the Father's will, he and his brothers will obey.

Those that harbor war in their hearts bring war to their lives. And the second gate is aptly under the watch of the second horsemen, War. Atop his red horse, who some say is because it was bathed in blood, the second general of hell's legions lives for its own purpose. War is only satisfied with loss and suffering, it thrives on the sorrows of those that are lost in battle. The only thing that War savors more than this, is the victory over those that shouts out against the Father. When this gate opens, War will unleash such a strength of despair and anguish that it will be akin to seeing the entire world burn for leisure. With his mighty sword, he blazes a trail of destruction in his path.

As an engineer puts the final touches on a weather console used primarily to study the air density in extreme cold weather conditions, he is startled by the shadows in the sky on this unusually sunny day. While the sun is out, temperatures in Umiat, Alaska can plummet to minus thirty degrees below zero with its inland tundra climate. Known as one of the coldest places in the United States, Umiat is located on the Colville River, 140 miles southwest of Deadhorse in the Arctic Circle. The town is not accessible by road or rail, only by

182

air or river. The engineer, who works for the United States Geological Survey team stationed here for this period of the year, looked up and dropped the calibration tool that he was holding. While Umiat has no permanent residents, the USGS camp operates from the middle of May to the middle of September where they have access to the internet and to news and entertainment by satellite. It was clear however, based on the engineer's reaction, now running furiously to the main camp station, that the arrival of the angels hasn't yet been acknowledged by this small band of researchers. The camp is run by a locally owned company that provides oilfield services in the area. Their crew consists in the summer of approximately ten people who work on a two weeks on two weeks off schedule. Add the handful of project teams from the USGS, at any given time, there are between twenty to thirty people lodged and fed here.

As the engineer disappears into the main station building, Metatron arrives devoid of the cold that exists around him. In 1944, the Naval Oil Reserve was set up here and it later became an air force base, which is now closed. So the wide open space is now filled with Metatron's company. As the angels land on the wide open cold tundra, Metatron looks to see where the third gate is. As he narrows his vision to a specific range of open fields just west of the installation, he feels the compulsion behind this gate's sin. In this desolate place, where only the hardened few can survive, lives the desire to take that which makes one idolize the power of treasures. In this land, where people come from all walks of life to try their hand in prospecting for gold, the heart of man is driven by greed and money. The ultimate prize for those that have no wish to live eternally is the shortsighted allure of riches. They spend their lives looking not realizing that the true nature of this life is being taken away from them, being stolen. As such, the Gate of Theft serves to make them acquire the subject of all their earthly desires.

The horseman of Famine guards this third gate. Riding a black horse and holding golden scales on which to weigh the riches that one has acquired, Famine not only spreads the seed of scarcity but perpetuates the need to hoard that which needs to be shared among others. With the sole purpose of making the wealthy have more and use the destructive power of a class gap on a society, Famine wreaks of selfishness and want. Where those that are wealthy continue to acquire what the poor cannot, Famine will happily take those that have hope in their hearts. He cares not for those that starve in their bellies but rather to starve man of their faith.

Metatron reaches out to his brothers and is informed that the vessel is safely in Michael and Gabriel's care. He prepares his brothers as in a little over one day's time, this place will not be so barren. He then proceeds to walk towards the main station building where about a dozen people have been standing and watching him for a while.

Sandalphon gets word that all three of his kin have taken their positions over three of the four gates. He gets the last of them, and the worst of them, as this gate brings all the other gates in union. Through all the three gates, all things that comes from each one ends up here. And Sandalphon knows that this is the main gate out of the four, the gate that serves only one purpose, this is the Gate of Death.

Much like with his brother Jophiel, the mere sight of Sandalphon exacts fear to those who saw him. But it is not fear for what they represent, it is fear that they will no longer be in this state of power. For over two decades, Somalia has been the face of civil unrest. The constant fighting between the Islamist rebels and the Transitional Federal Government, which is supported by the United Nations. The government seeks to control the fighting in the capital of Mogadishu where regular fighting have occurred to gain control of the capitol. As a result, thousands have fled the country out of fear and even more thousands have died fighting. As Sandalphon approaches just outside of Merca following the Shebelle River, they are greeted by shouts of scorn and disrespect from those that saw them. Descending just outside of the city limits, Sandalphon had to brush off soldiers that attempted to attack them. So much death in this place, as Sandalphon deflects the bullets off his wings and gives the soldiers a strong thrust from his majestic wings which was enough to fling them off their perch and into the dark buildings that they use to ambush those below.

This gate is where the bulk of hell's legions will emerge, as death permeates throughout this entire region, it only awakens the desires of its keeper. Some call the fourth and last horseman by the same name. Some call him the bringer of the end, the pale rider or simply Death. Riding an ashen steed and armed with his enormous scythe which he uses to impale those that he slays, it is Death that the Father's son had faced during his time in hell. To have conquered Death, the Father knew that Death would want recompense so as a soul dies, and if it belonged to hell, Death would be the one to collect it.

Fittingly, the last gate from which hell will be unleashed on this earth, the sin that feeds it goes hand in hand with Death. For those that deserve death have impure hearts, so shall those impure will be cast upon the fire to be cleansed. Impurity of one's soul leads to death, the death of the spirit and the death of the body. Because it flatters, this sin makes us fall at once into the habit that we so strenuously try to avoid. A habit which some carry with them even to death but realize it at the very end. Husbands, and decrepit old men, indulge in the same impure thoughts and committing the same sins that they committed in their youth. Because impure sins are so easily committed, they become multiplied without number in one's heart.

If the Father were to ask the sinner how many impure thoughts he has consented to, he will say that he cannot remember. But behold, if you cannot tell the number, the Father can and you know that a single immodest thought is enough to send you to the depths of Hell. How many immodest words have been spoken, in which man has taken delight with and by which you scandalized a neighbor? From thoughts and words you proceed to act them out, and to those innumerable impurities which those wretched souls roll and wallow in like swine, without ever being satisfied. Such vice is never satisfied even in death.

As Death uses these impure thoughts to muster his minions behind him, Lucifer has given these four horsemen dominion over this holy war. As it was in the past as it will be in the future, the four horsemen, generals in Lucifer's army, keeper of four gates shall once again try to make this world their own. Sandalphon reaches out to Michael, to let him know that they are in place and ready to do what is called of them. Michael reaches back to them to let them know that he and the vessel are near their destination. He lets them know that Gabriel has spoken to the son and had explained the truth of his purpose to him. Michael then tells them that as they are called to the hour, when these four gates open, they all know what they must do. As the Father wills it, it shall be done.

Sandalphon now hears peace around him with the fighting and shooting halted for a moment. He then realizes that the government soldiers are there with him, and they kneel before him. He quickly lifts them up and looks them into their eyes. The lead soldier barely manages to speak.

"My lord, what must I do to be saved?"

As Sandalphon looks at the soldier and all those other behind him, he is once again reminded of man's nature. There is an inherent trait in all of men that cannot be removed. Which is why the Father and all the angels of heaven do this for the worlds they fight for. The power of choice is the single most powerful weapon that Lucifer has no hold of. As long as man can choose to do what is right, to choose to do good rather than evil, then there is always hope. He looks back at the soldier and smiles.

"Repent of your sins and have faith, for the truth shall set you free."

186

The truth has a whole new meaning to these men. And as Sandalphon feels his brothers do the same thing where they are, countless souls are drawn to the cause for good.

As they army of heaven prepares for what is to come, they look to those that will be part of a new world, a world that will be filled with love, joy and peace. And of all these, love is the greatest and most powerful of all, for the Father so loved this world that he gave up his Son for it. And now that love is here, now, in front of these soldiers, these men and women, these people who may have not known the Father at all. Choice is what makes Sandalphon have hope, it is what makes him joyful.

* * *

As Michael receives word from all his other brothers, he senses that the vessel stirs in her thoughts. His back was turned against Elizabeth but he knew that she was there, looking at him, sensing that she wanted to ask something.

"Ask what your heart would like to know Elizabeth, I will tell you only the truth."

As Michael turns around, Elizabeth was already pondering her thoughts. Michael knew this but wanted to have Elizabeth ask her question.

"Once the Son is born, what will happen Michael?"

Michael had anticipated this question, which he knew Elizabeth would want to hear the answer from him. He walked Elizabeth back to her seat and buckled her up. He then proceeded to kneel in front of her and cupped both of her hands into his.

"When the second coming is at hand, this world will cease to exist."

Elizabeth's eyes widened as she heard this from Michael, and Michael understood the reaction which he promptly corrected.

"Not in a bad way Elizabeth. You see, all things have a beginning and an end. What is happening now is simply another step towards what is to come next."

As Elizabeth relaxed in her seat, Michael continued.

"A new world will come to be, a world where there is no more pain or sorrow. Where there is no sickness or persecution, it is a world filled only with those you love and is filled with only joy and peace."

As Elizabeth took comfort in this answer, she sat up and snapped back at Michael.

"And love?"

Michael smiled at her, such a pure heart in this child.

"And love."

Then Michael sensed another thought in Elizabeth's mind. This time, it was unexpected, and to him, it was a surprise. For someone who can commune with the world around him, Michael was not one to be surprised by anything. But this vessel, the chosen one to bring the Son of the Father once again into the world, the one from the blood of that of the first mother, intrigues him.

"Is there something else you would like to ask me Elizabeth?"

As Elizabeth looked up at him, she had a face that could only be described as curious. As some turbulence shook the plane, Elizabeth shifted in her seat and tried to form the question she had. Of course, by now, Michael had already seen her thoughts.

"I am wondering how Zachary's presence makes me feel safe. Even now, when I know that he is with your brother Gabriel, I feel that I need him to be beside me. Why is this?"

As Michael tries to give Elizabeth the answers that she needed, Michael in turn thinks back to the time when this was a question he never knew he would have to answer. But for now, Elizabeth deserved an answer, even if it wasn't the complete one.

"Zachary is bound to your fate Elizabeth, just as you are bound to the Father."

As Elizabeth tried to understand Michael's response, Michael knew that at some point, the truth about Zachary will have to be revealed. Not only to Elizabeth, but to his father and to everyone.

"You see, in the beginning, as with the virgin mother, someone had to be there to make sure that she was safe, and that she was able to go where she needed to go."

Elizabeth was intent on her listening, looking straight into Michael's eyes.

"As then, as it is now, Zachary will stay with you and make sure that you get to where you need to go. And I know that he understands this as well."

Now Elizabeth goes back to her curious face which Michael understood as her way asking for more answers. As the transport banks left, an announcement comes from the cockpit and provides a brief update to the passengers and crew.

"We are inbound to Delta Zulu, ETA 22 minutes. Secure all stations and prepare for arrival."

As the announcement jostled me from a somewhat deep slumber, the transport banks hard and General Mancuso turns to me.

"Ambassador Stevens, once we land, the Joint Chiefs will be there and they will expect a debriefing."

As I straighten up in my seat, and look over to Zach who was now back in his seat with his eyes closed, I look back to General Mancuso and gave him a brief grin. It was always ridiculous to me how the military has the need to know everything that's happening, even though it something that's completely out of their control. I

189

wanted to tell the general that there were no more strategic points to be taken here, no more political or any kind of socio-economic angle that the United States government can use. This is not something that anyone on this planet, let alone this country can hope to control, and I was looking at Gabriel as I was thinking all this.

In all of the history of the world, these past days have heralded a new age of reality. One that calls for people to accept what is in front of them. I've often heard the religious expression that implies the truth is something that you need to believe in your heart and not to be seen with your eyes. For someone like me, it's not a hard concept to embrace, I've always put my faith in those that I can see, touch and feel. But since Loretta died, I've lost the need to believe in anything any longer, in anything much more divine than my loss. I was no longer going to be held hostage by the pain of suffering when those that I believe in, those that I love are taken from me.

And yet, with the arrival of heaven's army, with the message that was delivered throughout the world, with the impending end of all that is, I cannot help but believe in the very thing that I'm seeing before me. These angels are real, and so I deduce that heaven is real. And if it is, then perhaps Loretta is there, waiting, and hoping that after this war ends, that we can be together once again. I looked back at the general to give him some sort of response.

"Look around you General, what else do you think the Joint Chiefs need to know? What's happening here is not just about the United States, it's about every living person on this globe. If the Joint Chiefs want answers, they can ask them."

As I nod my head towards the handful of angels in the cargo area, still standing, still and quiet, the general looked at them and looked back at me. He knew I was right and he knew it was something that came down the wire, but from what I've learned from these past few days, is that the hearts of men can be persuaded to believe in something larger than themselves.

"Fear not, for behold, I bring you good news of great joy that will be for all the people. For unto you is born this day in the City of David a Savior."

I looked at the general as he recited this passage, a little surprised that someone in his line of work would know what I expect to be a verse in the holy bible. I had a question on my face and he sort to clarify it.

"It's from the Gospel of Luke, chapter 2, verse 10. You see the angels revealed themselves to the shepherds when Jesus Christ was born, and told them of the change that was coming."

As I looked into his eyes, the general strained to say what was in his heart.

"Whatever's coming, it'll change everything we know Ambassador. In fact, it already has."

As I felt the landing gear grind underneath us, I realized that we were on a slow descent. Earlier the general told me that the President, Vice President and Secretary of State were secured underground and has left the Joint Chiefs as well as the Defense Secretary above ground to conduct operational and tactical efforts. The general also said that NATO has been out on high alert as well as the security council of the United Nations has been alerted, along with all nation members.

With the presence of the angels in virtually every corner of the globe, all military forces have been ordered to provide unwavering support to the angelic corp. If this war is to be won, it will be won by both divine and earthly soldiers, and the general has indicated his wholeheartedness in being part of it.

"Once we land, a secure convoy will take the asset to an undisclosed location. I'm afraid that from there it is above my clearance level. But be rest assured you and your company will be

191

taken care of but once you're off this transport, that's where my command ends."

I looked at the general and from what he said, it almost sounded like a warning. As the pilot announce the landing procedure was about to begin, I looked back at the general and wanted to make sure I understood him correctly.

"Is there something that I need to know general? This woman, this child was entrusted to me and I will do what I need to in order to make sure she is protected, by any means."

The general nodded to me as if he was saying it was the only thing that I could do. But I knew that he was also telling me to be wary of where Elizabeth may be going. I then looked to Gabriel, who was now looking at me, and with all of my will, got out of my seat and walked up to him. I had seen him talking to Zach earlier and I wanted to let him know now of what Zach told me. It may have been the wrong time since we were landing but I felt it was now or never.

"Gabriel, I saw you earlier speaking to my son. Did he tell you what he saw?"

Gabriel nodded to me and I was relieved to know that it was something he knew about. Surely it is something that he can understand better than me but I continued to speak, thinking of the general's warning.

"You must promise me Gabriel that no matter what happens to me, you will look after my son Zachary. I don't know what's going to happen when we land but I need to know that you have his back."

Gabriel then looked at Zach, who was now looking at both of them. He knew the love of a father for he has felt it all his immortal existence. This is no different and Gabriel sees the love in David's heart. He put his hands on David's shoulder and as the plane touched down, the landing made David shuffle his feet, but Gabriel caught him by the side of his shoulder.

"I say to you David, son of Elliot, on my honor that I will do all that I need to make sure your son remains safe."

As the plane taxis and the speaker announces our imminent arrival at the main hanger, I look back to Gabriel as he and his kin get ready. I then notice that Sarah and Patrick has unbuckled themselves and began walking towards Zach and General Mancuso begins to bark orders to the marines that accompanied us on this flight. The transport then comes to a slow jolt, and the sound of compressed air begins to fill the air. A moment later, the rear ramp of the transport begins to come down and I had forgotten that we've been in this windowless plane for so long that the daylight blinded my eyes for a minute.

As I adjust to the brightness, I hear commotion outside of the transport. The ramp came down completely and I see a slew of activity outside of the transport's perimeter. Finally, as we walk out, I saw the base soldiers, surrounded by media and then the official convoy that I only assumed were the Joint Chiefs arrived in unmarked black SUVs. There was media present and as they snapped photos, along with all the commotion, I managed to see our sister transport right alongside us, generally in the same state of deplaning. Sarah, Patrick and I walk towards them and immediately Zach goes to Elizabeth's side. Gabriel meets up with Michael and as a group we all begin walking towards the convoy that has been waiting for us about thirty meters away. As we did, I looked back at General Mancuso, and he simply nodded to me and proceeded to meet the convoy ahead of us as his men took positions around us.

CHAPTER FIFTEEN

JOINT BASE ANDREWS

MARYLAND

As the convoy pulled up, the Chairman of the Joint Chiefs, General William Moorer, was on the line with Defense Secretary Dempsey. He was given enough time to assess the tactical risk and advantage of having the asset brought over from Italy into the United States but still unaware of the operational strength of the threats they face. The defense secretary had instructed him to make sure that General Mancuso provides a complete debrief of the last sixteen hours so that they can have the most updated intelligence of what they are, or will be dealing with.

"Yes, Mr. Secretary, we're meeting them now and will provide a situation report within the hour."

As the driver stops the black SUV, the Chairman, accompanied by the SEAC, or the Senior Enlisted Advisor to the Chairman, Sergeant Major Craig Henderson, was creating defense scenarios on the possible outcome of the engagement. Given that this kind of force is something that the combined military force of the United States, and with that, the world, has never seen before, the scenarios, which were specifically designed to project percentages of loss and acceptable collateral damage was, to say the least, inconsistent. General Moorer wanted the Sergeant Major to create a more realistic assessment scenario from first hand intelligence. And the only way that it would happen is to get it from the newly arrived force of the angelic corps.

As both the chairman and SEAC looks at the two groups coming out of the two transports, the sight of the angels struck them the most.

While the angels had arrived a little over two days ago, and have since been a permanent fixture in the landscape as well as the open skies, neither the chairman nor the SEAC has had an opportunity to see one up close, much less meeting them. And from the manifest from Camp Darby, these were not mere angels but the Archangel Michael and Gabriel. Only had the general dreamed of meeting such figures, of myths and legends, in this very real and sudden series of events.

"General, with your permission, upon completion of protocols, I'd like to begin the debrief starting with the two angels."

As General Moorer nods to the SEAC, he prepares himself as he sees the group now walking towards them, just passing the media line that has been authorized by the President itself. Overhead, the rumble of jet engines fill the air as General Mancuso ordered the fighter wing to remain on ready alert while the asset was secured on the ground. The Chairman then gave the SEAC the cue, and as they exited the vehicle, the security details from the two other SUVs, at this point on standby jumped out and began to form a perimeter around General Moorer and the SEAC. About twenty meters ahead, he clearly saw General Mancuso walking towards him, followed by a group of civilians and the angels walking behind them with a complement on the sides as well. In addition, Mancuso's marines also have created a five meter spread pattern surrounding the main group.

As Mancuso came up to the Chairman, he stopped and gave the customary hand salute and announced himself.

"General Mancuso, Garrison CO, Camp Darby, Italy."

The Chairman gave back the salute and as they both put down their hands, Mancuso reached over to shake Moorer's hand.

"General Mancuso, welcome to states side. Your orders will be given to you by Sergeant Major Henderson, but well done on getting the asset back here as ordered."

Mancuso just nodded and then sidestepped in order to introduce the party behind him.

"Ambassador David Stevens, Chairman of the Joint Chiefs of Staff, General William Moorer."

As David stepped forward and shook the Chairman's hand, he then quickly joined Mancuso on the side to introduce everyone else.

"Mr. Chairman, this is my son Zachary. Miss Sarah McKenzie, my executive administrator and Patrick Roberts, my chief of security."

As the group goes to the other side of the Chairman facing Mancuso and David, it was clear to David that the General was anxious to meet the person which all of this is for, or about. As the two archangels approached, the Chairman strained to see the asset which was behind both figures as they came face to face with him. David saw the general swallow a subtle gulp, which he took as his cue to break the awkwardness and to introduce their newly found allies in this war.

"Mr. Chairman, may I present to you the Archangels Michael and Gabriel along with their kin."

The mere presence of both angels, much less the combined aura of divinity with those that accompanied them, was impressive. The Chairman was a seasoned military man, but his gaze into Michael's eyes faltered as he bowed his head and reached out a hand. Michael stepped forward and instead of taking the chairman's hand, he grasped his entire forearm with his and gave it a firm shake. As General Moorer looked back up at Michael, he also looked to Gabriel as well as the other angels and felt a sense of calm. Once Michael felt it was the time, he slowly reached behind him and shuffled Elizabeth out to his front, but not far enough from arms reach.

"William, son of Richard, I present you the living vessel of which the Father has chosen favor with. Her name is Elizabeth Scarpello."

196

General Moorer was taken aback, this was no woman, and this was a child. But there was something about her that made her look older, whether it was the gentle smile that she had or the kind of soothing way she looked at him. This was the asset that will ensure the outcome of this war? He looked at David, who was somewhat empathetic to what he was thinking right now. However, time was running short and they must get the information they need in order to prepare for this holy war.

"Everyone, we have no time to lose. Ambassador Stevens, your party will be escorted back to the Pentagon where Defense Secretary Dempsey is waiting for you. Elizabeth, you will need to come with us so that we can take you to a secure location."

As the words rang out in the air, Michael and Gabriel pushed back Elizabeth behind them and their wings tensed up, as well as the soldiers around us.

"The vessel stays with us, it is the will of the Father and my divine responsibility to protect her. Your assistance is admirable William, but they are not necessary. We are capable of keeping the vessel safe from those that wish to harm her."

With that, the angels with Michael and Gabriel began to hover and as calmly and slowly as he could, General Moorer spoke back to Michael.

"Michael, if I may. Far be it for me to question your mission, as we are both soldiers, and I understand that which you need to do. But if this vessel, Elizabeth, holds the fate of the world within her then don't you think we should do all that we can to keep her from being found?"

The words rang true to Michael but it also made it clear to him that the General's thinking was still of this world. Whatever thoughts they may have, ideas or strategies, all of these will fail against the hordes of hell. For this enemy does not want, it takes. Willingly, cruelly and without remorse. An enemy that has nothing to lose and everything to gain will always have an advantage over those that have something to lose and someone to protect.

"I say to you, there is no place that you can take her that the enemy will not find. No depths or crevice nor secret chambers will keep her from those from the pit."

General Moorer realizes this and looks to David for confirmation. The attack on the plane on their way to Camp Darby made its way to David's head. It's true, as he looked back to General Moorer to nod in agreement. Having served for most of his life in the military, General Moorer knew the time when a plan can no longer sustain the expected results. As he pondered the scenarios that the SEAC had presented him, with possible locations of safe houses that are highly secured, it had dawned on him that these scenarios are all but of mortal enemies.

And what can they do against the power of hell? It would be wise to heed those that has fought an enemy before, as they would have the tactical experience on how to fight them again. For what it's worth, General Moorer knew that his command, his entire career in the military ends today. Today he becomes a private in a new kind of army, in a new kind of war and he will have to listen well to those that have fought it before.

"I understand. Then in this case, all of us will proceed to the Pentagon and provide an assessment to Secretary Dempsey."

He looked back to Michael and Gabriel, and saw that they knew he understood. He couldn't say how but he knew they were there to help, and he was going to make them do so.

"Michael, I would like to ask you to address the men and if at all possible, provide them some intelligence of what they will be up against."

Michael nodded, as did Gabriel.

"We shall assist you and your brothers in all that we can. Elizabeth shall ride with Zachary whilst we follow above."

With that, Elizabeth walked over to Zachary and both of them, along with David stepped into the SUV that General Moorer came in. Patrick and Sarah went with the SEAC into the second SUV and General Mancuso followed in an army Humvee.

Michael reached out to all his brothers, now stationed at the gates across the world. The vessel was safe, and our earthly brothers are taking the war to heart. However, Michael also reminded his kin to be aware of those that turn as when the hordes of demons and reapers and all things evil is unleashed in this world, the hearts of men may falter quickly. He has seen it before, and he has no doubt he will see it again.

As the convoy sets out, Michael, Gabriel and the others follow aloft, staying no more than thirty feet off the ground and keeping the convoy in full sight. As the sun sets, Michael thinks to himself that the end will come soon, and as the moon is filled with blood, so shall it be as well here on earth.

* * *

As Defense Secretary Dempsey puts down the phone, he then picks it up once again and runs an encrypted protocol to secure the line. As the line goes clean, he then dials a number that he has only used for two times in his life. This was the third time. As the other line rang, he looked out of his office on the north side of the Pentagon where he could just see the lights come on to illuminate the Washington Monument.

As part of the President's cabinet, as well as a member of the National Security Council, the Secretary of Defense is the principal defense policy adviser to the President and is responsible for the formulation of general defense policies and any policy related to all matters of direct concern to the Department of Defense. Under the direction of the President, the Secretary exercises authority, direction and control over the Department of Defense and works in conjunction with the Joint Chiefs as well as other Executive and Strategic Command Units in enabling all defense initiatives under the United States government.

As the line picks up, Dempsey heaves a huge sigh and does not try to hide his acceptance of the situation.

"The vessel is safely here your Holiness, I have informed the others. Now that this time has come, hopefully our preparations will not be in vain."

On the other line, across the pond, Pope Nicholas VI offers a calming voice, as well as advice to his fellow brother of the order.

"Samuel, we all are blessed to witness such a thing. I myself never thought that it would happen in my lifetime. But now, as I look out across St. Peter's Square, I see people, and I see the angels, and I feel hope my friend. Have hope Samuel, have faith in what we were called to do."

As Samuel Dempsey, appointed Secretary of Defense to the President three years ago but a member of the Order of Light through generations of Dempsey's never thought that this day would come. But now he knows that the vessel is on her way here, along with none other than the Archangel Michael and Gabriel, and will be witness to what will be the crowning entry in the history books of man.

"I know Ricardo, and I am grateful for it. I know we have prepared for such but it's quite difficult to comprehend that it truly is happening."

As Secretary Dempsey continues to look out his window, his attention was caught upon a company of winged figures flying over the monument. It was so surreal for him that he looks twice every time he sees them. By now the world was witness to these celestial beings that have only been present in the teachings of the holy bible.

He remembers the most vivid image of an angel in his mind when all of this began. He was about ten years old and growing up in Princeton, New Jersey from a wealthy family, he had sat down one night by his grandmother when she started telling him a story.

It was close to Christmas then and because he didn't really have much of an understanding of religion, his grandmother was a member of the local Baptist church and she told him all about how the angels appeared before the shepherds to tell them of the good news. It was something that he remembered to this day and a little over forty eight hours ago, that vision became true.

"Have you met them Ricardo?" he asks the Pope. And as the Pope recounts the initial encounter with Michael, and how Uriel had stayed behind to provide the much needed reminder to those that have faith of what is to come, he said it was the single most inspiring experience of his life. When Dempsey heard this, he again let out a huge sigh and he knew that in less than an hour, he will come face to face with these magnificent servants of the most high.

"I heard that you have encountered an attack."

As the Pope recounts what had happened, the magnitude of what these demons can do became apparent to Dempsey. It was not enough that they protect the vessel, they had to make sure that wherever she was, she would always be surrounded by those that will bless her.

"That is unfortunate. This is something that we've never faced before Ricardo, but I swore to defend and protect her with my life. I have every intention of doing what I promised."

As Dempsey turns around from the window and now looks upon his desk, he opens up a folder that simply had an emblem of a dove on the cover. He thumbed through the pages until he saw what he was looking for and studied it a while before continuing his conversation with his brother in the order.

"I've told the others to be ready when the time comes. We may need to move quickly when things go astray. On another note, tell me about this Ambassador Stevens."

As he listened on, he thumbed through more pages and then finally closed the folder and put it in his attaché case. The light on his phone indicating another line was active and an incoming call was coming, he quickly said his goodbye.

"I will be in touch Ricardo, be safe my old friend. Pray that we have the strength to endure the coming days until the end, until His coming."

With that he quickly released the encryption protocol that opens up the communication service back to his desktop phone. As the line rang, he picked up knowing fully who it was based on the light indicator on the phone, which blinked red.

"Hello Mr. President. Yes sir, they are en route. I expect them to arrive here in about thirty minutes. Yes sir, that's the plan. I will contact you once we've secured the asset and will ask the Chairman of the Joint Chiefs to join you for a status report. Understood sir."

As he looked at his computer monitor, he pulled up the tracking monitor and saw that the convoy, being tracked by satellite, just got onto 695. He estimates that they will be at the lower level in about fifteen minutes. He picked up his phone and rang his assistant. A young airman came into the room and promptly waited at the other side of his desk.

"Please make sure that incoming Alpha convoy gets situated in Level 6. Inform me when they are here and I want maximum security around this. Do you understand airman?"

The young airmen promptly said yes and then left the room. Dempsey then looked at the tracking monitor again and started to get ready. Above all he was quite excited to meet the angels that accompanied the vessel. He must remember to use the word 'asset' but have been thinking about whether to divulge his true nature to the Ambassador. It wasn't clear to him yet at this time what role this Ambassador Steven will play in all this but one thing he does know, is that there's a reason why he's here.

But he also wants to meet this Elizabeth Scarpello, as the Pope had been quite impressed with the girl's resolve. How does one react when they are told that they hold the fate of the world in their hands? He could only imagine what it must have been like when she received that personal message from the spirit. It takes courage to accept things that are beyond one's control. Coming from a bloodline that was meant to fulfill such a happening, it was worth the commitment that he made when he was asked to join the order. And now that time is here, it is real, it is going to happen, and there's nothing anyone on this earth or above it can do to stop it. We must find that courage in ourselves now, more than ever.

* * *

As the convoy crossed the Potomac River, the SUV carrying David, Zach and Elizabeth along with General Moorer turns into the Jefferson Davis Highway which is restricted only to official Pentagon vehicles. The highway has a series of exits that branch out into four distinct entrances to the lower levels of the Pentagon's main building structure and the convoy takes the exit that was marked "Level 6".

As the convoy, along with Michael and Gabriel approached a driveway that led underground, Michael, Gabriel and the others landed behind the convoy and proceeded to hover inside the complex. As the lead SUV went through a series of electronic gates, each one opening through credentials that were provided by the Chairman, the convoy arrived at a loading port which served as the main building garage for Level 6 personnel. There was a company of soldiers waiting for them, led by a young airman that was in Secretary Dempsey's office about twenty minutes ago.

Each of the SUV's then parked in a diagonal pattern beside each other and as they did, the company of soldiers surrounded each one in the front, sides, and rear. After shouting an all clear command, the doors opened and everyone came out and proceeded to walk towards the elevated platform where the young airman was standing patiently. At the heels of this, Michael and Gabriel, along with the others descended slowly and the power from their wings rustled up some of the soldiers. As they made their way to the same platform, the soldiers were following them with their eyes. Even the airman was a little flustered when they finally made it to the platform, so the Chairman actually had to clear his throat to snap him back.

The airman led them down a brightly lit corridor and after flashing his badge to open a large silver door at the end, the corridor opened up to a massive situation room that seemed to track the entire movement of operational military facilities in the entire globe. As the group filed in, the silver door closed behind them with a distinct blomp sound that indicated it was sealed shut. As the group was led further into the adjacent space where a conference room was located encased in glass, the airman showed each one in.

"Please take a seat and Defense Secretary Dempsey will be with you shortly."

Michael and Gabriel remained standing right behind where Elizabeth sat. As David looked out to the situation room, he could make out some distinct labels on the giant monitors in the room. He saw that there were some attacks in Syria that involved ISIS trying to demolish a mosque that had welcomed the angels in that region. Another monitor reported some fighting that broke out in Israel, in Bethlehem between factions of Jewish and Nomadic believers.

David shook his head, and looked back at Michael and Gabriel. He felt ashamed, ashamed to be called human, to be part of such short-sightedness, even in the midst of clarity. But this is why this world is being judged. Even in the face of being plunged into the pits of eternal fire, man's nature was still going strong. The self and innate nature to preserve himself, to put his wants in front of others. Then General Mancuso spoke.

"And you will hear of wars and rumors of wars. See that you are not alarmed, for this must take place, but the end is not yet. For nation will rise against nation, and kingdom against kingdom, and there will be famines and earthquakes in various places."

As his words broke the silence in the room, Michael and Gabriel looked at General Mancuso, somewhat surprised and happy. For those that know the word as it was, are those that can see hope above all else.

"Mathew chapter 24, verse 6 and 7." Mancuso added.

Everyone in the room pondered on the verse that Mancuso just recited. Indeed, the nations have taken arms against other nations, and all over the world, drought, earthquakes, storms and floods have inundated areas high and low. But this is not yet the end, as it is only the beginning. Then everyone looked to the door as a man came in and stood there, looking at them. Of course the Chairman knew who it was, but as Secretary Dempsey surveyed the group of people in this room, he could only smile.

He started to walk around the room, still not speaking and looked intently on each person sitting around the table. Then as he came around to where Elizabeth was sitting, he looked up to the two angels behind her, majestic, magnificent. He then circled back to the head of the table and put down his brown attaché on the table. Putting both hands palms down on the table just on the sides of his bag, he bowed his head and began to say a prayer.

"Heavenly Father, I stand before you as your humble servant. I lift up those in this room, for you have chosen them all to be here, and for each to fulfill a purpose. We know not your will, but we seek to obey it, as it is revealed to us. Amen."

Secretary Dempsey stands up straight and clasps his hands together.

"I am Defense Secretary Samuel Dempsey. On behalf of the President of the United States, I thank you for being here. We have much to plan for, and very little time to do it. So, shall we begin?"

He pulls out the folder that he was thumbing through earlier, and began rustling through the pages. As images of explosions and attacks blared over the monitors outside of the conference room, it was an eerie thing to see as no sound carried through the sound proofed glass walls. Every now and then, someone's attention will be taken by a specific image bright enough when it's on the main screen in the situation room.

"So, Elizabeth here is the key to our salvation. She bears the living spirit and when the second coming happens, this world becomes part of the heavenly kingdom."

Except for the angels in the room, as well as myself, everyone else gasped for air. I had forgotten that this piece of information was imparted to me selectively by the Pope and the Monsignor, and along the way, I've treated it as common knowledge. However, Sarah, Patrick, Mancuso and the Chairman are hearing this for the first time.

"So our mission is clear, protect Elizabeth until the second coming happens, yes?"

Again, everyone around the room was taking this in quite slowly and as the realization hits each person, the facial expression turns from fear, anger, frustration, and confusion to that of understanding. It was hard to face the mortality of one's life, even if there was a chance for life to continue eternally. It was another part of human nature that dictated self-preservation, it was, by large a reaction based on fear.

The other thing that I realized was how Dempsey knew about this is such detail. Then it dawned on me and as I looked to him, he gave me a quick look and a curt little nod, as if to confirm my suspicions.

So he was a member of the order as well, as the Pope did say there were a handful of them in the world. Now it made sense why he asked me to take Elizabeth. The Pope probably knew that I would inadvertently wind up with Dempsey here in the United States.

"Michael, if we are to fight this war, can you perform the unction of our forces?"

Michael looked to Gabriel, and as Gabriel nodded, Michael stepped forward and stood beside Dempsey.

"The blessing has since been granted to all in this world that chooses to fight for the kingdom. My kin will do what they can to prepare your men for what is to come."

I looked to Zach as this was said and I could see that Zach had already decided to be part of it. If it was going to be so, then I will be right there beside my son. But then Patrick asked a question, which was something that stirred more his worry than his faith.

"What about those that cannot fight, what will they do? I have family, as other do. Women and children, surely they cannot be expected to be part of this war."

This time Gabriel spoke as he went right beside Michael.

"This war will define the end for all. When the second coming happens, all souls in this world will be saved. However, if we fail, every single soul will burn in chaos."

So there it was, clear and precise. No options, no alternatives, no chances of changing anything. The end will come, it's only a matter of how it will be at the end.

"The moon runs with blood in a day's time, Samuel, son of Joshua is correct, we must prepare. Right now four of my kin place their forces and guard against the four gates. When the blood moon fill the skies, these four gates shall unleash hell. And they will spread like famine across this world."

As everyone thinks about this, Michael continues.

"But do not lose hope my brothers, for there is a greater glory to be had. I am here with my kin, sent by the Father, so that together, we can make this world part of the heavenly kingdom. There is no greater calling, and when the Son comes again, the kingdom will be for everyone, and forever."

Those in the room pondered that statement. For everyone, forever.

CHAPTER SIXTEEN

THE BLOOD MOON

Secretary Dempsey lays out a plan that will involve a multitude of things to be completed. And there's not much time to do it. As Michael and Gabriel keep in touch with their kin that has stayed outside of the building, both ponder the thoughts that the secretary has proposed. While Michael had instructed them to provide any kind of assistance to the a small group of special forces that was sent out by Dempsey, Michael was keen to point out that whatever it takes, the vessel is their primary responsibility.

Dempsey, having pointed out that the vessel, Elizabeth, would be the primary target, the first order of business is how to make sure she is surrounded at all times by both divine and earthly forces. And yet, as Dempsey looks at Zachary, the Ambassador's son, he wonders of this is the person that the order has been foretold of.

In the year 44 A.D., the mother of Jesus Christ, Mary had since moved from Jerusalem to the outskirts of Bethlehem. While popular teachings put Jesus Christ's death at 1 A.D., scholars estimated that the death of Christ actually happened between 29 and 36 A.D. Other scholars have studied scriptures and have deduced the exact time, day and year that Jesus Christ died. Catholic traditions, including Easter and Holy Week points to some truth in the time and day, which occurs at 3 PM on Black Friday but through researching specific timelines that involved those that were at hand during the crucifixion, the year that it happened was pegged at 33 A.D.

Mary and her family, including Joseph, her cousin Mary Magdalene, as well as other followers of Christ have secluded themselves after witnessing the resurrection in Jerusalem. Hence since, the formation of the modern church, based on the four canonical gospels that referenced the life of Jesus Christ, it became the foundational truth of the now modern Christian church.

But in between the years after the resurrection, and when Jesus Christ came back to address the disciples for the last time and stayed on earth for forty days before his ascension into the heavenly kingdom, to sit at the Father's side, accounts have been sparse on what has become of the earthly mother and father of Jesus Christ, Mary and Joseph.

It was believed that after the resurrection, some of the disciples, namely Paul, Luke, and Matthew, joined Christ in his stay. The accounts have also pointed that Mary and Joseph were also part of the party that travelled temporarily with Jesus while he wandered throughout the region, even with people saying that he had been sighted as far out in Africa, as well as in middle Asia and in the region of the Adriatic Sea. It was believed that after a decade from Christ's death, Mary and Joseph had since settled into a small rural area just outside of Bethlehem where they had lived out the remaining days of their years.

However, born to Joachim and Anne from Nazareth, Mary had another sister. A younger sister who was also named Mary. This however was never divulged to the public for several reasons. In the early times of Jewish tradition, the eldest daughter had by right the means to marry first. The younger or youngest sister was to remain under servitude to the family until such time that she becomes betrothed under law. After the now famous passage from the angel's visit unto Mary, Joachim and Anne had declared that their younger daughter of the same name was to remain outside of the scandal of how Mary became pregnant outside of marriage. Then, this was constitutional and there were heavy laws that governed adultery. The punishment ranged from burning, to hanging and to public stoning. So fearful that this would affect the family name, Joachim and Anne had concealed the existence of their daughter, the younger Mary, from all accounts going forward since Joseph took Mary to Bethlehem.

But this also became the single bloodline where all throughout the years starting from that time; this was where Elizabeth had come forth. The younger Mary, now believed to have left the region and travelled through the Roman Empire under cover of a different name, went through the Avars and the Antes Mountains, and headed to the Polanes region, now known as Poland. Further records show that the younger Mary had since started a family and that family then spread over the Finnish Alps, and made their way into Guntram, on the border of now modern Germany and France. Elizabeth's ancestral roots had begun in Italy, presumably with the immigration of her great, great, grandmother from the Frisian Coast.

During this time, there were those that knew of the younger Mary's relation to the mother of the messiah and have since followed her progress in the hopes that like her sister that she would be chosen to be a messenger of the Holy Spirit for another messiah. This was the earliest known existence of the To Tágma tou Theíou. Then, it consisted of a scribe that made sure the lineage of the younger Mary was chronicled accurate but over the centuries became a much more secretive organization, changing with the economic, political and cultural challenges in the coming of the modern world, so that it has the power to protect and conceal the whereabouts of those that are from this specific bloodline.

Secretary Dempsey, who was inducted into the order after his father before him had kept this mission close to his heart for all his life. The preaching and teachings of the traditional beliefs surrounding the end of days was something that over the past centuries was influenced in some way or form by the order. The sole purpose of this was to make sure that when the bloodline received the blessing from above, that it will herald in a new world for everyone.

Which was why when Dempsey heard Michael say what he did, he knew in his heart that this was where he should be.

As the early beginnings of this order found out, in scriptures that has long since vanished, there was mention of a protector. A guardian that will usher in the second coming. This guardian will be of both worlds, and shall be the one to walk amongst those in the light as well as in the darkness. Having studied the bio of each of the civilians on the transport prior to landing in Andrews, he paid particular attention to David and Zachary. He had asked the Pope the same question. Why them?

* * *

I was looking at Zach and the way he was with Elizabeth. I also noticed that he seemed to have some sort of connection with the Archangel Gabriel. When they were talking on the transport on the way here, it didn't seem like they were saying much and yet it seemed they were. I couldn't put my head around it but knew that there was something that Zach knew that he wasn't telling me. Call it father's intuition but I wanted to give Zach a chance to do it in his own time. I've given him all this time after his mother died, and I could've reached out to him more but chose not to. So I don't want to appear overly concerned now as it might make him feel strange. I want to make sure he is safe, but honestly, I'm not sure if any of us are, at this point. I tried to focus back on what Secretary Dempsey was saying. He was talking about details over a map, which I understood to be major locations for where the concentration of forces should be at.

"So, we will send the European contingent, along with your brother Raphael to engage the first gate."

On the monitor behind Dempsey, there was telemetry readings tracking the cycle for the fourth and final lunar tetrad. The blood moon marks the sign when the gates open, and the strategy was to make sure that both angelic and earthly forces are ready at each location to meet hell's legions head on. I had thought of something and raised my hand like I was in school.

"Yes, Mr. Ambassador, you have something to say?"

Dempsey looked at me like a teacher would look at a student who seemed unsure of what he was about to say. Michael and Gabriel were also looking at me, calmly yet with an alarmingly indifferent expression.

"Do we know exactly how many will be coming through these gates?"

I didn't know what word to use, demon, devils, or minions. I guess I was trying to understand the scale of this all as this was something that no one, and I mean no one has ever experience before. Dempsey looked at Michael and Michael paced a few steps towards me with the intent to provide an answer.

"Each gate is kept by a horsemen. These generals in Lucifer's forces each lead legions of demons. Their numbers are not infinite, but more precisely, their numbers are all those souls from the beginning of time that has been consumed by the flames of the hellfire below."

I looked at Zach and he looked back at me knowingly, and Zach understood that this was something that the world has never seen ever before.

"And what of your army Michael, how strong a force did heaven send down to aid us?"

Michael looked to Gabriel and both of them did not hide their expression.

"David, heaven's army has been sent here to help you and the rest of the world. Yet we cannot completely abandon the heavenly kingdom without protection. All in all our angelic corps consist of five thousand legions of angelic warriors."

I was no expert but a legion, if memory served me correctly from early history classes, was about five thousand strong. Give or take a couple of hundred depending on where and when you have defined the term, we're looking at approximately twenty five million warriors of the angelic corps now present on earth. Based on the map that Dempsey has where these gates were located, each Archangel commanded one thousand legions while the rest are dispersed all over the world.

So five million angels, give or take, are in position at each of the four gates. Dempsey, working with NATO along with other military branches from every major nation in the world that can spare a fighting hand, in addition to those civilians, now being called militias that have been formed around the globe has begun sending troops to these locations as we speak. Based on the numbers that I'm seeing on the map, the five million angels will be joined by no less than about two million men from the combined forces of the world for each gate. But Michael still hasn't answered my original question. And I was afraid of the reason why.

"We have faced this menace in the past, and from our knowledge, each gate will unleash three thousand legions of minions from hell."

Three thousand legions, from each gate. If my math is correct, that's fifteen million individual demons from each gate with the sole purpose of destroying the vessel. Our combined forces are outnumbered almost three to one at each gate. As I put that into perspective, Michael continued.

"However, while their numbers more than triple that of the angelic corps, we have your forces to help us with this war. As it was in the past, so shall it be now. Also, hell's hordes have one disadvantage when they come to the surface."

Dempsey seemed to straighten up, and judging from his somewhat agreeable expression, he knew exactly what Michael was talking about.

"You see David, we were sent here through divine intercession, so myself, along with my brother Gabriel, the other twenty five million of the kin we call the angelic corps have all but inherited our immortality from the Father."

As Michael looks to Elizabeth, Gabriel continues to explain what Michael was saying.

"You know us as angels, but the term we use in your tongue is much closer to the word Eternal. As Eternals, we have been given the supreme responsibility to protect the kingdom of heaven, and to aid those worlds that are going through judgment. As such, we have been in existence since the beginning of time."

I looked to Dempsey who was smiling now, obviously enjoying this swarm of firsthand information coming from an Eternal.

"But those that are banished to the pit, which seeks to make this world part of their misery and sorrow, have no divine intercession. Their powers during the normal course of a world's history lies in their deception and corruption of the will and hearts of men. Once judgment comes, their desire to corrupt and enslave the will of men serves them no more which is why those reapers attacked us as they did. Their only means now to exact their agenda is to become real, in a sense. When they come to the surface, they become corporeal."

As Michael began to walk around the room, Gabriel continues to explain the basic difference between them and the demon horde that we will face.

"As Eternals, we are immortal. This, however, does not mean we cannot be slain. The only way we can be struck down is when a demon is able to take our own weapons and use them against us."

Immortals, and yet they can be killed. But only with the very weapon that they use to deliver their righteousness. I should imagine that trying to take an angel's weapon then would be no easy task.

"Although the gates are where the majority of hell's legions will be unleashed upon this earth, it is not what worries me."

Dempsey now started thumbing through the folder that he's been using the entire time. When he found the page, he slid it across the table and it slid towards me close enough for me to stand up and reach it. On it were five different names, names that I didn't comprehend nor wanted to. Beside each name was a marked symbol.

"Lucifer has his personal guards, demons of the highest rank. These five, also known as the hand of hell is what Lucifer will send forth to go after the vessel."

As Michael said this, Elizabeth gasped and looked at Zach. Zach was beside her and put his hand on hers. Gabriel also walked over to Elizabeth and put his hands on her shoulders.

"This has always been their calling, and they will not stop. Each one will try to attack using the inherent power that has been given to them. This is why Gabriel and I will stay close to Elizabeth."

Trying to make sense of all this, I had finally one thought that someone in the room still hasn't asked about. It seemed obvious to me and yet it was something that I felt was being avoided at all cost. I decided to ask the question and for whatever reason, will accept the answer that I get.

"Michael, what of your fallen brother Lucifer, what does he have at hand in all this?"

The room was dead quiet, as Michael heaved a heavy sigh which conveyed so much despair in his voice that I immediately regretted asking the question. Not because of the answer but because of the pain I see it causing Michael. I've seen it in small doses in the jet while we were headed to Camp Darby, but now, it's in full view. It was clear that this was a subject that Michael had been carrying with him, for all eternity.

"Lucifer's contempt for me fuels his rage and anger. It is the reason why this war has to happen."

As he walked over to the head of the conference table, he takes something out of his waist belt and turns around. What he was holding was a golden sheath with a knife in it. He put it on the table.

"This dagger was forged in the heavenly armory for but one purpose. When I come face to face with Lucifer, I shall use it and that will be the end of the dark lord of the fiery pit."

Now Dempsey was looking at the inscriptions on the dagger and wanted to pick it up, but Michael stopped him and put it back into his waist belt.

"No mortal can wield the Dagger of the Spirit. Only an Eternal can do so, and only an Eternal can use it against the fallen."

The maps was now indicating that the European contingent has reached Giza and have now met up with the forces of Raphael. Similarly, forces from the Asia Pacific Military Alliance had made its way into North Korea and now standing by with the forces commanded by Jophiel. Canadian and United States Regional Command forces have arrived at the remote Alaskan site where Metatron welcomes fleets and fleets of heavy lift helicopters, VTOL transports and C-130s that used the old air force base in that location as a staging point.

As the Fifth, Sixth and Seventh Fleets arrived in the Arabian Sea, accompanied by Task Force 20 and the Submarine Force U.S. Atlantic Fleets, thousands of amphibious and air lift units heads towards the coast of Somalia. Joined by twenty other multi-national fleets from across the globe, the task force designated Omega Zulu was taking a permanent station just off the coast of Somalia, and in total consisting of approximately six hundred and twenty ships.

The map was an indication of the most massive military deployment ever seen in the history of mankind. And it shall also be the last of its kind. As David stood up and walked towards Michael, he felt the genuine loss that this being is going through.

My wife died over a year ago and I've just truly moved on a few months ago so to see this being, this Eternal still feel a scar over the loss of someone dear to him throughout all of time was humbling for me. As I stood beside him looking out of the conference room, I felt I needed to ask him something.

"Have you come close to fulfilling the dagger's purpose?"

With his eyes closed, and still pondering the memories that this question had brought upon, he opened his eyes and was clearly in tears.

"I had come close plenty of times, but have had the heart to only strike once. The scar, which Lucifer now bears on his left chest, serves as a reminder to both of us that life is never eternal. At some point in this vastness of time, existence for one of us will end."

We were both jolted by a high pitch alarm that filled the room, as we walked back to the conference table, the main monitor tracking the lunar tetrad had begun an automatic countdown clock.

It started from ten hours and was now counting down in hours, minutes, and seconds. Secretary Dempsey quickly went over to the communications panel and picked up the phone. Not having the need to dial a number, the other line picked up and Dempsey began his report.

"Mr. President, all joint forces are moving into position and on standby status. Based on our calculations, which was directly corroborated by NASA, we are now under the ten hour window until the Omega protocol."

I walked over to Zach and sat beside him. I turned his chair to mine and looked him dead in the eye.

"I know that there's something going on with you. I know that you know that it's something you can't tell me right now. But whatever it is son, know that I support you and trust you, alright?"

I gave Zach a big long hug and then I looked to Elizabeth who was equally nervous of what she has just heard. I cupped her hands and wanted to make sure that she knew this was something that all of us was willing to do for her.

"We are all here for you Elizabeth, every last one of us. Don't be afraid."

As Michael and Gabriel reach out to their kin, outside the building, to those in the skies around the globe and to the four waiting at each of hell's gates. The message was to be ready, and to be righteous. Welcome those that join you as they have chosen to fight for the light. Do what you can for them as you would do it for your kin.

Dempsey continued on the phone, and with each remark, the reality of the end becomes clearer and clearer.

"Yes, Mr. President, we have both Michael and Gabriel here and they have given us their tactical and operational knowledge of the forces we will face. It will be sent out to all commands sir. Yes sir, I understand Mr. President."

As Dempsey puts the phone back into its cradle, he looks at all of us in the room. He breathed a deep sigh and then tried to make his message clear.

"The President has lost the first lady to an attack. Reports indicate that the reapers were destroyed by both the angels and secret service agents that were with the President's company. There were a total of five reapers that came. All were destroyed but not without taking out a dozen and a half secret service agents."

Then Dempsey looked to Michael, and under the President's authority, addressed him formally.

"Michael, on behalf of the President of the United States, I've been asked to request from you confirmation that the First Lady is at peace."

As Michael reaches out to the souls that have departed this earth, ready to enter the kingdom, he opens his eyes and looks back at Dempsey.

"She is now within the kingdom of the Father. She knows the joy that can only come from being within His grace."

Dempsey pursed his lips and then went back to pick up the phone. I looked to the countdown clock which now was being broadcasted in some way or form all across the globe, to both military and civilian networks, I began to think about seeing Loretta again.

* * *

As the appointed time drew near, so was the furor over who gets to unleash their forces on the world above first. Also, each of the five demons that make up the hand of hell, one was eagerly looking forward to bringing suffering to the earthly realm. Lucifer is pleased, as any king would be, with the willingness of his warriors to exact his will among those that choose to fight for the light.

"My lord, allow me to draw first blood. I will find this vessel, and bless her with my lecherous charm."

Satanachia has been eager to get his hands on the vessel. To him, it was the ultimate prize. During the golden age of darkness, Satanachia spread his wickedness into the hearts of those that lived in the cities of the plain. Three of these cities, Admah, Zeboim and Bela

220

are obscure enough in theological history that no regular person would associate it with the despicable acts that this demon has unleashed. But the other two cities were the pinnacle of sin that was obliterated in what scholars now estimate happened on or about 4000 B.C.

Sodom and Gomorrah, mentioned in the Book of Genesis and throughout the Hebrew Bible, the New Testament and in other deuterocanonical sources, as well as in the Qur'an was situated on the Jordan River plain in the southern region of Canaan. Sitting just north of the modern day Dead Sea, Sodom and Gomorrah was compared to the Garden of Eden, being a land well-watered and green, but as Satanachia's handiwork gripped those that dwelled in these two cities, divine judgment was then passed on both cities, which were consumed by fire and brimstone. Not until Satanachia's fervor for unnatural and soulless acts were satisfied, did the vile demon leave his mark upon those that had witnessed its destruction. Throughout history, the brazen disregard of those that were punished in Sodom and Gomorrah had made it synonymous with insolent and abominable sexual acts and have since been the reference that spawned the phrase "crime against nature".

The demon revels in his own voraciousness and wishes it upon any victim he can molest with his black heart, especially those women who exhibits purity and moral cleanliness. When he learned of the vessels existence, the drool could not be wiped off his two faced lips as he desired mostly to destroy the pureness of a woman's soul.

"You shall have your chance my dear Satanachia, you must savor the hunt, as it brings more pleasure to your heart planning what you intend to do with this woman, and make her your unwavering servant of the flesh."

As Lucifer said this, Satanachia howled into the depths of the chamber where the fire burned hotter as he stroked his entire being, bringing him to what most people would assume as a climactic ecstasy of satisfaction. The others around Satanachia rejoiced in a wild and disturbing response to the demons seemingly self-inflicted fleshly joy. As the demons looked to Lucifer, they knew their time is at hand for the blood moon is upon them.

"Upon this time, as the moon flows red with blood, we will take this world in the name of all things wicked. We shall persecute those that fights for the light and we welcome those whose hearts are filled with malevolent and malicious desires, and make them our own!"

Once Lucifer said this, the entire chamber, which looked like the interior of what can only be described as molten lake of fire and oil with ominous and jagged rock from the chamber ceiling being met by space upon space of empty barren rock where Lucifer's minions' roost like hunters waiting upon its prey, filled with a deafening roar. All manner of shapes and forms that only serves one purpose, the demons that inhabit the pit live their existence with the purpose of exacting pain, suffering and hatred to all that they can. Over the centuries of modern and ancient history, the dark kingdom that Lucifer keeps as his own have been seeking to destroy lives through possession of those that are close to the Father's heart. Lucifer aims to take those away from the one he used to call Father, as he was taken away from the grace from above. The day that Lucifer was cast out of the heavenly kingdom, it was the day that the seed of vengeance grew permanently in his heart.

"Abaddon! Prepare the horsemen, so that when the hour is at hand, that hell is to be unleashed so as to kill all hopes on the world above."

As Abaddon bows to his master, the five demons that make up the hand of hell get much more specific charge.

"I expect you all to know what I wish."

As Lucifer talks to his five most revered wreakers of havoc, they all smirk in the thought of what they will do once they find the vessel.

222

They also savor the chance to slay an Eternal, which is the foulest and most disgusting being to exist in their eyes. The hatred for an angel is only matched by the evil in the hearts of each demon. Each one will not think twice to cut down an angel, for no reason and for mere amusement.

"The one they call the vessel, is protected by non-other by those that had banished me.

When you find them, I expect you to show no mercy, if you do, you shall get none from me."

Lucifer's gaze sealed the intent of his threats; the five dare not disappoint their master. Punishment in this kingdom was a way of existence for demons, when punishment is given, one should not take it lightly.

"They travel with these mortals that seek to protect them. Fools! Bathe in their blood but make sure you bring the vessel to me! And I assure you Satanachia, I will leave some for your satisfaction as well."

Once again, the demon writhes in such expectation from this that it makes it reach a climactic orgasm. The other demons begin to laugh and began to walk away from the rock and rubble throne where Lucifer sat. As the five depart, Lucifer sinks into his throne, and snickers to himself as he looks at his five lumber away. His thoughts, always reaches a fever pitch during judgment, filled with the same malice that he has had for an eternity while he stroked a scar that was just below his neck and going downwards to his left rib cage.

"This time my dear Michael, I shall make you suffer for what you and the Father have done."

CHAPTER SEVENTEEN

ZACHARY'S DESTINY

The Special Forces outside the Pentagon was busy training with the company of angels that came with Michael and Gabriel. The team's commander, Major Henry Krakowski, was a veteran SEAL as well as having served in the military for almost his entire life. He prided himself in being able to have seen what war could do to those that fight in it, but tonight, in this time face to face with this angelic corps, he has nothing to compare it to. The angels were pure, and not only in the common sense but their movements and actions, so fluid yet so powerful. It was hard not to admire the totality of good that emanates from each of these mystical beings.

As Krakowski went through the introductions of his twelve man team, all highly trained and skilled military professionals, the angels in turn introduced themselves to the team. The head angel that Krakowski was talking with was called Iliah. He stood tall at over six feet, as did all of the angels and while Krakowski was not small himself, the stature of the angels were augmented by those strong and graceful appendages on their backs.

It was one thing to imagine how these beings moved, it was another to see them actually do it. With the grace and power of a bird of prey, they can deploy their wings in a moment's notice for a slew of configurations base on what needed to be accomplished. During one of the demonstrations of how Iliah could vertically take off in one powerful flap with a full extension of his wings was nonetheless quite impressive. Not only does the wings provide so much power, the wake of wind that can only be described as a quick gust of compressed air enough to knock down anyone within the radius of its affected area was also a formidable offensive tactic.

Iliah was explaining to Krakowski the nature of the wings of an angel and how it's part of the whole being and not simply an external part. An angel's wings are all but indestructible, and this was proven by a quick demonstration that Iliah asked the Special Forces team to conduct. Iliah had five of Krakowski's men line up in a row and asked five of his kin to line up in a row opposite them. The hesitation from Krakowski's team was quickly reassured by Iliah saying that whatever will happen, it will not affect or injure the angels in any way. Krakowski told his team to line up and get ready. Iliah said that when they are ready, they are to shoot at the angels in any way, angle or trajectory. The angels facing Krakowski's team was still and unfazed as Iliah said this aloud. As the team prepared, Krakowski gave the sign to his team to go full round, which in military term means to let loose.

As the SEAL team members drew their breath and raised their weapons, the angels, keen on every sense was way ahead of the incoming fire that was unleashed by the five man team. As each SEAL team members randomly unloaded a full clip of nine millimeter armor piercing rounds at the angels, each angel deployed their wings as a sort of shield around their bodies and as the bullets hit them, sparks flew as each bullet was deflected away from the targets. The angels saw each of the bullets coming towards them with their heightened senses and adjusted their wings accordingly. In the end, after a barrage of fire spent the magazines in the MP5's, the smoke cleared and the angels were back at their stance with their wings behind them as if nothing happened. Krakowski had never seen anything like it. The speed and accuracy of the angel's movements were so perfect that it seemed to the naked eye that they didn't moved at all.

The angels approached the five man team and patted them on the back somehow to signify the camaraderie that was expected to exist from those that fight with the same cause in their hearts. The team was dumbfounded, and humbled at the same time. Not a matter of training or skill can atone for the simple perfection of these beings. Krakowski was then happy to tell himself that they were here to help.

As Iliah continued to converse with members of the team, he showed them maneuvers that could help coordinate an attack consisting of airborne and ground assault troops. When the gates open, it will take both armies, angelic and earthly to do what's needed to keep them from devastating the world until the second coming happens.

Just then, Iliah receives a message from Michael within the structure. As the angels were given instructions to prepare and be ready, they all look towards the one direction that made the team momentarily stop their activities as they look at the angels listening with their eyes closed. As the angels open their eyes, they know that the time is at hand and soon, the fallen will begin sending his demons to the gates. But Iliah had received a specific message, and it was simple. Beware of the five.

* * *

Within the conference room, the countdown clock now read six hours ten minutes and forty eight seconds until the last lunar tetrad happens. As Dempsey keeps the President apprised of troop movements which now have made their way to all locations and are on standby status, David looks to Zach as he and Elizabeth sat together and held hands. He then looked to Gabriel and as if Gabriel knew the very thought in his head, Gabriel looked back and gave a look of reassurance. David stood up and walked over to Michael.

"You need to tell me how Zachary is involved in all this. I know he is, I can feel it, but I just don't understand it."

Michael felt the genuine pain in David's heart, one that a father would feel for a son. Was it not how the Father felt when he gave up His Son for these souls? He was there and he felt the Father's anguish, but the Father so loved the world He had created that He had saw it fit to sacrifice part of Himself, His own Son given up in order for those that are on earth to be one day saved. Michael looked at David and saw the grief in his eyes, and as David struggled to accept the fate of how things will be, he would not remove his fatherly love towards Zach.

"David, there are things that were set in motion long before Zachary was born. The Father knew this, as we did. I am afraid that you will not understand even if I explained it you."

David looked at Michael with a strained face. He closed his eyes and then tried to calm his mind and his heart. He was never one to leave anything to fate, but he knew at this point in his life, he can only accept the things that are happening. He looked back at Michael with resolve in his heart.

"Try me."

Michael felt that it was time for David to learn of how Zachary has been part of this plan all along. He gestured for David to sit down beside him as he knelt on one knee in front of him.

"Very well."

As Michael pondered where to begin, David settled into his seat, preparing his heart and mind for what he will hear. He felt like he was back at the Pope's office almost three days ago when he was told of what is to come. Here he is again, in the exact same situation, but now it involved Zach.

"Being immortal, we Eternals have lived since time and space had been forged by the Father's hand. Given the gift of everlasting life, we were also tasked with the divine responsibility of protecting the kingdom to whom all will come to during the Day of Judgment. For this world, this is happening now."

As Michael said this, David looked back at the countdown clock, which was now under five hours until, in his mind, all hell breaks loose. He thought that that was quite clever and yet he felt the accuracy of the statement and realized that it was the reality of things to come.

"But in order for this world to be saved, and be part of the heavenly kingdom, it needs to herald in the second coming. In your scriptures, this was represented as the Father's Son coming back to save the world. In reality, the essence of the Son, in this case the child which is in Elizabeth's womb represents the second coming. For this world to be saved, the life that comes during judgment must be from the Father Himself."

David, who was listening intently was trying to understand what Michael was saying. He had done some quick reading and looked at the part of the Holy Bible where the second coming was to happen. There was no mention of angels coming from the heavens to fight a holy war. There was no mention of four gates that would unleash hell on earth. And there was definitely no mention of the world physically being part of heaven or hell depending on the outcome of this war.

Michael, sensing his thoughts understood David's confusion. As he continued, he would hope that his words would ring true in David's heart.

"This is why Elizabeth's bloodline was spared. For being the chosen in the past, it was up to the Virgin Mother's descendant's to herald in the newborn king. And like in the first instance of the holy family, the Virgin Mother was given a guardian. A man that would have the heart and mind to protect and keep the vessel that will bear the Father's Son. In your scriptures, you know this man to be Joseph."

David was slowly beginning to realize what Michael was telling him. And a certain truth sank deep in his heart, a truth that could no longer be denied. He looked to Michael in a pleading way but yet Michael was stern in his countenance as he continued.

"Zachary is Elizabeth's Joseph David. He is the guardian of the vessel. They were destined to meet. Which means that you were destined to be here."

It was like a light bulb. There it was, David was just now connecting all the dots. He stood up and ran his hands through his hair, the others looked over but David was oblivious. He then realized another truth, a truth that he did not want to confirm but needed to. He looked back at Michael and with eyes wide, asked the question that Michael already knew was in his heart.

"Was it in His plan that she die?"

Michael saw the hurt on David's face, but more importantly, felt it in David's heart. Michael knows that the ways of the Father is not devoid of loss and sacrifice, and yet, in some ways, it was still something that was difficult for Michael to understand himself. But he had faith, and he was sure that when David sees the end of it all, he will understand everything, at least to be able to find peace in his heart.

"David, the path to the kingdom is never easy. Know that for all those that have lost someone they loved, it shall be like new again in the Father's kingdom. I mentioned before that your wife Loretta was special. Do you remember?"

On the plane, right before the reaper attack. When Michael and David were talking and he mentioned her and said that she was a special woman.

"Yes, why did you say that?"

Michael stood up, and looked up to the skies, seemingly through the concrete ceiling and he smiled. Then he looked back at David.

"Because she was one of us David. She was an Eternal."

* * *

Dempsey dropped his coffee mug on the floor, and it shattered, it broke the silence in the room. What Michael had said seemed impossible, but after all the things that has happened, nothing seemed impossible anymore.

David was still looking at Michael but now Zach was up from his seat looking at Michael as well. Gabriel stood beside Zach and putting one hand on Zach's shoulder. As Zach looked at Gabriel, he simply nodded and gave Zach a reassuring nod.

"What are you saying, that Loretta was, she was an angel?"

David was on the brink of losing his mind, he had no response to what he was just told. He had so many questions and Michael felt it in his heart. How was it even possible, David's mind was racing but Michael then swiftly went to his side and held his hand to David's heart.

"David, feel the truth in my heart as I let you find peace in yours. Feel the truth flow from me to you."

As Michael began to soothe David, it became clear to David that whatever it was that Michael was telling him was true. He felt it was true and he knew it was, however, his humanness was getting the better of him. David then began to calm down more and he ended up sitting on a side table against the wall of the conference room. When Michael felt that it was time to have David release his heart, he let go and David gasps a mouthful of air as if coming from a deep, deep dive.

At this point Zach was ready to know more about his mother. And he wanted to know why he saw what he saw.

"Tell me about my mother Michael." Zach said as Gabriel took his hand off his shoulders.

"Zachary, your mother was once a general in heaven's army. Her name then was Shalim. She was glorious and wondrous in her nature, and she was faithful. But every millennia or so, the time of the channeling happens. This is when those in the service of the heavenly kingdom gets to ask one thing from the Father."

Zach was taking this all in. Her mother was an angel named Shalim. From how Michael described her, she was quite a warrior in the angelic corps. But why did she leave heaven?

"The one thing an Eternal cannot have is offspring. This is the price of immortality. But there are those that feel the longing for such, a family of their own so to speak and Shalim was one of the ones that crave it so. At her behest, she asked for her life to be channeled out of the kingdom and into the earthly world below. Granting her wish, her essence, her soul was then sent to a womb of what you know now as her earthly parents."

It made sense to Zach now. Her mother was always so happy, she always seemed peaceful. Now he understood why. He always said that her mom could never hurt a fly, and that was the truth. Zach felt a warm sensation in his heart, and as David came close to him to give him a hug, both of them broke down in tears as they realized this truth about the most important woman in both their lives.

"There are Eternals that have chosen to participate in the channeling over the course of creation. Their offspring retain the divinity that was once that Eternal's birthright. This is why you were chosen Zachary, this is why your destiny is intertwined with Elizabeth's. Both of you have been favored by the Father, and both of you must see this through."

Just as Zach was going to ask another question, Michael held up his hands and Gabriel began to spread his wings. They looked at each other and then to Elizabeth and Zach.

"They are here."

With that, the alarms began blaring as monitors began showing external and internal feeds all across the Pentagon. Michael looked to

Gabriel, and Gabriel nodded and swiftly took Elizabeth and Zach outside of the conference room.

"Wait! Where are you going?"

David yelled but Gabriel did not look back. Michael then held back David as he began to go after them.

"David, Elizabeth and Zachary will be safe with Gabriel; he will extinguish his own life before he will have anything happen to Elizabeth or Zachary. Do you understand?"

They began to hear screams and yells from the monitors, and as a dark figures filled the screens, they blew out each image but David thought he saw a glimpse of horns.

"I've instructed my kin to go with Gabriel to protect the vessel and your son. They are joined by the team that was assigned to train with my warriors outside."

An explosion rocked the building and all power was down for a moment. As emergency generators kicked in, the lighting in the conference room became earie, as lights blinked on and off and the monitors flashed with random images. Then the silence was broken by a woman's scream as she was impaled with what seemed like a thin saber like tooth but about ten feet long. However, it was not how she was impaled, it was where. From the dim lights, it looked like it went into her genitals and was now protruding out of her mouth. Michael knew this demon well, and was not going to stand idly by.

"Satanachia! You defile those that serve the Father! You shall meet your doom here demon!"

As the woman's body, still writhing, was then flung to the far wall. A loud chuckle filled the air and Satanachia made sure that everyone could hear what it was he had to say. In a heavy laden growling voice, he spat back at Michael's threat with contempt and ridicule.

"Michael, you fool. These worms are mine to defile, and you are free to stop me if you choose. However, I have something in store for your precious vessel!"

Another boisterous laugh filled the room and as Satanachia began killing those around him. Michael then flung out of the darkness and struck Satanachia right in the middle of his forehead. Michael then spread his wings in full and drew his sword back as he flew over the demon. Satanachia let out a blood curdling scream as black ooze came from his forehead. Michael then swiftly flew around the high ceiling room and dove straight down with both wings and sword pointed at Satanachia's head.

But before the blow could reach him, Satanachia parried with his saber like tentacles and hit Michael in midflight. This caused Michael to go through several walls in the structure as the force almost crumbled the entire command room into rubble. As David moved to escape from the debris that was falling, he and Dempsey ran down a corridor behind the conference room. Patrick and Sarah was behind then and as they cleared the conference room, the corridor lights began to blink and Dempsey continued to lead them towards the main interior section of the building. They past a section where it seemed where Michael had gone through but he was nowhere to be found. They continued running.

"Is this all the might that the Archangel Michael can muster?"

Satanachia then began plowing through the walls of the building. All the while sniffing and licking the walls and chairs and once he had found the chair that Elizabeth sat, he licked it with such excitement that it almost drove him mad.

"She sat here, I can smell her insides. I will use her to my heart's content before I kill that which lies in her womb!"

As he flung the chair out, Michael came from the shadows and dug his sword, now in flames, into Satanachia's shoulder. The demon screamed loud enough that the entire building heard it and as Michael dug his sword deeper, he spoke words into the demon's heart.

"You shall not have one inch of her demon, for I will send you back to the pit where you belong! And face judgment for your failure and to once again remind your master that he cannot win against the light!"

With those words, Michael pulls out his sword as he flies off the demon's back and with a swift change of wing configuration, he made a twirling action, still with his sword in hand and chopped off Satanachia's head. The eyes on the demon blew out as the head flew towards the monitors and hitting them with an explosive force. Then the body of the vile demon crumbled to the ground and became as black as coal. It then disintegrated into a pile of heaping dust then burst into flames.

Michael then reached out to Gabriel, who had taken the vessel and Zachary into the center of the building structure where they were joined by the others, as well as the company of angels outside along with the Special Forces team. Michael had informed his brother that one finger has been chopped off, but four remain. Be on the ready as they will try to strike before the gates open.

Michael then looked at the head of the demon that he had just slain. Knowing that its darkness will make its way back to the pit, he knew of the judgment awaits it. However, this was the first time that his fallen brother had done such a thing. If Lucifer was desperate to start going after the vessel even before he unleashes his minions onto the world, there must be a reason but Michael is blind to his fallen brother's thoughts. The only thing he knows is that their mission has not changed. He looked up and spread his wings and with one strong flap, was airborne and shot through the ceiling and was out in the open above the building. He then saw where Gabriel was and swiftly headed towards them. However, he also saw something moving towards his kin and the vessel, swiftly and with intent. Two demons,

234

part of the hand was making their way from opposite sides of the building. The team was going to be trapped in the middle, he quickly sends word to Gabriel and his kin. The message was to fly!

CHAPTER EIGHTEEN

A FATHER'S LOVE

As Belial and Angul smash through walls upon walls through the Pentagon, they both feel the darkness snuffed out from their brother Satanachia. This only fuels their rage as they seek to exact the kind of revenge that brings them joy as they pummel through the buildings to get to the vessel. As they did, bodies of those that they run over in their unstoppable charge get butchered by their hands. The screams and howls of their victims are heard by the group in the center of the building.

Gabriel quickly gets Michael's message and he and his kin prepared to take flight. But as they did, the two demons break through the inner walls and now had them surrounded from each side. To protect the vessel, Gabriel separated Elizabeth and Zach. As Michael landed in front of Belial, Gabriel went to face Angul as well. When Zach saw this, he ran towards Elizabeth and grabbed her hands. Then the rest of the angels broke in two groups, one group protecting the vessel and Zach while the other group protecting the civilians which included Dempsey, David, Sarah and Patrick. The Special Forces team spread out to create a perimeter just behind the Archangels. With wings spread and ready, all the angels held their weapons towards the two demons that now stand before them.

As Belial and Angul filled with hatred in seeing these angels, they let out a deafening roar that affected all except the angels. Gabriel, with his spear held fast, points to Angul and returns with these words.

"Go back to the pit you came from willingly, or face the judgment that will befall you demons!"

Gabriel, who amongst the seven enjoys the fruits of combat the most, relish the opportunity to exact the righteousness of the Father. Michael looks at Belial with familiar eyes and provides a similar warning.

"Go back to your master and tell him that he will not covet what he seeks. As it was the end for your dark brother, so shall it be with you."

The two demons roar back with even more malice and as they did, several minions now uprooted themselves from the ground beside each one. Reapers, hellhogs, half breeds, and other manner of forms that cannot be described. They are now outnumbered two to one and Elizabeth now felt genuine fear for the first time since she was chosen. As each of the two demon rallies their own forces, Belial addressed Michael.

"You wreak of righteousness Michael, which is why your head will be my master's prize! As for the rest of you, and especially you little girl, you will know pain like never before and you will all beg the master to end your puny worthless lives!"

With that, with a flick of his hand Belial sends the minions to clear a path. Michael and Gabriel stands fast on their ground as the minions approach and was surprised when they were joined by Krakowski's men on the line. Both Archangels quickly say a prayer of protection for these men, who have embraced the fight for this world. Krakowski, using his comm radio started telling his men to hold as the minions drew near. Krakowski had never seen anything move so fast in his entire life and against such a foe, sheer force is not enough, they needed a way to maintain the line without being overrun.

Some of the minions, mainly the half breeds takes to the skies and this was Michael and Gabriel's area of defense. As both angels take to the skies, the SEAL team form a two man back to back pattern that allows them to have contact with the minions as they approach from any angle.

Michael strikes first, cutting a half breed in half with his flaming sword as well as chopping off the wings on another half breed that looked like a cross between a bat and snake. Gabriel's spear impales two demons at once, and with a swift turn throws his spears and impales another demon to the ground. Krakowski's team, now engaged in fire fight below fire at the charging hellhogs, but their bullet ricochet off the stony outcrop on where its horns meets it head. As it charges through the line, one of Krakowski's men gets impaled in the hellhogs horns and is dragged with it as the hellhog shakes its head and cuts the man in half. After trampling over the remains of the severed victim, the hellhog then comes around for another charge. Krakowski's team forms up and fires again but the same happened. This time, they had enough time to get out of the way and regroup closer to the center. Iliah then flew over to Krakowski and the angels begin to thwart the advance of the other minions, Iliah gives Krakowski some advice.

"The beast's back is its weak spot, try to find your mark there."

As Krakowski heard this, he sees three hellhogs now barreling towards them. He quickly radios to all his team members and as they prepare for the incoming charge, a couple of angels then came in and scooped up the members of Krakowski's team and had them follow the charge of the hellhogs. With a clear line of fire, the team then unloaded a full barrage of bullets from above on the hellhog's back and upon impact, the spines of the hellhogs burst into a heaping pile of disgusting innards as each of them went down and then turned to black dust.

With Michael and Gabriel finishing off those demons that have taken to the air, they plummet back to the ground to aid the remaining forces that have been protecting the vessel. Michael also calls out for any other kin; they have to aid them in this battle. Now the reapers advances and as the members of Krakowski' team fall back, the angels step forward to face this menace. The reapers now in full corporeal form, floating black abysses of darkness circle the angels like a fog of black death. However, the angels were familiar with these creatures know full well how to deal with them.

As the reapers expel sharp dark dagger like spikes from their form aimed at the angels, these are easily deflected by the angel's wings. Then the angels spread their wings open and with one powerful flap, sends a gust of air towards the circling black fog and as it hits each reaper, it almost blows them out of existence leaving the core of the reaper exposed. As the angel swiftly thrust their swords into the reapers with one fluid motion, the reapers scream in agony as they disintegrate into nothing.

That was the last of the minions and after the short intense battle, three of Krakowski's men are down. One angel had ascended back into heaven when it was charged by three demons during the initial charge. A half breed was able to crimp the angel's wings as the other two held its arms at bay. The reaper then forced the angel's sword from his hand and drove it into his heart. As the angel faded into a bright blue light, it quickly shot up towards the sky, back into the Father's kingdom.

Now they faced the two demons, Belial and Angul, and Michael and Gabriel knew that this was something only they could handle. These were no ordinary minions, but part of the personal death squad of Lucifer himself. Even with his battle with Satanachia victorious, Michael knows the power these demons possess and they will not stop until the vessel is destroyed. That is just something that Michael cannot allow.

Belial and Angul wanted to wither down the numbers so as to give them an advantage over their foes. They don't care how many minions get sent back to the pit as long as the upper hand is something that they achieve. Looking at the weary angels, both demons relish their plan and is filled with the kind of dark hope that their success will bring them much praise from their master. But both remembered what they were told. Bring Michael and the vessel back unspoiled. The rest can be slaughtered. Both demons summon even more minions to the surface. As they see the terror in the worm's faces, especially from the vessel, this fills their hearts with desire beyond hatred. It fills their hearts with the sheer delight for the suffering they bring.

Michael and Gabriel along with Iliah and their kin now stand before the two demons. As more minions claw their way from the pit, Krakowski realizes that they need to get out of this place. He quickly surveys the surroundings and sees a wall where the demons have broken through from the outer sections. He quickly radioed his men coming up with a quick extraction plan. While doing this, Belial charges to strike Michael, and with claws extending a foot from his hands, the demon swipes at Michael. Michael leans back as the claws comes within inches from his face and then as a countermove, he jumps to the air in a quick hover, and then spins around to gain speed and charges head first into Belial. The demon braces itself with both arms and as Michael's sword impacted the demon, the result of such force, a wave of energy cascades outwards like a ripple in a pond that knocked everyone off their feet and shook the very foundation of the building structure.

Gabriel, facing the disgustingly wretched demon Angul was dodging the demon's spitting attack. As each shot from Angul's mouth missed Gabriel, it burned whatever it touched, wherever it landed. Grabbing heaps of flesh from his own body, Angul began flinging these at Gabriel much like Molotov bombs. Except the difference is when it exploded, it created this black patch of death instantly killing those around it. One such attack landed close to one of Krakowski's team members and as the ooze ate its way from the feet upwards, the team member screamed in agony and was engulfed within seconds.

240

The energy wave that was caused by Michael's blow opened up a closer exit to the group and Krakowski immediately made a bee line for it. As his men moved quickly, they saw the minions coming out from the ground and as they passed them over, one minion was able to grab Elizabeth's ankle and caused her to fall to the ground. Immediately Zach yelled out and went back to get Elizabeth. As Krakowski saw this, he ordered his men to continue on as he headed back to help Zach out. The minion was almost clear of the ground and Elizabeth was screaming while Zach tried to pry off the black root like hands that held Elizabeth in place. Now that the half breed was out, it salivated as it saw its prize and as Zach covered Elizabeth as the minion reached down to take them, a salvo of bullets quickly dropped the minion back and to the ground. Krakowski then slid beside Zach and both of them pried off the now lifeless hand that left a bloody bruise on Elizabeth's ankle. Krakowski handed his weapon to Zach as he lifted up Elizabeth into his arms and began to sprint towards the exit where the others were now waiting. Michael and Gabriel saw this, and as both continued to battle with the two demons, the rest of the angels dealt with the new wave of minions. However, momentarily distracted to make sure that the vessel was safe, Michael gave Belial a split second to come around and strike him with a blow that knocked Michael back into the far wall of the inner structure which caused it to crumble. Belial quickly went to where Michael had struck, clear the rubble and found the one who is like God, out cold. He then took Michael's sword and with a moment's hesitation wanted to plunge it into his chest. But he remembered the master's command, and he dared not disobey. So he bound Michael and as Gabriel saw this, his heart was filled with anger.

"Let him be Belial, you have no claim on him!"

Still fighting Angul, Gabriel could not go after Belial who was now descending into a hole with Michael over his shoulder like a prized animal freshly caught. Gabriel screamed in terror.

"Michael!"

His shout was met with a strong impact of one of Angul's spit attacks and it threw Gabriel down to the ground.

As the group waited for Krakowski and Zach to get to the exit, David was eagerly looking at his son. From the corner of his eye, he saw a hellhog sweeping in from the side and both Zach and Krakowski couldn't see it coming. David started yelling but with everything that was going on he knew they couldn't hear him. He then lunged forward, passing one of the team member and grabbed his sidearm. David began running towards the charging hellhog. As the other members of the team saw this, they tried to stop David but it was too late as he was already out in the open. David was waving his arms up and down and then began to raise his weapon to bear on the incoming hellhog.

Zach saw this and realized what his Dad was doing. Krakowski stopped and tried to grab Zach and egged him to keep going. But Zach started yelling towards his father, and as the hellhog changed course going directly towards David, Krakowski had a clear line to the exit. Zach was looking at his Dad, still firing the gun at hellhog but had enough time to look at Zach. He was waving Zach to go and while Zach knew he had to, he stood there looking at his father.

"Dad no!"

Knowing that they were out of danger, David stopped running with the hellhog still coming at him at full speed. He lowered his gun, and looked to Zach and mouthed off the last words that he would ever say to his son.

"I love you Zach.....always."

As David smiled and looked at the hellhog just mere seconds away, he closed his eyes and felt genuine peace in his heart. Yes, all things have a purpose, and yes all things happen for a reason. As the hellhog hits him and cuts him down, his last thought was that of seeing his beloved Loretta once again.

"No!!!"

As Zach saw his father die, he broke into tears and fell to his knees. Just then, the hellhog turned towards him and began to charge but was quickly put down by Krakowski and his men. At this point, the demon Belial had taken Michael hostage, and the other demon, Angul had since blasted Gabriel to the ground. As the other angels fight off the minions, which were now slowly retreating since they have gotten half of their prize. Sarah was headed to Zach while Patrick, with panic in his face ran to his old friend, lifeless on the ground.

As Sarah knelt beside Zach, she gave him a tight warm embrace that offered little comfort. He stood up and walked over to where his father was and put his hand on his head and broke down into more tears. At this point, Gabriel joined the group and offered a prayer for Zach's father.

"I am sorry Zachary, he gave his life to save you. There is no greater love."

He then felt a hand on his shoulders, squeezing. He looked up and it was Elizabeth. Then he looked at his father again and knew that it was not going to be for nothing.

"I love you too Dad, and I hope you are with Mom right now. Know that I'll see this through, and I'll see you both, soon."

Yes, we all had a purpose. This was planned from the beginning. Who are we to ever question life? We are here to fulfill a purpose, and there is no higher calling in doing so.

As more of Gabriel's kin arrive to drive off the remaining minions that Belial and Angul called upon, both demons have disappeared into the dark pit.

All the worlds suffering at the hands of man will compare to nothing at the hands of Lucifer, this is to be sure. Looking at the nature of how man treated each other from the beginning of known civilization, it was a wonder that we ever made it to the twenty first century. And yet with all of man's transgressions, he has also brought forth an unprecedented time of love, of culture and of self-sacrifice. Now faced with the two options, to be part of the kingdom of light or be cast into the hellfire underneath, all of man's doings come to a single point in time. It all comes down to the faith that he has in his heart and what he is called to do. With all the tragedies and sorrows, all the disappointments and failures, man has now been given the ultimate choice to remove all that has happened in the past and start anew.

But such an opportunity does not come without loss. During this holy war, this war that will be the last ever fought on this earth, people will be lost, loved ones slain and friends divided. The chance to attain everlasting life, ironically enough, invites the very prospect of ending one's life. But there has never been such a prize before, never has it been possible to think of eternal peace and joy. But now it is at hand, and those who choose and by their faith can and will be saved. But not without loss, not without pain, and not without sorrow.

All the angels, on earth and in the heavens grieve in their hearts. Their supreme general, the one who is like God, the one that does what the Father asks, has been taken. Never has it been in the history of time and space that an Eternal has been removed from his Father's grace. Within the pit, the light cannot see, and for all those that share in his plight, they can only pray for their brother Michael.

Gabriel now has reached out to the others and have told them of what has happened. All of the angelic corps lifts Michael up with resounding prayer to the Father. Gabriel is reminded that all things happen in His will and His time. There is a purpose to all this and

Gabriel will not question it. It does not, however, ease the pain that they all feel in their hearts.

I look at Gabriel and now feel his heart for him. I reach into his mind to see if he has any need for comfort.

"Gabriel, what will become of Michael?"

The question I pose almost seems too hard to answer, but the truth has always been painful, always.

"I am afraid that Lucifer will now rain his wrath upon him. In all of the times that we've faced Lucifer, this is the first time he has done anything like this. I fear for Michael's essence, I know not what waits for him in the pit."

Gabriel did not hide his sorrow, nor did he try to convince me or himself that it will be alright.

"I cannot reach him Zachary, none of us can. He has been cut off from the Father's grace as with all of those that goes into the fiery depths of hell. I am afraid that Michael is lost to us."

Then I remembered my encounter with the beast in Italy. I felt that there was a connection between that and what was happening now.

"Gabriel, the beast that I saw, why did it reveal itself to me? There must be a purpose, a message, something."

Dempsey, listening intently on the wayside, made his way towards me and Gabriel.

"There will be one, a guardian that will be of both worlds."

As Dempsey said this, Gabriel pondered something in his mind, which he then realized was something that was made unto the Father's purpose.

"The beast Zachary, it revealed itself to you and yet did not attack. I think I know why."

Dempsey was now thumbing through pages upon pages in his folder that he desperately gripped on to and then upon finding the page he was looking for, handed it over to me. I read it in my head and then aloud.

"The guardian of the vessel has a choice, to embrace the light or be part of the darkness. Until the second coming, the guardian may choose between these two paths."

Gabriel understood it clearly now, and he knew more than ever why Zach saw the vision of the beast.

"I don't understand, what does that mean for me?"

Zach looked at Gabriel and Dempsey began to nod his head in agreement, as if knowing what Gabriel was about to say.

"Zachary, the beast you saw was a mirror of the choice you could make. Lucifer sent it to you in order to show you what you may become."

Now Zach understood, when he looked into the eyes of the beast, there was something familiar, something he knew but couldn't put his finger on. Now he did, he was looking at himself, far into the void where he had made a choice to accept the darkness within him. But this still didn't make any sense to him and how it can possibly be part of any purpose for protecting Elizabeth.

"Okay, so I can make a choice that will turn me into this thing. But I haven't and I wouldn't so I still don't understand how it affects me."

Dempsey was now pacing back and forth and as Sarah and Patrick listened, he knew that there was a slim chance if at all, to save Michael. Gabriel knew what was in Dempsey's mind and had to agree the merits for it. But he also realized that it will involve having Zach put his life in harm's way.

"Zachary, what this means is that someone like you can go into the pit. You may choose to fill your heart with the darkness and become the beast that you saw but you also have the will to control it so it does not overcome you. As the beast, you will freely wander within the depths of hellfire, long enough to be able to find Michael and free him from his bondage."

I couldn't comprehend what Gabriel just told me, but knew it to be true. I've just been told that I have a chance to go into hell as a demonic beast in order to save the Archangel Michael. I had to repeat that sentence in my head again and again until it actually made sense. Once I've gotten past this part, we spent the rest of the time talking about the details and what I needed to do. As insane as it sounds, I've accepted the fact that I'm going to hell.

CHAPTER NINETEEN

THE BEGINNING OF THE END

With all the armies of the world poised as the clock counts down to mere minutes of the blood moon, all across the world those that have chosen to believe and have faith have been in prayer for the entire time.

In Saint Peter's Square, the Pope has been leading an all-day vigil with thousands upon thousands of Catholics within the square.

Across all the churches all over the world, the pews are packed brim to brim with believers. Having no more time, and accepting the judgment that will be defined by this holy war, all those that believe in some sort of faith have been praying for one singular thing. That those heavenly and earthly forces defeat that of the darkness.

Even in the Middle East, Muslims have been in deep prayer since the arrival of the angels. Along with those in China and Tibet, where all hostilities once existed, now there is only a call for prayer.

The families and friends of those that have chosen to put their lives on the line in order to protect the ones they love, with the chance to attain eternal peace, joy and life was enough for anyone to join the cause.

All over Europe, people have created make shift shrines where they are in order to pray for those that will defend this world. In Africa and South America, people have looked to the skies and have given praise for the angels in that region of the world. They have sent blessings up to them so that they may be victorious in their task.

In North America, the Native Americans offer spirit blessing up to the stars in order to guide those that are fighting the forces of evil.

All over the world, as the blood moon comes, everyone has given up their lives in a simple act of prayer. With all things that come to an end, all that can exist beyond it is faith.

As Dempsey, Sarah and Patrick along with Zach and Elizabeth and the company of angels now led by Gabriel arrive at the National Security Agency Headquarters in Fort Meade, Maryland, the hour is almost at hand and Dempsey quickly pulls up the tracking protocols and quickly advise the NSA's S33 Global Access Operations Directorate of what had just transpired on the grounds of the Pentagon.

Proceeding to the main control facility in OPS 2 building, the mission protocols have been loaded and the countdown clock now read T minus fourteen minutes before the last lunar tetrad occurs. Mission orders fly through the digital airwaves to all major military stations surrounding and in the direct vicinity of the four gates. All mobilization have been given the green light and all commands have been given regional jurisdiction on their combat readiness. All of the combined forces of the globe now faces the most lethal and deadly force that is about to be unleashed on this planet.

Land, sea and air forces have amassed from all across the world where opposing forces now fly under the same flag of truth. Once enemies, fighting decades old wars, soldiers now from both sides stand shoulder to shoulder. Putting aside whatever fight or dispute they have had, which they have committed their lives to upholding draws no more reason now. There are no more nations, no more political agendas, no more profit and no more ambition. The only thing that draws everyone to do something now is for those that they love. To protect those that they would spend the rest of their lives with. To be able to enjoy the fruits of a promise that once was just an ideal, but now have become a very real reward.

As Dempsey looks at the countdown clock, now just two minutes from the lunar tetrad, Gabriel sends out word to all the angelic corps.

At each gate, each of the Archangels, commanding their millions of kin, prepare themselves for the gate's opening. The four Eternals, Jophiel, Sandalphon, Metatron and Raphael quickly converses with their earthly counterparts. As each regional commander of the forces assigned to support each of the four Eternals send word to their forces to begin enacting protocols for battle, each of the Eternal conveys a message to all of them.

"As we stand here, in the breach, waiting for what vile and gruesome things will emerge from these gates, know that we are with you all, as brothers in arms as well as children of the Father. Do not fear, and have faith in His will. As you fight in His name, you shall receive His protection and grace. If the Father is for us, who can be against us?"

As this message resounds through the ranks and multitudes of those that have chosen to fight for the light, they reply with a deafening voice of their own with two words.

"No one!"

As each of the Eternal prepares their forces, Dempsey and everyone else at the mission control room look at the countdown go to zero. Dempsey then shouts to one of the terminal officers.

"Give me a visual of the lunar tetrad!"

As the main monitors in the room change their image to what was now the moon over the black sky, all in the room pauses to see it finally change from pale white to dark red. The kind of red that can be compared to blood running in water. Suddenly, alarms begin blaring off in the main control room. As mission officers hurry to ascertain the source of the alarm, Dempsey already knows in his heart what it was.

"Give me a global map overlaying the four gate locations with the geothermal trackers."

As the global map was put up in the main control screen, each point where a gate was located, a steady surge of thermal activity began to intensify. Sarah was holding Elizabeth's hand while Patrick and Zach looked intently on the screen. The tracking monitors are now showing major geothermal activity on each of the gate locations, and according to the readings, the temperature have been steadily climbing to impossible levels. As the map showed more and more red and yellow temperature status, it also began swelling, starting at a hundred meters and now growing wider and wider. Dempsey then realized that each gate was now looking more and more like a volcanic eruption, and looked at the troop mobilization and its inherent position to where the center was from these temperature readings. He quickly went to the control panel and issued an immediate order.

"Send word to all stations, all commands. Evacuate and remove the troops from each of the gates. There is imminent activity that will result in a catastrophic geothermal explosion. The gates, they are like volcanos and the impending eruption will take out our forces. They need to get outside of the blast radius."

Dempsey was running his hands through his head. It made perfect sense, lure all the lamb to the open field and then slaughter them in droves. The devil is cunning indeed and if we are to win this war, Dempsey was telling himself that we needed to start thinking outside of human engagement. As the terminal officers blare out communications to all four regional military commands, Dempsey looks at the global map and slams his fists on the table. They waited too late, not everyone will be evacuated to a minimum safe distance. He looked to Gabriel, as to find some comfort or knowledge that this was something that could have been averted. Gabriel looked back, with only acceptance in his face.

"Did you know about this Gabriel? Did you know that this was their first strike initiative?"

Dempsey was clearly irate, and given all things equal, he felt he had every reason to be, even if the person he was irate to was a divine being from heaven.

"Each war is different from the last, each gate decides its evil in its own way. I'm sorry but this was something that no one, not even us could have foreseen."

Gabriel had already sent word to all his brothers, the message was to help as much as they could to save as many lives as they could. But the first priority is the gates, once they are open, the blackness will pour out into this world and this holy war would begin.

Alarms began blaring as the levels of geothermal readings went off the charts, eruption was impending and based on a quick look at the mobilization of troops, only seventy five percent of the troops are outside the estimated blast radius. Thousands upon thousands will be incinerated by fire.

"Damn it, God Damn it!"

As Dempsey said this, Gabriel shot him a quick glance, but Dempsey, unfazed by it looked back to Gabriel with equal disdain.

"We're fighting an enemy that we can't possibly defeat. Yes, your corps of angels will be of great value Gabriel but so many people, at this initial stage will be lost. How? How can we have faith Gabriel? We've already lost so many, and Michael, has been taken. Tell me Gabriel, are we doomed to fail?"

Gabriel has heard all this before, and it is the way the darkness works. Lucifer will try to break the hearts of those that fight against him. From all his arsenal, his greatest weapon is and will always be fear, anger and hate. If his enemies lose their hearts, then he has already won. And this is why Lucifer loves man's nature. So easily dissuaded, and so very fast to judge, which was why Gabriel knew he can only say what he felt was true.

"You will find faith, if you know what it is you are fighting for. The only failure we face, is that of our own design. Those that have given their lives for the light are now part of it. Is this not enough for you, for anyone to seek to believe in what we do here, now?"

Dempsey, with both hands still on the table, breathed a deep sigh, and then stood up. He knew that Gabriel was right. He knew that this was to be expected. And if we falter now, there will be no hope, for the vessel, for Michael, for the entire world. As the global map shows each of the gate erupting in succession, Dempsey picks up the unmarked phone line by his console and waits for the line to be picked up.

"Mr. President, it has begun."

* * *

At each of the four gates, evacuation was being carried out but time was no longer available as the gates burst open in a fiery explosion. Molten lava shot up as high as four hundred feet with debris of liquefied rock spewing from the gate's opening. As those within the blast radius were instantaneously destroyed by the smoldering heat, those that were able to escape the opening were in awe of its venerable destructive force. The angels, having helped move man and machine at a safe distance now began to rally around the eruption. As the flowing magma settles out into the perimeter of the gates, the forces felt the ground rumbling, steadily. At first it felt like an earthquake but the shaking wasn't side to side, it felt like something bubbling up from the depths were burrowing upwards towards them. With panic in their hearts, the soldiers begin to cascade away from the open gates as the angels formed a circular pattern over it. Fear was in the hearts of those that have seen what just happened, and fear of what is to come.

The rumbling, now coming to fever pitch suddenly silenced itself to the confusion of the combined forces. The silence was eerie and disturbing. It was an unwelcome sign to what everyone was expecting to be the most horrible of enemies.

With a second more of silence, it was suddenly broken by a colossal expulsion of what can only be described as a mass of evil. From out of the gate, hordes upon hordes of wretched forms and beings that cannot even be described begin to fill the air and the land. The blackness looked back at all those that stood before it and relished in their destructive desires as they charged into the forces awaiting them.

The four Eternals, having seen the same thing across all of the four gates brandish their weapons with one heavenly cry.

"By His will!"

A cry that was heard across the globe, all the way up to the welkin in the heavenly kingdom, the cry of the righteous will always be heard. The angels then head into the black swarming mass of darkness and begin to cut down any and all things that came from the pit. Their attack was swift and precise, simple yet graceful, as each angel found a target, that target was eliminated into black dust. Armed with the heavenly weapons bestowed upon each of the Eternals, they all make good use of it in the fray.

Raphael's Bow of Light strikes multiple demons with one arrow. Jophiel wields his axe with strength and honor, striking it in the center of the blackness and cutting through row upon row of minions. Metatron's hammer crushes those that finds themselves underneath it and Sandalphon's mace delivers a blow that shatters all those demons around him. As the rest of the angelic corps, led by the four Eternals fought with their hearts, the earthly forces resound a battle cry of their own. Going through all communication channels, the command to attack is given.

"All stations, engage the enemy, fire at will, fire at will!"

A barrage of firepower that can only be describe as earth shattering was let loose towards each of the open gates and all manner of ordinance, from the land based forces to those from the air forces from above to the ballistic shells of battleships situated far away from the shore, the amount of conventional explosive fire power that was directed towards the gates shook the earth's very core. You could feel the earth tremble as each shell, missile and bullet find their mark and the minions that have sprouted from the gates burn in the scorching fields.

Heavy bombers flying at high altitude release bomb payloads that when it impacts the gates, shakes the very mountains around them. Civilians, hundreds of miles away in fallout bunkers feel the concussive force of the war that has begun to save this world. After about fifteen minutes of continuous firing, the regional commander for the Somalian gate ordered a cease fire to perform an assessment. It took almost five minutes for the smoke to even clear enough for them to even have a visual at the gate. As initial reports come in, the swarm of hell's minions are nowhere to be seen. The global command officer at the NSA asked for confirmation that the impending first wave was destroyed. With smoke clearing up more and more, the gate did not show any movement and all those in the vicinity of the gate were taken out. Upon reporting this, a roaring cheer went out among the troops as well as those in the command room as it would seem that victory, for now, was achieved.

Dempsey however knew better. He looked at Gabriel as Gabriel reached out to his kin. This was no attack, this was a mere probe. There is more to come and celebration is premature at best. They all knew what followed next and prayed that those in battle would have the strength of heart to face it.

The troops cheering in the field were reaching a new height as rumbling once again started under their feet. As the angelic corps regrouped around the perimeter of each of the gates. Silence gripped the troops and the gates seemed like they were now pulsing with new life. Suddenly a blast of red hot light shot through to the skies piercing the heavens above. Everyone shielded their eyes from the intense heat and brightness that can be only described as liquid sun. Upon the cascading eruption, one after the other, the explosive force now seeped back into the gate, however, what it revealed left all those gasp with fear. The Archangels knew these figures well, atop their steeds, the generals of each gate looked upon those that they will conquer. Before Jophiel and the others could attack, a thunderous voice swelled from each of the gates.

"Behold the Horsemen, as they lay waste to your wretched earth. Know that they will show no mercy in doing my bidding. Prepare yourselves for this is where you meet your end!"

The entire world gripped in fear as each of the horsemen stared down on their victims. As Jophiel, Sandalphon, Raphael and Metatron knew this was their calling, they could feel the fear of their earthly brothers who they are fighting alongside with. In a show of faith, each of the four Eternals cried out towards the sky and then headed the charge towards each of the horsemen at each gate.

Followed by the legions of angels behind each one, the gates now once again flowed with legions of its own, like ants coming out from their hills. As the earthly forces saw this, conviction gripped their hearts and each command, made up of those that were old enemies, now cried in unison and joined to aid the angelic corps. If this was the end, let it be such an end worthy of what everyone was fighting for.

Each army at each of the four gates clash in numbers never before seen in the history of man. Thousands upon thousands engage the minions from below and both angelic and earthly forces rally to fight for the utmost common cause. The gate spews out more and more minions, now allowing the most vile and despicable demons out into the world. The forces at the gates cannot contain all of them as they spread beyond the battle sphere and across the globe. In all areas of the world, people now began to panic with the impending attacks from below.

However, angelic forces not at the gate stand ready to face the hordes that spreads across the land. Civilians have also armed themselves in order to protect those that they love, men and women, and sometimes barely men and women, take up arms so that this world can be part of the heavenly kingdom. The initial attacks begin, in places closest to the gates. Dempsey gets reports that the West Coast has now engaged in isolated attacks from the gate at Umiat.

Several reports also indicates both the European and Asian contingent have started to see attacks in populated areas.

As the battle of the four gates begins, Dempsey, looking at the global threat map and seeing the entire globe consumed by the evil that has now been unleashed on the world, he looked to Gabriel and picked up the phone. The other line picked up and Dempsey, sullen in his voice did not hide his distress.

"Mr. President, the battle for our souls have begun. Yes Mr. President, God help us all."

About The Author

Myles Gorospe, born in 1968, was originally from the Philippines until he immigrated to the United States in 1997. Upon arriving in San Francisco CA with only fifty dollars to his name, he began to seize the opportunities that were presented to him in the US, his new home. Having lived in parts of the West Coast, Colorado and eventually settling in the East Coast, he worked numerous jobs in the technology and business  management industry. While finding success as a professional in these industries, he also remembers his first job ever, where he worked as a janitor for a local trucking company in San Jose. While this is his first book, he had the idea for this series for almost ten years. In 2014, his best friend who had listened to the story's concept encouraged him to finally finish writing it. He now lives in New Jersey and in his spare time enjoys reading a wide range of books, over a wide range of topics and areas and also an avid collector of Star Wars memorabilia from the original trilogy. He is somewhat of a wine connoisseur and loves to travel around the world. Finally, as a Christian, he believes that all things come in God's time and that we have it in ourselves to do what God calls us to do, we simply need to have faith.